Wicked

Somerset University

Ruby Vincent

Published by Ruby Vincent, 2020.

Copyright © 2020 by Ruby Vincent
Cover Design: Covers By Combs
All rights reserved. No part of this publication may be reproduced, stored in a retrieval system, or transmitted in any form or by any means, electronic, mechanical, recording or otherwise, without the prior written permission of the copyright holder.
This is a work of fiction. Names, characters, businesses, places, events, and incidents are either the products of the author's imagination or used in a fictitious manner. Any resemblance to actual persons, living or dead, or actual events is purely coincidental.

Prologue

I got in the car and set off for home. Twenty minutes in, I squinted at the rearview mirror.

"Is that...?"

I picked up my phone and called Jaxson.

"Hey, baby. What—"

"Jaxson, I think I'm being followed." My eyes darted to the mirror and the same white car. "They were behind me on the way to your beach house and now they're following me back."

His tone sharpened. "Do you recognize them?" he asked. "Dad? Dad! Call the police."

"No, I— Hold on. They're getting closer."

The glare off the windshield made it nearly impossible to see. As the distance closed between us, I made out a green hood and white hands clutching the wheel.

"I'm not sure who it is," I admitted.

"It could be one of your security team."

"No, I told them not to follow me. I had to do something in private and—"

Suddenly, the car accelerated.

"Jaxson!"

They rammed my bumper. The force sent me and my phone flying. The seat belt snapped, biting into my neck, and I gasped from shock and pain.

"Val," I heard. "Val, what happened?"

"They hit me," I screamed. "They hit me on purpose."

The car came for me again.

The impact knocked me sideways and the car veered off the road. My screams tore the silence as I sped off the embankment headed for the trees. The last thing I saw before the impact was a squirrel scurrying out of the way.

Chapter One

Valentina

"And you didn't see their face?"

"No," I repeated for the dozenth time to the sixth person. "I saw white hands, a green hood, and a small, white car. That's it." I sighed. "It wasn't enough for the police to go on either."

Jacob and Elliot shared a look. The three of us were in Ryder's study going over the details of my attack once again. The boys insisted on it after weeks of investigating brought the Evergreen Police Department no closer to finding the culprit who ran me off the road. I didn't know what they thought my memory would shake loose after all this time, but I sensed them pacing outside the door, wishing just that.

"We have more resources than the police," said Jacob. "We also have the men and time to devote solely to the search. We'll find the person who did this. But if there's something else we should know, please tell us now, Miss Moon."

"What do you mean?"

Jacob gazed at me steadily. "You told your guards not to follow you to the beach house. Why? Did you know you were in danger?"

"I didn't know I'd be followed or someone would try to hurt me," I said. "I went to the beach house for a break. It's been an awful few weeks for me... which I don't have to tell you."

His expression didn't change. "Of course, Miss Moon. I'd like to apologize again for betraying your confidence. All the same, I trust the matter was handled appropriately."

I nodded. "It was."

"This one will be as well," Elliot spoke up. "We're using your description of the car to match against students, classmates, and others in and around your life. In the meantime, I'm sure you agree that your guards must be with you at all times. Kennedy and Hadley will maintain a distance, and Juliet remains at your side. Their presence will ensure no one attempts to harm you again."

"Thank you," I replied. "I sincerely appreciate all that you have done and continue to do, but it's hard for me to feel comfortable surrounded by people reporting my movements to Caroline."

"Our role is not to spy on you," said Jacob.

"I understand," I said. "I also understand that you signed contracts and the person you work for isn't me. I just need to know if I tell them not to follow me somewhere or to keep information to themselves, they'll listen."

Jacob opened his mouth to reply. I held up a hand.

"I also know this is something I have to take up with Caroline," I added. "And I intend to. Thank you, gentlemen, let me know if there's anything else I can do to help."

The men knew a dismissal when they heard one. They inclined their heads and turned to go.

I sank into Ryder's chair and dropped my head on the desk.

How can I help? I don't have anything useful to tell them now or five weeks ago.

I genuinely did not know who tried to run me off the road. All of my known enemies were dead or in jail. The police ruled out retaliation from the gang, and the men who attacked me in the shed were in no condition physically or mentally to come for me—the boys assured me. The only place for my mind to go was the Sallys.

But it wouldn't stay there for long. No matter how I looked at it, there was no reason for Leighton, Reagan, or Patricia to want to hurt me. I kept their secret even now. Something they knew because

Leighton wasn't dead and pictures of the wreck and the death certificate wouldn't sway me otherwise.

"Val, what did Elliot and Jacob say?"

I raised my head as the guys filed into the room. Jaxson, Maverick, Ezra, and Ryder. The loves of my life. Each one more different than the last and it struck me whenever they were in the same room together.

Ezra in his buttoned-up shirt, black slacks, polished shoes, and slicked-back hair did not look like a man who only weeks ago lay in a hospital bed with a gunshot wound. His rehab was slow, but his return to my perfect Ezra was not.

Maverick kept it simple. Jeans and a loose t-shirt that he imagined hid his sculpted body. He was wrong, of course, but I wouldn't tip him off lest my introverted love work harder to accomplish the task.

Ryder, on the other hand, did not try to hide anything. Tousled raven locks hung in his silver eyes, drawing everyone's attention for the barest moment they could look away from the toned physique his leather jacket and designer jeans accentuated.

And then there was my Jaxson, who did not let wealth, side-eye, or veiled comments sway him from baggy pants hung low on his waist, band shirts, or the collection of piercings he'd been adding to his ears since eighteen. He was up to five altogether.

I hummed. "Go outside and walk in backward. Let me see those asses shake."

"Yes, ma'am." Jaxson spun around, making me laugh.

The other boys collectively rolled their eyes.

"Be serious, Val," said Ryder. He swiveled my desk chair. "Up."

Grumbling, I did as ordered, only for him to take my place and drag me onto his lap. "What did they say?"

"They're stepping up security on me and redoubling efforts to find my attacker," I replied. "Everyone is doing the best they can do. We just have to wait for them to turn something up."

"I'm sick of waiting," said Maverick. "We know who it was. Leighton Lewis."

I cut eyes to Ezra. He spilled everything I told him about Leighton, the Sallys, and Logan after the car crash. I didn't blame him. I walked away from the crash sore, but unharmed. Nonetheless, the stretch of time I was too disoriented to pick up the phone and call Jaxson back, was enough for a terrified Ezra to let them know what I'd truly gone out to the beach house to do. The five of us were now strictly on a no-secrets rule.

"If she's alive, I can find her." Maverick bore over the desk. "I will find her."

I shook my head. "We've been over this, Maverick. Somehow Aiden found out you were digging into him. I'm assuming that's how he was able to cover his tracks because there's no way that boy doesn't have skeletons in his closet. If Leighton and her *friends* can fake her death, make Reagan and Pat disappear into thin air, and... Logan, then tipping our hand that we don't believe the official story is the worst thing we can do."

"I messed up before," he said. "If I'd known who I was dealing with, I'd have hidden my tracks better. I do now—"

"We don't." I placed my hand on his balled fist. "We don't know anything about this cult or whatever it is. But I do know Leighton liked me," I admitted. "She wanted me as a Sally so badly she broke rules and *laws* for me." I lowered my voice though we were the only ones in the room. "She returned the one thing she could have used against me. Why do that only to kill me?"

Ezra adopted Maverick's position. "I thought Aiden liked Sawyer too. The president went on about him being the one we should look up to. What if the person in the car wasn't trying to kill you?" His dark eyes pierced me. "What if that day you weren't supposed to die? You were supposed to disappear."

I rocked back on Ryder's lap like I'd been smacked over the head.

"Because I want you, Valentina," Leighton whispered. "I wanted you from day one."

"Could that be true?"

"You shook your guards loose," said Ezra.

I hadn't realized I said that out loud.

"You were alone with no one around for miles," he continued. "The driver might not have noticed you were on the phone until the last second. Then they had to hit you again and run you off so they could get away."

"I don't— Ugh," I cried. "All we have are theories and guesses. We don't know anything because we still don't know what's going on with the Sallys and Sams."

"Someone else can figure it out," said Jaxson. All joking was aside. "You changed your mind about dropping out. Change it back, Val."

"We're not having this argument again," I said. "Teagan is gone. Sawyer is gone. And although I'm not shedding any tears over Logan, he was killed and a person or people connected to Leighton covered it up. Any situation where people go missing and a dead body can be hidden on speed dial, is not a good one. Someone has to do something or this won't stop. Who knows how many people they've done this to over the years?"

Ryder had been silent up to that point. "How do we know this has been going on longer than Leighton and her friends have been there?"

"Something Brian said," I replied. "Ezra, Brian told you he didn't rush the Sams because they were too intense. Guys who washed out of Nu Alpha Theta would leave Somerset to get out from under the black mark. But doesn't that seem an extreme reaction to getting kicked out of a fraternity? Somerset is on the level of an Ivy League school. Everyone has clawed their way to an acceptance and they wouldn't give up their place for the Sams." I smacked the desk. "I bet those guys were taken too."

"We're back to theories and guesses," Ryder said.

Jaxson knelt in front of me. "And none of them tell me why you have to be the one to prove it," he whispered. "This is getting fucking twisted, Val."

I stroked his jaw. "Believe me, I don't want to be involved, but someone has to get close enough to the Sallys and Sams to find out the truth. It can't be Ezra because Aiden named him public enemy number one.

"It can't be Maverick or Ryder because they missed their chance to rush. It can't be you because you're not even a student. And it can't be our team of bodyguards because they pass for college kids as well as I pass for a capuchin monkey. I'm already in. The girls like and trust me. It has to be me."

"You're not a freaking undercover agent," Maverick burst out. "I've said it before, why don't we tell the police everything that's happened and *make* them listen."

I got to my feet. "And I said before that we can't make them listen without proof."

"Whoa," Jaxson cut in. "Let's not kick this shit up again. Val, we get that we can't ignore what's happening, but this is dangerous and we almost lost you and Ezra. We have to handle this a lot smarter."

I opened my arms for him. Jaxson wrapped me up tight and warm. I called him my goofy one. It didn't come close to describing the multitudes that was Jaxson Van Zandt. He was the glue. He kept us together. He kept me together.

"It's been a long day, mama," he said in my ear. "Come with me to the studio. We'll listen to some music, sneak beers out of Dad's office, and fool around in the sound booth," he said to my giggle. "Just what we need."

"I can't. Adam has his playdate." I pulled back. "Speaking of which, who is watching the kids?"

"Caroline," said Maverick.

"You left that poor woman alone with four preschoolers?"

Ezra shrugged. "Jacob will protect her if they attack."

"But we should give her a break," said Ryder. "I'll take over watching the kids. You guys go to the studio."

"I'm not leaving you to handle them yourself either," I said. "Adam's teacher went through the trouble of setting this up for me. Besides, I want Adam to introduce me to his friends."

I kissed Jaxson's cheek. "Next time, baby. We'll fool around in the studio all you want."

"Next time."

I picked up on his disappointment as well as I did my own. We'd been saying next time for a while. Between work, school, Adam, Ezra getting hurt, the attacks on me, and everything else, I still hadn't made it to the studio for our technically forbidden date.

I'll make it up to him tonight when he comes back from work. Make us a special dinner and surprise him in our bedroom.

Downstairs, Caroline read her book in the armchair. Cara curled up in her lap, purring under Caroline's stroking loud enough for me to hear from the other side of the living room. She certainly didn't appear harassed. And the children coloring quietly on the floor were putting the stereotypes of young kids to shame.

Especially this one.

I eyed the little boy in suspenders, a bow tie, and tiny leather shoes. He looked like a grown man hit with a shrink ray.

"Adam, baby."

"Mommy!"

Adam bolted for me, arms out. He wasn't the only one.

I almost went down when Adam and the little blond boy tackled my legs. He beamed at me, showing off his missing front teeth.

"You must be Cole," I said. Adam described his friend Cole as looking like Daddy Jaxson. He must have gotten that from the blond hair.

I tapped Cole's nose. "Aren't you a cutie?"

"Yes," he said. Cole twisted around and pointed to the third boy. "That's my best friend, Michael."

"Hi, Michael."

Michael waved, but didn't get up.

The boy in suspenders got up and reached for my hand. "I'm Landon."

"Nice to meet you, Landon."

Landon blinked up at me. "I'm hungry. Can I have an apple, please?"

"I've got an even yummier treat. Would you guys like some chocolate chip cookies?"

I got three yays and one headshake.

"Henrietta says chocolate is mean to your face," Landon said matter-of-factly. "I want an apple."

"Who is Henrietta?" I asked.

"My mother."

"Of course," I muttered under my breath. *This is what happens when you send your kid to a preschool for the rich. You get four-year-olds watching their complexion and calling their mother by their first name.*

"You can have all the apples you want, Landon."

He gave me a million-dollar smile. "Thank you."

Adam took my hand and led me to the carpet. He climbed in my lap and happily went back to coloring with his little group.

I pressed a kiss to his mop of curls. He could have as many friends in bow ties as his heart desired. Seeing my son happy reminded me that no matter the craziness going on in my life, at least I was doing one thing right.

JAXSON

"Go right through, sir."

"Don't call me 'sir,' Paunch," I said. "It's Jaxson."

The security guard flashed me a sheepish look. "Sorry, sir. Mr. Meyer heard me call you Jaxson last week and wrote me up. I can't lose this job."

I swallowed my irritation. Cursing out Daniel Meyer wouldn't do any good for my probation.

"I get it," I said. "Sorry about that."

"It's cool."

I saluted and continued on to the elevators. I dropped my smile as the doors shut.

I wish Dad would get rid of that fucker.

But a wish is all it would be. Daniel Meyer, vice president of Interstellar Records, had been haunting this place long before I was born. He wasn't going anywhere anytime soon.

My phone went off in my pocket. I moved the food to one hand and fished it out. I knew who it was before I checked the screen.

"On my way, Papa VZ."

"You know, Dad or Father would do just fine." His amusement bled through the reprimand.

"Nah. A man of your stature needs a proper title befitting your fatherhood."

He barked a laugh. "A man of my stature also needs black coffee, a bacon cheddar wrap, and an everything bagel."

"Got it."

"Did you also get the bottled water and Cobb salad?"

"Oops. Must have slipped my mind."

"Jaxson." The reprimand was clear this time.

"Papa."

He heaved a sigh. "I had a feeling you'd forget, so I sent Gwen to get Daniel's order. You've certainly helped me see the wisdom in having two assistants."

"You gotta stop calling me your assistant, old man. These people won't respect me by the time I kick your ass out and take over."

"How quickly a man of my stature devolved into 'old man.' That's why my plan is to make sure they don't respect you."

"Crafty fucker."

He cracked up. "Get your ass up here with my food while I'm still in the mood to give you good news."

Dad hung up.

I put my phone away, chuckling. If Meyer didn't like the staff being informal with me, he one hundred percent blew his shit at the way Dad and I talked to each other. It was just our thing. My dad was a tattooed, leather-wearing, bourbon-swilling, ex-guitarist/songwriter who had enough sense to funnel his royalties into business, but not enough sense to refrain from dating the talent.

He found Mom in a dive bar, signed her band two weeks later, and then got her pregnant five months after that. He liked to call me his happy accident after a few too many. But I knew he loved Mom and the picture-perfect life the three of us had for a short time. I didn't question why he never got remarried.

I stepped out onto the silent top floor. This was Levi Van Zandt's domain. This is where he signed the biggest names and brokered the best deals in the industry.

And soon it'll be mine.

Daniel and Dad cut off mid-conversation when I walked in.

"I know y'all were talking about me."

Dad laughed. "That's what we do all day, my boy. Sit around talking about you."

"He admits it."

Dad patted the desk, demanding his food. I handed it over and then plopped down in the chair and put my feet on the desk.

"Off," said Dad.

"Make me."

A sharp intake of breath sounded on my right. Dad just smacked my feet off and went back to eating.

"Hello, Jaxson," said Meyer, disapproval laced his tone.

Of course it did. His three spawn were perfect, smiling automatons who "yes, sir" and "no, sir" him to death. If Daniel and Dad did talk about me all day, it'd be to argue about my manners.

Dad was the president, director, and CEO of Interstellar Records, but everyone had their second-in-command. Enter Daniel Meyer, vice president and the man who was with him when Interstellar was an idea he scribbled on a bar napkin.

From their college photos, Daniel rocked ripped jeans and band shirts even harder than Dad. Until law school chewed him up and spat out a three-piece suit and five-hundred-dollar haircut that used to have a personality.

I skipped the greeting. "You wrote up Paunch for calling me Jaxson. Last I checked that was my name."

He flashed me a too-white smile. Val said the touch of silver at his temple and strong, stubbly jaw made him handsome. I don't see it.

"Interstellar is the biggest music label in the country," he said. "How does it look to outsiders if we don't maintain a level of professionalism? Especially in regard to the future president of the label."

I grinned. "Did it hurt you to call me that?"

Dad's eyes flashed. "Jaxson."

He started it, I wanted to say. But it wouldn't win me any points.

"Sorry," I said instead. "I just think if I'm taking over the place, I should decide what my employees call me."

"They're my employees, you overpampered brat," Dad announced. "So I'll decide everything from here on until I'm dead. Got it?"

Just like that, Dad put us both in our place. *That's why he's Levi Van Zandt and I'm the one fetching his coffee.*

"Got it," I said. "So, you have a present for me?"

He cracked a smile. Dad never stayed mad for long. "I said I had good news. You tell me if it's a present."

I cut eyes to Daniel and noted his pinched expression. If he didn't like it, it was definitely good for me.

"What's up?"

Dad leaned back with his coffee. "Over the past year, I've moved you around the departments, letting you get a feel of what it takes to run this label. The heads have kept me informed on how you're doing, and while all of them have nothing but good things to say, Bianca is most impressed with you.

"She says you've never complained about staying up all night listening to demo tapes. You've got a way with the artists, and Gael of Cosplay Meltdown asked for you specifically to sit in on sessions. She wants you to spend the rest of your internship working for the artist and repertoire department. Are you inter—?"

I bolted up in my seat. "Yes."

He smiled. "Good. You start now. She's already got a band in her sights that she wants you to scout."

"I'll get them. This is great, Dad. A and R is exactly where I want to be. I have to play you the last two demos I listened to," I said, voice rising with excitement. "One has this great R and B sound. It's kind of a Sam Cooke—"

"I'm sure Bianca would love to give them a listen." Daniel moved behind Dad's chair. "We wouldn't want to go over the head of the department."

"I wasn't—"

"No, he's right, J," said Dad. "Can't have Bianca thinking we're putting her out of a job."

I got another peek at those loathsome teeth as Daniel smiled. "While you're agreeing with me, Levi, I'd like to discuss the internship again. We agreed he'd spend time in every department and his next destination was legal. I personally think he'd benefit from a more thorough grasp on contracts, copyright infringement... theft."

I clenched my teeth hard enough for Dad to see my jaw tic. He must have because he spoke up.

"Give the kid a break, Daniel. He's learned his lesson." His eyes so like mine pinned me to my seat. "Right, son?"

"I'm not a kid anymore. I know what I did was wrong and nothing like it will ever happen again."

"There you have it," Dad said.

"Levi, we agreed," Daniel gritted out.

"Jaxson will have his time in legal. For now, he works under Bianca."

If Daniel planned to argue with him, he was cut off by a knock on the door.

Dad's second—only—assistant pushed into the room with a *Tim's Bistro* bag hanging off her fingers. Her blinding smile pierced the tense atmosphere. Gwendolyn Sandoval had that kind of effect. And that kind of smile. She flashed it in my direction as she crossed the room.

I could admit it. When Dad introduced me to the blonde, blue-eyed, freckled twenty-four-year-old sporting ripped shorts that did nothing to hide her shapely legs, or ass, I straight-up thought he was gunning for a sexual harassment lawsuit. No way was he not trying to get in those shorts.

Then Gwen opened her mouth and hit me with the musical equivalent of drinking me under the table. She knew bands and artists not even I had heard of, and she dealt with the most temperamental of them under our label with a smile. I didn't question she earned the job.

"I've got your order, Mr. Meyer."

"You can take it down to my office. Good day, Levi. Jaxson."

He blew out of the room and Gwen spun around, hurrying to catch up.

Dad ripped his wrap in half and slid it to me. "You gotta stop roasting Daniel's nuts, J."

"Nice image."

"You did wrong and you have to earn his trust again. Whether you like it or not, you both work together. Petty shit tanks businesses as fast as they do great bands. You're not breaking up Interstellar Records."

I snatched the food, kicking my feet up on the desk despite him. I tore off a bite to save me from answering.

Dad was missing one fact: Daniel did not want to work with me. Dad's reaction to the leak was to ban my cellphone. Daniel's reaction was to ban me. He didn't want me near the artists, near the sound booths, near the building. He told my dad he wanted me gone and all talk of me taking over put to bed. He said as much to my face.

He wasn't interested in my apologies—and I gave plenty. He ignored my clean track record since that day. And he barely acknowledged me unless it was to get on my case for my clothes, speech, or existence. Along with his monogrammed mother-of-pearl cuff links, Daniel wore his dislike of me as his second signature.

"I'll try, Dad," I said since that was the only answer he'd accept.

"Good. Now go. Bianca is expecting you."

I didn't move. "Can I play you those demos later?"

Dad crumpled his wrapper. He reared back and sent it sailing over my head. I heard a soft *ting* that told me he got his target.

"Sure. But not too late. I'm taking a friend out to dinner."

I heaved myself out of the chair. "Whoever this *friend* is, I'm not calling her mom."

Dad's lyrical laugh rolled out of his chest. Every sound he made was music. "Get your ass out of here and report to Bianca. Some of us get paid to work around here."

Every sound was music, but that music wasn't always pleasant.

"We could all get paid around here if you slid me a salary," I mumbled.

Dad just laughed me out of the door.

I stepped out of the elevator and almost ran into Bianca. She stood in Artist Alley like she was waiting for me. Behind her, platinum records covered nearly every inch of the walls, hence it was dubbed Artist Alley.

"It wouldn't kill you to bring me coffee too," she said, pierced brows arched. "It might even get you on my good side."

"We both know I live on your good side, mama. You love me."

"I don't remember pushing your skinny self out of me," she shot back. "So don't call me mama."

"Ma'am, yes, ma'am."

She gagged. "Somehow that's even worse." Bianca draped her arm around my shoulders and led me off. "Did your dad tell you the good news? You're mine for the foreseeable future."

Daniel's wish to turn the label into a haven of pantsuits, pencil skirts, and blazers hadn't penetrated far outside of his domain—legal. Bianca sported jeans that were ripped from wear and tear, not style. Her plaid top was rolled up to the elbows, revealing her ink. And the tight tank top underneath showed off everything else. With her messy bun, coffee mug perpetually in hand, and shadowed eyes from late-night gigs, you wouldn't peg her for a department head in the biggest label in the country. But Bianca put everyone who underestimated her in their place.

"That's alright with me," I said. "Throw me at any band you can think of."

"Remember you said that."

We walked into her office. Bianca pushed her sleeping bag on the floor and gestured for me to sit. Sometimes we were recording so late she crashed on her couch. I'd feel bad for her if I wasn't the poor sap snoring in her spare bag on the floor every other night.

"They're called Beyond Berlin," she began. Bianca poured us both coffee. "They play every weekend at this bar downtown and fans have been posting their sets online. They're good. Crazy good. The lead singer's got this voice that haunts you long after the song ends." She surged forward in her seat and liquid splashed out of her mug. "They're signing with us, Jaxson. We're the label that'll catapult them to the stratosphere. Drop by the bar tonight and tell them their dreams are coming true."

"Yes, ma'am."

"Ugh." She slapped my knee though a smile played on her lips. "Stick to Bianca."

"That's my night booked up. What do you need me to do now?"

"I've got a stack of demos with your name on it. Grab Gwen and get to it."

I left and went off in search of Gwen. I found her in her usual place, hovering around the art department. She was a music and graphic design double major. Working for a record label designing album covers and posters ticked off each box in her dream job listing.

It was pretty sweet down here. The employees decked out their work stations with touches of their personality. Band posters they designed decorated the walls, and couches and beanbag chairs took up a corner of the room. They'd get comfy on breaks and toss ideas around. I enjoyed the time I spent here but I wasn't an artist. I wasn't meant to work with them.

"More demos," Gwen said when she saw me.

"You know it."

"Want to grab some food of our own first?"

"My chef made paninis. You also know I brought you one too."

She clapped. "If I knew one of the perks of working here were five-star lunches. My roommates are wicked jealous of me."

Gwen picked up her tote bag and followed me to the elevator. She never went anywhere without that thing. It was covered in green and white school pins and scribbled-on designs. She looked like a fresh-out-of-university intern living with four roommates. Thanks to my clothing choices, I did too. It made it even funnier when I told people who tried to dismiss me my last name.

We rode the elevator up to my office, talking about nothing in particular.

I called it my office. But the windowless broom closet I claimed for my own was better described as just that—a broom closet. All I could fit in here were a couple of chairs, a small table, and a mini fridge and microwave that claimed almost half the space but was worth it.

I threw our paninis in the microwave while Gwen booted her laptop. Bianca was kind enough to drop off the stack of demos and there would barely be room for her computer and mine on the table.

"Have you started looking for a new place?" I asked.

"Maxie and I can't decide. He wants the place we can afford someday. I want the place we can afford *today*. Cottonwood may not be as bad as Evergreen but it's still pretty pricey."

Maxie, or Maximiliano, was Gwen's boyfriend. The guy was in med school and one day, when he was a doctor and she was heading up the art department, they'd live anywhere they wanted. Until then, Gwen refused to tell me how much they owed in student loans because it'd make me cry.

I took out our food and passed hers over. "I heard Jayden mention in the breakroom that he found a nice one-bedroom in a place called Verden Courts. Have you looked there?"

"Verden Courts." Gwen whipped out a pen and wrote it directly on her arm. "I'll check it out after work. Thanks, J."

She reached out to ruffle my hair and I swiftly ducked her. "Must you? I'm not your kid brother."

Gwen chuckled. "You're even cuter than my kid brother. I was worried working with Levi's son meant I'd be doing all the work while you took the credit, but I was so off. You're the sweetest little thing."

"What every guy wants to hear."

I was cracking her up. Apparently, a four-year age difference basically made me a toddler in her eyes.

"What are we doing after this?" she asked when she finally got herself under control.

"I'm heading downtown for an open mic night. Bianca's got Beyond Berlin in her sights. Ever heard of them?"

She gasped. "Oh my gosh, yes. Maxie and I have heard them play a few times. I'm the one who sent her the link. Can I come with you?"

"Yeah. If you want."

Smiling away, Gwen put in her earphones and queued up the first demo. If it was possible for someone to love this job more than me, then that someone would be Gwen.

I settled back in my uncomfortable seat as a jazzy, rhythmic bass filled my ears.

But it's not possible. No one loves this more than me.

VALENTINA

Landon streaked across the lawn, uncaring of the expensive clothes he was getting grass stains on. Michael was leaving him in the dust but that didn't stop him from giving all he had in their race.

I glanced down at the newest addition to my lap. I brought the boys out to run around in the sun, but after plopping down on the patio chair, Cole climbed on top of me without a word. He tugged on my earlobe while he contentedly drank from his sippy cup.

"Don't you want to play with your friends?" I asked.

"No. I'm sleepy." He rested his head on my bosom. "I take a nap."

I bit back a smile. *If only Adam went down this easily. I've got to lure him into running around the yard knowing he'll pass out afterward no matter how much he complains about his nap.*

Cole soon drifted off to sleep. I relaxed, watching the boys play.

My phone buzzed in my pocket. Carefully, I shifted Cole and fished it out.

"Hello?"

"Hey, Val. Whatcha doing?"

"Adam has a playdate. What about you?"

"Getting ready for a date of my own," said Sofia. "Hudson is taking me to a reading of one of his favorite writers. What do you wear to those?"

"Whatever gives you an excuse to snuggle into him all night."

"The grumpy ass would probably throw his jacket at me and say to occupy my own personal space," she muttered.

"At least he'd give you his jacket."

"It's like I'm a princess."

I laughed. Sofia grumbled about her sarcastic, opinionated Brit, but he'd proven a thousand times over he was the best of men.

"That's not the only reason I called," she said. "The girls have been all over me since Leighton's death. Reagan and Pat are gone and they don't want us to leave too. I don't know what to tell them."

I chewed my lip. *I didn't know* what to tell Sofia. How do I explain my decision to stay in the Sally house after all?

"You want to stay, don't you?"

There was a pause on the other end. "Not if it isn't safe for us," she said after a beat. "But if it truly isn't, I don't feel right about Palmer, Keily, Mai, and Blair being left in the dark."

"I don't feel right about it either," I admitted.

One thing I was sure of is they were normal college girls looking to have fun, get good grades, and snag nice internships. I could only assume Leighton, Reagan, and Patricia started that way too. There must have been a series of events that changed those women into what they were now. If left alone in that house, would Keily, Palmer, and the girls be forced through those events?

Not possible. My mind rebelled against the thought. *Whatever is going on, I can't believe all of the Sallys are in on it or they recruit every sister into their sinister web. It wouldn't have stayed secret for so long if that was the case.*

"Val?"

I blinked back to the conversation. "I honestly don't know if we're safe. I believe Leighton, Pat, and Reagan were involved, but if it ends now that they're gone, there's no way to be sure. Which is why... I'm not dropping out."

"You're not?"

"No. I can't if I'm ever going to find out what's truly happening in Zeta Rho Sigma and Nu Alpha Theta."

"You realize this means I'm not dropping out either. I won't let you deal with whatever this shit is alone."

"I do realize that but I'm hoping I can persuade you otherwise."

"Nope."

I sighed. "It wasn't a strong hope."

"I'll call Keily back and tell her we're not going anywhere," she chirped. "Love you."

"Yeah, yeah. Go get some off your hot British dude."

She laughed. "I intend to."

I hung up, not feeling nearly as chill as she sounded.

"Hello," a sweet voice said. "I see my little one took his nap early."

A woman the spitting image of Cole stepped out onto the porch. On her heels was a guy who quickly adjusted my image of the most well-dressed man I knew. A tailored gray plaid suit and cream overcoat matched his shockingly silver hair so perfectly, I understood why it was the only thing he could have worn that day. Nothing else would have made sense.

"I'm Mrs. Reed." She held out her hand. "You must be Valentina. Sorry we missed each other earlier."

"Completely my fault," I said. "I had a meeting."

The man shook my hand next. "Declan. Nice to meet you."

"Did the boys give you any trouble?" asked Mrs. Reed. She gathered Cole in her arms and dropped kisses on his face as it scrunched up in sleep.

"They were angels. We should do this again sometime."

Declan waved for his son. "I'll have to check Landon's schedule, but I'm sure we can fit something in."

He has a schedule?

"Michael, sweetie," Mrs. Reed called. "Time to go."

Soon the boys were gone and it was just me and Adam. I brought him upstairs, bathed him, and then turned on his cartoons as we curled up in bed. He was out in twenty minutes.

Quietly, I tiptoed out of the room and went down to the kitchen.

I'll cook Jaxson's favorite to make up for our missed date. Roasted chicken, mashed potatoes, and whatever he wants to drizzle on me for dessert.

It'll be perfect.

JAXSON

"Look it up on your phone. Mine's about to die."

"I know the way," said Gwen. "I go there all the time." She held out her hand, a grin stealing over her face. "This means I drive."

"Sure." I tossed the keys over the hood. "It's Ezra's car. No loss for me if you ding it up."

She rolled her eyes. "Why would I do that? I'm a great driver."

I glanced around. "Who are you lying for?"

"Shut up."

Howling, I slid into the passenger's side. Gwen made herself at home pulling up the seat, adjusting the mirrors, and then messing with the radio.

"I miss your old car," she said. "What happened to it?"

"Mama, I know you heard the rumors."

"Been waiting for you to confirm them."

"I sold it to pay off a cartel and Papa Van Zandt was so pissed he refused to buy me another." I reclined the seat back and folded my hands behind my head. "Until he gives in, I'm riding around in this Porsche. It's too bad. The speakers are shit."

"Man, I wish I had your problems." She cut me a look. "Except for the cartel part. How did you get mixed up with them?"

"That's a story for later. Crank the volume up."

"Ima let you get away with that because this is a seriously good song."

She turned The Script up as high as it could go. We belted out the lyrics, tearing through town for the bar. Out of nowhere she turned it off.

"What the hell, they were getting into the chorus," I protested.

"You can sing," she stated. "Why don't people know?"

"My girlfriend and the imaginary audience in my shower knows. Who else do I need to tell?"

She whacked my arm. "I'm serious. Why aren't you in a band?"

"My boys don't play. Except for Ryder but he only does classical."

"You are allowed to form a group with people other than your boyfriends."

"They're my *boys.* Notice the lack of a compound word."

Gwen smirked. "In my imagination, you're getting naked with those hotties."

I hummed. "But if I'm your kid brother, do those fantasies count as incest or pedophilia?"

She whacked me again. Thanks to Gwen, I went home bruised most days.

"You should start a band," she said.

"Look, it's like this. I like eating, not cooking. Driving cars, not building them. And listening to music, not making it. Dad gave me the real growing up. Being crammed in a van zipping all over the country to sing the same songs over and over again isn't as fun as it sounds. And the whole time you're sweating that if you stop for one second, you'll become a has-been."

"You're too young to be this cynical." Gwen pulled the Porsche up to the curb and killed the engine. "Sing because you love it. Don't worry about anything else."

"I just told you I love confining it to the shower. Is that good enough?"

She groaned like I was the most irritating person she ever met. "We're here. The Taproom. The bands don't go on for another couple of hours. You can watch me knock back a few beers until then."

"It's my lucky night," I deadpanned.

The Taproom was the kind of smoky, shadowed dive you saw on television. Cheap upholstered booths lined the walls, and the middle was clear for the crowd to dance before the stage. I sat while Gwen ordered us drinks.

What a day this will be for Beyond Berlin. They woke up this morning thinking this place would be the highlight of their career. They'll end the night looking at a deal with Interstellar Records.

Gwen slid into the booth and handed over my soda. "You'll love Beyond Berlin. They match your style exactly. Something you can dance to but with a nice message."

"Way to simplify my complex tastes."

She grinned. "You're not that complicated, Jaxson Van Zandt. Sorry to be the one to tell you."

We passed the time talking music and inhaling greasy bar food. As the clock ticked closer to nine, the bar filled up. The pushing and shoving to get closer to the stage made it obvious who the crowd was here to see.

"Hello, everyone." A short guy wearing the bar's logo spoke into the mic. Behind him, the curtain lowered and a spotlight hit the stage. "Who's ready for Beyond Berlin?"

Shouts and whoops were his reply.

"They've got an amazing set for you guys tonight," he said. "Let's show some love to get them out here."

The bar burst into applause. Gwen got out of her seat and sat next to me. As the band jogged out, she whispered in my ear. Warm Guinness breath washed over me.

"The drummer is Rylan Sherman. He never gets a solo but the fans would go wild if he did. Their panties melt every time he tosses a wink their way."

A lanky guy in a leather vest took his place at the drums. Shiny, long black and gold hair hung down in his face. He pushed it back with his drumstick and grinned at the crowd. The screams ratcheted up to deafening.

"The guitarist is Chandler Kaufman," she continued. "Definite interview type."

Interview types were what Gwen and I called the artists with the charm and wit to handle themselves in interviews. Some artists could do a long set and then play to half a dozen reporters and cameras shoved in their face. Others ripped the microphones out of their hands and threw them at the sound guy. True story. We made sure the interview types were front and center.

Chandler Kaufman could for sure play to the cameras. He has that clean-cut boy-next-door look that Ezra insisted on.

"That's the bassist," she said. "Ty Boyce. He's Welsh. The accent isn't strong but still swoon-worthy."

"You're thinking the label should play up their sex appeal," I said, following where she was going.

"I don't make those decisions, but look at this crowd. It's eighty percent women. It couldn't hurt to bring the boys out from behind their instruments."

I nodded. Gwen didn't have to intern for every department like I did, all the same, I could see the head of the PR department agreeing with her. All that shipping crap could catapult a group to the top faster than their talent.

"But I'm all about the talent," I said aloud. "Let's see if they're as good as everyone says."

"Trust me," Gwen replied, "she is."

She emerged from the back on the wave of a rolling hush passing through the audience. She struck them—and me—dumb.

Glittering, fiery red hair flowed from her black beanie. The shade a perfect match for the ruby gloss on her Cupid's bow lips. As her eyes swept the crowd, she gifted each one of us a secret smile that wrinkled her sharp nose. She was the ethereal kind of gorgeous. A gorgeous that didn't seem real. If I reached out to touch her, surely my hand would pass right through.

"Thanks for coming out, everyone," she began. A low, throaty voice fell from her lips. "We're Beyond Berlin."

The screams kicked off louder than the cheers for the drummer.

"That's Serena Blackwood," said Gwen. "The band's singer and songwriter."

"Stage name?" I asked without looking away.

"Probably. But it suits her."

"We're starting off with a favorite of mine." Serena wrapped herself around the microphone stand, caressing it with long, thin fingers. "Stuck In Your Nightmare."

The band launched into the song and the world fell away. The screeching fans. Heavy cloud of smoke. Lingering scent of wings and burned barbecue sauce. All of it disappeared as Serena Blackwood sang.

Haunting.

The word Bianca used and its accuracy was frightening. It slipped through your ears and laid claim to your mind like a poltergeist. Weeks, months, years would pass, and I'd never be rid of the memory of her voice. It'd haunt me for the rest of my life.

Serena's song led the audience through the pain of love lost. Loving a man who couldn't love and experiencing a pain worse than indifference or hate—invisibility. He never saw her at all.

How could you not see Serena Blackwood?

Gwen described them well. Beyond Berlin had a good beat. People swayed on the dance floor, bobbing their heads to the tune. They gave a little something to dance to, but their lyrics had depth. Serena had something real to say.

An elbow in my gut pulled me out of my reverie.

"What do you think? Interstellar material?"

"Yes," I replied. "They're incredible."

Not just Serena. The entire band was on point. These weren't amateurs skipping notes or dropping their sticks. It was clear all we needed to do was get them in a studio and their magic would take over.

"I can't believe I've never heard of them," I breathed.

"Spend all your time in Evergreen and you'll miss a lot. Join me, Maxie, and our friends on the weekends. We're always checking out local bands."

"Can't do the over twenty-ones," I reminded. "But take video the next time you come across a group like them. We'll get them in front of Bianca sooner."

Serena wrapped up the song and transitioned straight into the next one. They did an excellent job mixing slow and upbeat, sad and heart-pounding, deep and fun. I loved every song they played, and that never happened. I was the kind of picky bastard that savagely tore apart a weak bridge.

"Good night, everyone," Serena crowed. "You've been amazing."

I rose as she jogged off the stage. Chandler took her place and talked up their website and where they'd be playing next. I made a beeline for backstage.

"Hold up." The guy that introduced them intercepted me in front of the door. "You can't go back there."

"You'll find that I can, playboy." I flashed him my card. "Jaxson Van Zandt. Interstellar Records."

His mouth fell open. "But you can't— You can't be— The band's going to freak!"

I winked. "Want to witness the glorious moment?"

The guy tore off, leaving us behind. "Ty! Serena!"

Gwen and I followed at a more dignified pace. We spotted him in time to see him dart through the door at the end.

"—believe who's here!"

We walked inside their makeshift dressing room. The space was even more cramped than my office, and made smaller by Serena's presence. She filled the entire space. Every eye was on her, even the furniture was angled to face the woman perched on the stool. But she looked back at me as Rylan dabbed her damp chest.

In a blink, her lips twisted. "Who are they? My biggest fans?" she scoffed. "Get the fuck out of here, kid. No autographs."

The guy made a choked noise, the opposite of the laugh that came from me.

"What is it about my look that screams scabby-kneed child on the playground?" I closed the distance between us. "I'm not here for your autograph, though I suspect it'll be valuable one day. I'm Jaxson and this is Gwen. We're from Interstellar Records."

Rylan stilled, eyes widening.

"Are you serious?" The voice came from behind me. "Did you just say Interstellar?"

"That's right, Chandler," said Gwen. "You guys have a minute to talk?"

"Do we? I can't believe this. Did you guys hear our set? Did you come to hear us play?" His voice rose with excitement. "This is insane."

My eyes locked with Serena. Ty, Chandler, and Rylan were buzzing. She had yet to utter a word.

"You were amazing up there," said Gwen. "I've actually been following you guys for a while. I'm excited Interstellar is offering you this opportunity."

Serena cocked her head. "What opportunity would that be?" She spoke in response to Gwen, but the question was for me.

"We'd like you to come in and record a demo," I said. "We can have you in the studio as soon as next week."

Rylan and Ty seized each other, jumping up and down and carrying on like they were going to burst into tears. Chandler's hug was for me.

"Yes, yes, yes!" he cried. "We'll be there. Thank you so—"

"No."

Rylan and Ty came down so fast they stumbled into the couch. Chandler slowly released me.

"Serena?" he said.

She stepped off her stool, green simmering pools zeroed on me. The closer she came, I noticed her glittering red hair was the result of real glitter.

"No," she repeated in my face. "We're not wasting our time recording a demo that you'll throw on a pile and never look at again. If you want Beyond Berlin, then bring us in to sign a contract."

"Serena," Chandler hissed. "What are you doing?"

"Be quiet, Chandler." She shoved him aside.

Up close, the spell of the music, lights, and hazy room faded. She was not ethereal. And if I touched her snarling mouth or the furrows between her flashing eyes, they'd be very real.

"We want a contract, tour dates, and a recorded album in the next few weeks. Not a damn demo."

"I'm afraid it doesn't work like that," I said evenly. "You're a local hit averaging two thousand views a YouTube video. You're good. Extremely good. But at this point, still a risk. We'd record the demo, run it past the manager and director, and then we can talk contracts. From what I heard tonight, you won't have a problem getting one." I held her gaze. "But we can't skip the steps."

Serena slinked into my space. It took herculean effort not to tense as she pressed herself against me. "You must not have heard me." Her hot breath tickled my skin. "Skip the steps or you can't have us."

"Serena!" Chandler burst out. "Jaxson, please. We'll do it. We're happy to record the demo."

She spun on him. "Really? How the fuck are you going to do that without me or my songs?"

"They're Interstellar Records. We can't turn them down."

"Oh, please. The days of them being the biggest name in the industry are over. Why else are their scouts sulking around shitholes like this?" I was granted the favor of her attention once more. "Isn't that right? After that cock-up a few years ago and all those albums leaked, no one wants to sign with you. Suddenly a local hit averaging two thousand views a YouTube video is worth your time, and if you want to be worth ours, you'll stop pretending like we're the risk when *you* are." She reached for me. "Got it, kid?"

I caught her wrist before her fingers touched my lips. "I'm going to need you to stop that, mama. My lady doesn't take kindly to other women putting their hands on me."

Her self-satisfied smile twitched.

"As for the rest." I shrugged. "If you don't want to record a demo, fine. I was looking forward to passing it along to Papa Van Zandt, but our demo pile is loaded with talent. He won't miss what he never heard."

"Papa?" she repeated.

"Your info is outdated," I continued like she hadn't spoken. "We took a hit and came back stronger than ever. You noticed our biggest names didn't leave us and never will. Last year, we tracked more in revenue than our leading competitors combined." I opened my hand, letting her arm flop back to her side. "We don't need you, we want you— Scratch that. We *wanted* you."

I backed away, flashing the stricken members of the band a smile. "Y'all are crazy good. I'm sure another label will pick you up... eventually."

Gwen and I left. The door swung shut behind us and still we heard Chandler, Ty, and Rylan explode.

"What the fuck did you do?!"

"Is this okay?" Gwen whispered. "Bianca said you had to get them."

"Bianca mainlines coffee, sleeps in her office, and manages an entire department. She's got zero minutes for bullshit. She doesn't want a band that thinks they're too good for the label."

"It's not the band, it's Serena." She peered over her shoulder. "I didn't know she was like this. She seems so sweet on stage."

"She's an interview type. They know how to fake it when everyone is watching."

She nudged my arm. "Forget them. Let's grab some dinner. Those wings hardly hit the spot."

"I should get home. I'm always late nowadays and the others take their chance to lure Val to their beds while I'm out of the running. Tonight I want to fall asleep with my girl."

"You're so sweet." She ruffled my hair like a damn puppy.

"We talked about that."

Laughing, Gwen tossed me the keys. "I've been drinking. You should drive."

"Thanks for the permission to drive my own car," I said with a grin. Striding through the parking lot, we parted at the hood for our sides. "Can I wipe my ass too?"

"You've got a slick comeback for everything, don't you?"

"I—"

"Wait! Jaxson, wait!" Chandler raced out of the bar. He skidded to a stop, red-faced and cheeks ballooning. "We'll do it. The d-demo. Please, we want to do it."

I arched a brow. "All of you?"

"Yes. Serena too. She acts tough like that to warn off people who want to waste our time. The four of us are going to take Beyond Berlin all the way." He stuck out his hand. "Interstellar can get us there."

I let the smile spread across my face. "Then I'll see you next week."

We shook.

ADAM'S CAROUSEL LAMP cast dancing shadows on the walls. The little boy slept peacefully, and alone.

Val's sleeping in another bed tonight.

I trudged to my room. The smell of chicken and vanilla washed over me before I registered the scene. Flickering candles shed light on the small dinner for two prepared in the middle of the room. Val found a bed to sleep in that night and it was mine. Curled up on top of the sheet, she slept soundly in a slinky outfit I would have desperately loved to get her out of.

I swallowed a curse. Rushing to the nightstand, I plugged in my dead phone and received the rush of phone calls and texts asking when I was coming home.

After Chandler caught me up, I returned to the bar to discuss details with the band and their sullen lead singer. They had so many questions and gushing excitement to heap on me, I didn't leave until well after midnight.

"I'm sorry, baby," I whispered. "It won't be like this anymore. I promise."

Chapter Two

Five Months Later

Valentina

"Okay, baby. Pick up Cara."

Adam snuggled the fat cat to his chest and flashed his missing-tooth smile at the camera. I zipped around him, the shutter going off in rapid succession. He was the most adorable thing there ever was in his uniform and backpack.

"Val, I believe five hundred pictures is enough."

I narrowed my eyes on Ryder. He, Maverick, and Ezra posted up against the wall, smiling at me like I was oh so cute.

"It's my son's first day of kindergarten. I'll take a thousand pictures if I want to."

He put his hands up in surrender. "Fine, but if we don't leave in ten minutes, he'll be late."

I checked the time. We were veering dangerously close to eight and I had my own first day of school bearing on me. "All right. I'll get him as he's walking to the car on his first day," I said, squealing. "Where's Jaxson? Tell him we're ready to go."

"Val..."

I lowered the camera. "What? What's wrong?"

Maverick and Ezra shared a look.

"Jaxson's not here," Maverick finally said. "I don't think he came home last night."

My grip tightened on the phone. "No, he said he'd be there for our first day. We're dropping Adam at Evergreen Elementary together."

They didn't say anything.

Adam nuzzled Cara's furry head, the smile there to stay. "Where's Daddy Jaxson?" he asked.

"He's coming, my love." I kissed his forehead. "Ryder will take pictures of you going to the car. Mommy will be there in a second."

"Okay."

I dialed Jaxson after they were gone. It rang and rang and rang.

"Hey, this is Jaxson. Can't come to the—"

I hung up and tried again.

"Hey, this is Jaxson. Can't—"

Shutting off his voicemail, I took a deep breath and let it out slow.

His phone must have died. It's been crazy at work, but he promised me he'd be there, so he'll be there. I know he will.

JAXSON

"Jaxson? Jaxson? Jaxson!"

I shot up and tipped off the chair. It flipped and sent me to the floor, crashing on top of me.

"Shit! Are you okay?"

Gwen lifted the table off of me and helped me to my feet. I blinked blearily at her, swaying as I tried to make sense of what was happening.

"What the hell?"

"We need you back in there, Jaxson. Serena and Gage can't agree on song choice and she won't sing a fucking word until they do."

I patted myself down, looking for my phone. I slipped away to my office for an hour nap, setting an alarm to warn me when to drag myself back. It hadn't even gone off yet. Serena couldn't give me one flipping hour.

"I thought we settled this," I replied. "We're not using all of her new material. It's not ready. And where is my phone?"

Gwen scooted the upturned table aside and retrieved my cell off the floor. "She changed her mind. She and Gage have been arguing on and off for the last three hours because she keeps storming out."

Surprise stiffened my spine. "Last three hours? What time is it?"

"Almost seven thirty."

I snatched my phone out of her hand but the clock only confirmed it. "No. No, no, no, no! I set an alarm."

"What's wrong?"

"I have to go." Grabbing my jacket, I raced out.

"But what about Serena," she shouted after me.

"I promised Val I'd be there!"

I escaped the building, dialing Val on the way. The calls went straight to voicemail.

I cursed the whole drive. Cursed myself. My phone. My job. And Beyond Berlin. Five months ago, I walked into the Taproom looking for the next big hit. I found them.

Dad loved their demo. He ordered the contract written up and put in their hands before the ink dried. Their first album we recorded and released in two months and they took off like no band I've ever witnessed.

My summer changed in a blink. Forget chasing Adam around the yard, or slathering sunblock on Val at the beach. Beyond Berlin was back in the studio recording an album of new, original tracks that they would take out on tour. A process that we thought would go as smoothly as recording their first album.

We were wrong. Why?

Serena Blackwood.

She insisted on writing all the songs herself without help or input. Any suggestion that she tweak her lyrics resulted in her yelling, throwing something, or storming out. Most times all three.

If I had my way, I wouldn't have to deal with her at all. But I didn't have my way. Serena had hers.

She would deal with no one else but me. I had to hold her hand, talk her down, listen to her new material, and sit in on every recording session. All of this was in my job description, but it wasn't supposed to be for one band. Serena changed that.

Once she confirmed my father was the owner of the label. She declared she wanted my full attention and support. Then Beyond Berlin's album blew sale expectations out of the water and she had the clout to bend Bianca into giving her what she wanted—me.

I've missed too much this summer. I promised Val I'd be there on their first day, seeing Adam off to kindergarten. I punched the dash, frustration welling up on a tide of exhaustion, anger, and something else.

Val and I haven't had sex for three fucking weeks. Letting her down again won't help me change that. I just don't get it. I set an alarm!

I bent the speed limit to the breaking point.

Seven fifty.

Val and the guys would already be at the school with Adam.

Zipping in their parking lot faster than was safe, I squealed into a parking space and tumbled out of the car.

"Sir? Sir?"

I ignored the woman in the bright orange vest and burst inside the elementary school. Bulletin boards covered in garish designs streaked past me as I searched for Adam's class.

"—good day at school, baby."

Val.

I rounded the corner and there they were. Val bent over, peppering Adam with kisses and he giggled the whole way through. I mentioned once or twice that he was in serious danger of becoming a ma-ma's boy and got whacked upside the head for my trouble.

"Adam," I called.

The little boy beamed. Every day he grew more into his mother's looks. His mop of soft curls sprouted wild and untamed, and his green eyes lit up like Christmas trees when he saw me—a consequence of him not seeing me often enough.

"Jaxson! You're here."

I knelt down, slightly out of breath, and hugged him. "Hey, little man. Didn't think I'd miss your big day, did you?"

"No," he said confidently.

"Okay, everyone." A man stepped out of the classroom, addressing those giving their kids a last goodbye. "It's time to start class."

I pressed my forehead against Adam's. "You have fun. And make sure those kids know your dads are cooler than their dads."

"I will."

"Jaxson," Val reprimanded. "Adam, be nice and have a good day."

Adam took his teacher's hand. "Bye, Mommy. Bye, Daddies."

I moved next to Val as we waved him off. "I swear I set an alarm," I said out of the corner of my mouth. "I don't know what happened."

"You almost missed Adam's first day of school is what happened." The chill coming off of her filled my bones. Oh yeah, we wouldn't be breaking the three-week dry spell tonight.

"I'm sorry, Val. I—"

"Let me guess. Serena."

I glanced to the side. Maverick, Ezra, and Ryder were pretending not to listen and therefore making it obvious that they were. I gripped Val at her crossed elbows and drew her to the side. She stared at a bulletin board collage of Adam and his classmates' names rather than look at me.

"We stayed up narrowing down the song selection for the new album," I said. "I fell asleep. I'm sorry, baby."

"That's the second time this week and the sixth time this month. I thought your dad hired another assistant. Why do you have to take on everything?"

"Because Serena—" we said at the same time.

She scoffed. "I knew it."

Red stained her porcelain cheeks. Pointed away from me, twin lily pads boiled in their milky lake. Her pink, bee-stung lips were pinched tight. Steaming mad and she was still the most beautiful creature I'd ever seen. But then, this was the picture I fell in love with. Pissed and irritated with the brash idiot who called her baby and broke into her personal space.

I laced her fingers through mine and brought them to my lips. "No Serena," I said softly. "Not tonight. I'm taking the day off and spending it with you."

Val blinked. The lines around her mouth softened. "Really? But... I have class."

"I don't care. I'll wait outside for you. We'll have lunch at that place you like on campus. We'll duck into the bathrooms to fool around, and tonight, I'll make you a dinner that will most likely taste like shit but you'll reward me anyway by sitting on my face."

"Jaxson," she hissed. "We're in an elementary school."

My second reprimand of the morning but this one came with a smile. It spurred me on.

"The munchkins are in class and these parents know what I'm talking about." I nodded at a random guy passing by. He nodded back, looking confused as he did so.

Val giggled.

"After I've eaten you out to both our satisfaction, you'll suck my cock like a lollipop," I whispered. "You don't know how cute you look with a drop of cum right"—I kissed the corner of her mouth—"here."

Chewing her lip, Val's cheeks brightened for another reason. It amazed me that in spite of the freaky shit she's gotten up to with the four of us, the sweet innocence that drew me to her when we first met hadn't faded.

"Lollipops and eating out," she said. "I think you're just hungry."

"Starved actually. I haven't eaten since lunch yesterday."

Val's smile reached inside of me and flicked the lights on. My blood thrummed in her proximity. I was awake. Alert. Alive.

"Let's get breakfast. My first class isn't until ten." She lifted my arm and burrowed beneath. "I've been dying to spend time with you, baby."

"Me too. You have no idea."

VALENTINA

Jaxson kept his promise and rode with us to the campus. The five of us parted ways at the quad.

"I'm meeting up with Austin in the student union," said Ezra.

"My macroeconomics class starts in ten minutes," Ryder said.

Maverick kissed my cheek. "I'm joining the robotics team this year. I'm going to swing by the advisor's office and get more info about it."

"And then there were two," said Jaxson.

Burying my nose in his chest, I breathed in that intoxicating spicy-sweet scent. Now that we lived together, I knew the aroma came from an imported French cologne with black pepper, vanilla, and cinnamon undertones.

"What are you in the mood for?" I tilted back and brushed my lips along his stubbly cheek. "There's a yummy bagel place that has chocolate chip muffins and good coffee."

"Sounds good."

Jaxson and I strolled hand in hand across campus, talking about nothing and everything.

"How's Sofia?"

"She's good," I replied. "Her dad is back on his feet and working again. They hired someone to manage the overseas business though."

"Is she loving the family time as much as she thought?"

I laughed. "She is. They went to England to visit her grandmother over the summer and had a blast. She and Madeline have even made weekly nail appointments a thing."

"Good for her."

Snaking my arm around his waist, I pulled him closer. "What about you, my love? How's your dad?"

"I don't think I should say..." he returned. "You get weird about my dad."

I made a choked noise. "I do *not*."

"Don't think I forgot you wanted to be my stepmother."

"That was years ago. I've done too many naughty things with you now for it not to be awkward."

"Is that the only reason?"

I poked his side. "There's also the tiny fact that I love you."

"There is that." I picked up a trace of teasing. "In that case, I can tell you he just started dating someone."

I stopped dead. "He is? Who?"

"See," Jaxson cried. "You get weird."

I saved my reaction by capturing his lips. In the middle of the walkway, people streaming around, I nibbled his bottom lip and opened him up to a fierce, tongue-tangling kiss that made hooking up in the bathroom ten times more appealing.

"Are you sure you can't miss class?" he asked.

Boy was it tempting. "Not on the first day. Even if we did, I'd have to come back to campus. We have a mandatory meeting at the Sally house."

"You should've—"

"I know." I sighed. "I should have dropped out. I still have friends in that house, Jaxson, and people—actual human beings with families and lives—were kidnapped. I have a chance to find out what's going on with Leighton, Paisley, and Reagan out of the way. I'm taking it."

"Then I'm coming with you. We're spending the day together, I'll finally get another peek inside this haunted house of horrors."

The two of us got breakfast and then went to my first class, Social Psychology. I let Jaxson join me inside, wanting to soak up as much quality time with him as possible. This was quickly revealed to be a mistake.

We grabbed seats in the front row, all the way at the end. The professor's podium was angled away. He didn't notice Jaxson or his wandering hands. Jaxson tugged my jacket out of the way and stroked my nipple through the fabric.

"Jaxson, stop." My flaming cheeks were neon lights broadcasting what we were up to. I swatted at his hands, but he didn't take my weak attempts seriously.

I forwent a bra that morning, giving him clear access to tease the little nubs into hardened points.

Legs clenching, I pushed him away. Jaxson took my hand, kissed the palm, and firmly set it on the arm of the chair. Boldly, he reached under my shirt and tweaked them with abandon.

I didn't hear a word my professor said. Class ended with me dizzy, overheated, and my panties soaked.

"On Wednesday, we'll delve deeper into the theory," said Professor Something or Other. "Read the first two chapters so we can discuss."

I seized Jaxson's collar and dragged him to the nearest bathroom. I couldn't lock the door, so a few girls overheard the moaning and grunts coming from the middle stall.

Jaxson set a furious pace, plunging his fingers in and out of me, and pressing me against the door. One hand on my shoulder, the other driving me insane, and his cock digging in my ass. I came with a hoarse cry, not caring who heard.

My knees buckled. Jaxson caught me and turned me around. He locked eyes with me as he licked my arousal from his fingers. I nearly came again on the spot.

Gripping my thighs, Jaxson lifted me onto the dispenser. My hands were working fast to pull down his pants and reach the prize inside.

Jaxson lifted my shirt, drawing it over my head and bunching it behind my neck only to bury his face in it as I stroked him. Slow and languid. Then rough jerks as groans spurred me on.

He grunted and hot, sticky spurts covered my stomach and dripped down my sex. Jaxson went boneless on top of me.

"Damn, girl. We've got to stop meeting like this."

"You say that." I wrapped my arms and legs around him, stealing a slow, tongue-tangling kiss. "But we both know you love meeting like this."

"Got me figured out, don't you, mama?"

Jaxson cleaned me up and we stumbled out to an uncomfortable look from a girl bent over the sink.

He pointed over his shoulder. My lipstick was smeared on his cheek and he had a small rip in his collar. "Pro tip. The toilet paper dispenser can hold body weight."

She pinked, scurrying out of the bathroom with her hands covered in soap.

I dragged the silly goof out, laughing my head off. Wow, I missed him. Technically he was right down the hall, but I missed him.

Jaxson followed me to Psychology of Diversity. I stopped him at the door.

"Oh no," I said. "You're waiting outside, my love. You've proven you can't behave yourself."

"I was actively trying *not* to behave myself, so I'll take that as a compliment."

I kissed him. "The class is fifty minutes. There's a table over there. Sit, finish lunch, and find a way to occupy your time."

"Oh, I'll think of something."

Jaxson walked off, grinning that grin.

My butt hit the seat and I pulled out my textbook and binder. My phone vibrated as Professor Chadwick took his place.

Jaxson: After you suck my dick, I'm bending you over and

I abruptly stopped reading. The man was incorrigible. Determined to turn my brain to mush.

My cell buzzed all through class. I resisted the urge to peek, but imagining what those texts said had Jaxson's desired effect on me anyway.

I stomped out into his waiting arms. "Finally. I scoped out the bathrooms. The one on the second floor locks."

"I'm not rewarding your wickedness... until tonight."

He groaned. "Don't be like that."

"Come on." I wrapped his arms around my waist and led him off. "You wanted to go inside the den of evil, didn't you?"

"Ooh. Yeah. Can't miss it."

We crossed campus and arrived at the Sally house twenty minutes later.

"Valentina!" Keily launched out the door.

I fell against Jaxson carrying an armful of coed.

"I missed you so much," she gushed. "This year is going to be epic. I miss Leighton and the girls, but now there won't be pledging craziness or brutal initiations. We're going to have fun." She dropped to her feet. "Come inside. Sof and I made cookies. Chocolate chip slathered in Nutella for you."

Twisting around, I arched a brow at Jaxson. *Den of evil,* I mouthed to him.

He chuckled.

"We're just waiting for all of the girls to arrive," said Keily.

Jaxson and I wandered into the living room. Sofia was there, sandwiched between Hudson and Palmer, sporting a speck of brown on her lip. A glance at the cookie plate confirmed my suspicions.

"Did you eat my cookies?" I accused.

She cracked up, half choking. "You weren't supposed to know. I'll make you some more."

Sofia and I headed to the kitchen while Jaxson and Hudson caught up. The number of people my boys were fond of was a small, exclusive group. Sofia's boyfriend managed to shoot toward the top of the list before they officially met.

"What do you think the meeting's about?" I asked.

"I know what it's about." Sofia pulled a fresh batch of cookies out of the oven. "We had our mourning period and now it's time to choose a new president."

"Seriously? Right now?"

"Not today, but someone is coming to talk to us about it." Sofia set out the cookies to cool. "We don't have a president. Reagan, our vice president, left. And the other leaders, the treasurer and recruitment chair, don't want to move up and take on more responsibility. We got away with it for one semester. Now it's time to pick new leaders."

"Hmm." I hopped up on the counter. Snagging a cookie, I bit into the warm, gooey treat. "Who do you want for president?" I asked, mouth full.

"I heard Blair's gunning for it."

"As a sophomore? Can she get it?"

She nodded. "The only ones barred are freshmen and pledges."

"President Blair," I tried out.

Sofia leaned in, lowering her voice. "Gives you the heebie-jeebies, doesn't it?"

We snorted a laugh. We liked Blair a lot more now, but the girl was still intense.

"Some of the upperclassmen sisters are thinking of running too," she said. "But I think you should do it."

"Me? Why me?"

"You want to find out what's going on around here," she said, lips barely moving. "This is your chance. You'd deal with the local organization, the alumni, the officers, and Aiden. He has to plan things with you as the brother fraternity. This would give you a chance to get close to him."

"You make a very good point, Sofia Lorraine."

"I curse my mother for telling you my full name."

"But he knows I'm Ezra's girlfriend," I continued. "He's not going to slip up around me. Aiden is too smart."

"He'll be careful, of course, but being around and talking to him might give you a better idea of who he is. Who his friends are. If he's always running out of the room to take calls. Stuff like that. And as leader of the Sallys, no one could pull shady shit on your watch. You'll know everyone and be in everything."

I nodded along. What she was saying made a lot of sense. There was only one issue.

"Why would anyone vote for me? I don't—and can't—live in the house. I'm busy with my son, school, and boyfriends. And I actively avoided the Sallys for a while. All of that doesn't scream presidential material."

"The sisters like you, Val. They know you care about them. The girls who are just looking for fun, parties, bonding, and sisterhood know you'll provide. The sisters looking for something else... something shady... need to be watched by a president who isn't in on it. Only me and you fit that description."

"Why can't you do it?"

She shook her head. "Daddy's doing better, but they're still relying on me to take on more responsibility at Honey Hair. Plus, my classes and homework take up most of my free time while Hudson takes up the bit that's left. I can't squeeze this in."

"Neither can I," I confessed, "but you're right. As president, I can find out what's going on or at least stop it from happening again. If another Sam or Sally goes missing, you better believe I'm sounding the alarm through the whole state."

Sofia slathered the spread on a cookie and passed it to me. "And no matter what, I'll be here to back you up. These girls are my friends. I want them safe too."

"Val?" Jaxson came into the kitchen. He propped himself on my knees, opening his mouth for cookies. I fed him in between sweet, chocolatey kisses. "There's something I need to show you in Sofia's room."

"Oh? Is there?"

He nodded, face grave. "Urgently."

"If you're going to have sex in my bed," Sofia deadpanned, "put a towel down or something."

"Will do," said Jaxson.

"We're not going to—" I yelped as Jaxson threw me over his shoulder.

He took off running upstairs. Swinging upside down, I cracked up. A room full of girls peeked at us taking off and I'm sure they guessed why.

Jaxson set me on Sofia's bed and climbed on top of me. I draped my arms around his shoulders, sinking into the heady haze of Jaxson Van Zandt.

"Three weeks ends now," he whispered, voice husky.

I shivered. Three weeks since we'd made love. It hardly seemed possible. We let our lives get so busy.

"Promise me it won't be like this anymore." I kissed him softly. "I've missed you."

"I promise." Jaxson's gemstone eyes caressed my face and I could almost hear him think how beautiful I was. It's what I loved about him. His eyes said more than his words, and I could read it all. "Tomorrow, I'm bringing you to the studio. I believe we have a date."

"Fooling around in your father's office," I said, grinning. "You pull out all the stops. Careful or a girl will get spoiled."

"Nothing's too good for my baby."

The room was filled with our giggling, heated whispers, and hushed moans. Our plans for a romantic dinner and candlelit end to our dry spell in his bed were quickly forgotten.

"Val, you in there?"

I froze. Jaxson didn't. He carried on sucking the little bundle of nerves between my legs.

"The meeting is starting," Blair said. "Everyone has to be there."

"C-coming," I called.

Jaxson shot me a wicked grin. "Not yet."

"Jaxson, we have to go." I tried scrambling away and he secured my legs. Jaxson wore me like a beard.

"Where do you think you're going?"

"Baby," I cried, going for stern and ruining it with a laugh. "We'll pick this up tonight."

"What are we going to pick up? This." His tongue slipped past my folds.

I bit my lip hard. If Blair was still on the other side of that door, I did not need her hearing what was going on.

"Okay. Make it quick."

"I don't do quick."

"Jaxson!" I was definitely laughing that time. "Will you work with me here?"

"I am." Lowering his head, his tongue darted in and out of me, unraveling my resolve thread by thread. Pleasure rippled through my body, beginning in my lower belly, and spreading to infuse every cell of my being. His determination to torture me didn't work out like he planned. I was so starved for him, I came within minutes, body writhing into the pillows.

We made ourselves presentable and went downstairs. Jaxson veered off to the living room with Hudson and I headed for the dining room.

"Welcome, ladies." A woman I'd never seen before stood at the head of the table, motioning for us to take a seat. Sofia pulled out the chair next to her. I sat, studying our guest.

She was older, possibly mid-forties. She wore a classy, elegant air of wealth and status, a fact I knew from my new life in Evergreen. Her pantsuit and blouse were fitted and expensive. The shimmering pearls at her throat a stylish tie-in to the cream outfit. But the most telling feature was the massive diamond ring on her finger.

"Good afternoon, girls," she began. "My name is Ophelia Kessler. I'm the founder of Kessler's Kinder Toys."

That name was familiar. Adam rode through the house in his Kessler car almost every day.

"I'm also the head of the local organization of Zeta Rho Sigma." She swept her smile over us. Ophelia was quite lovely. Streaks of gray touched her brunette hair that she accentuated instead of trying to hide. A strong dusting of freckles graced her cheeks and upturned nose.

"As you're aware," she said, "Zeta Rho Sigma and Nu Alpha Theta are not like the other Greek houses on this campus. They were formed within this school in tribute to Sally Hollenbeck, and therefore are not governed by a national organization. Instead a local organization was formed to handle big-picture details." She gestured at herself. "I'm here to step in if there are problems, but my main function has been keeping in touch with alumni and organizing alumni events. The late and wonderful Leighton Lewis handled everything else, so there wasn't need for me to do more. She will be missed."

I'm sure wherever she is, she'd be touched to hear it.

"Today, I'd like to start the process of electing a new president and vice president. I aim to keep this simple and democratic. In a week's time, we'll return here and you all will cast your vote for your choices. First things to note are you cannot join executive roles as a pledge or freshman. A fact that won't hinder us as we're suspending the intake of new sisters this semester. The pledging process is too much to handle during this transition. Next semester, if the new president feels up to it, we can see about adding Sallys to the family."

I bobbed my head. It made sense.

"Now, let's get into the duties of the president," she went on. "First and foremost, you'll be there for your sisters. Solve problems. Arrange bonding activities. Handle disciplinary actions. You will also handle financial decisions such as funding any trips you take, and you'll meet with me once a semester. Any questions?"

No one raised their hand.

"As for the vice president, you will chair executive meetings and support the president however she needs. Take your time considering which position best suits you. These are not easy roles to undertake and I don't wish for anyone to be overwhelmed by the sorority and their course load."

Blair's hand shot into the air. "Do we put our names in for consideration today?"

"Yes," replied Mrs. Kessler. "All those who wish to run for president or vice president will throw their names in the hat today, giving you a week to show your sisters why you're the best choice. Then when I return, they'll vote."

"I want to run for president," said Blair.

Mrs. Kessler put up her hands. "One moment. We'll get to that. First, I want to answer any other questions."

A few other girls raised their hands. Mrs. Kessler went through one by one explaining in depth what the duties were and how much of a commitment it would require. The next thing I knew, my hand was up too.

"Does the president have to live in the Sally house?"

"No," she said. "We don't require any of our girls to live in the house. And we've had presidents who lived off campus and managed to do an excellent job running Zeta Rho."

"Still it would make more sense if they did live in the house." Blair smiled at me. "And if they had less responsibilities outside of the Sallys."

"It is for you all to decide who the best choice is," Kessler said simply. "I have no input in that regard. But I will say this, the sudden loss of Leighton and Reagan and the state it left you in, moved me to hire a house mother for the Sallys.

"We haven't had one for years, so to those who don't know, the role of a house mother is officially to manage the house. She will keep the kitchen stocked, handle maintenance requests, coordinate room assignments, and ensure you always have the little things on hand. Unofficially, Miss Ortega will be there for you emotionally. She is a licensed therapist, and if you ever need to talk, her door will always be open. Heaven forbid we suffer another tragedy, but if we do, I want you girls to have the support you need."

I nodded. Someone like that would be nice to take more off the plate of the president. *If that's going to be me.*

"This is how we're going to do this." Kessler reached behind her and picked up two pieces of paper. "If you'd like to run for president, write your name on this sheet. If you'd like to be vice president, put your name here. I stress upon you the informality of this process. Any campaigning done over the following week is up to you. Ladies, vet your future leaders how you see fit."

Kessler handed the sheets to the girl in front of her. Sofia looked at me as it went around, silently asking me what I planned to do.

I don't have time for this. I want to know what's going on and help Sawyer and Teagan if there's still a chance to do so, but I never agreed to do it like this.

Leighton's words suddenly shot through my mind. *"I won't talk to you or anyone. How I get my information is a presidential secret. If you want to know, you'll have to take over Zeta Rho Sigma."*

My nails scraped the table as I curled my fist. I wanted to know. Not only the truth behind the disappearances, but also how Leighton discovered what she did about me.

Mai slid the paper and pen over to me. I picked it up and wrote my name without hesitation.

Valentina Blythe Moon. President of Zeta Rho Sigma.

JAXSON

"We're catching a movie tonight," said Hudson. "Want to join us?"

"We can't tonight but for sure another time. It's been a while since I hung out with Sofia." I scoffed. "It's been a while since I hung out with anyone outside of work."

My phone buzzed.

"One sec."

I got off the couch and went to the other side of the room. Papa VZ flashed on my screen.

"Yeah, Dad?"

"Where did you go? Gwen said you ran out of here and never came back."

"I had to be there for Adam's first day of school," I said.

"Shit. I forgot. How is he? Did you give him the jacket?"

It was almost ridiculous how much our families loved Adam. Dad spent his life in his office or out on the road, so he didn't get to spend much time with him. But that didn't stop him from bringing home band gear as presents for the little guy.

"Yeah. He loved it. Adam wants to know when you're coming by next to swim with him."

"We can make it happen next week. I'm taking some time off. But don't leave it to me to be his swim teacher. The kid's like a fish in water. He loves it. Put him in lessons."

"Val's nervous about it after nearly drowning. We're working on her."

"Hmm— Damn," he cursed. "That's not what I called you about. Serena refused to do anything without talking to you and finding out you left didn't help the situation. It became enough of a problem that I had to step in, but understand, son, that this is your job. You can't walk out on your artist in the middle of a crisis. At the very least, you should have told Serena you were leaving."

I gritted my teeth. Yes, I ignored every call from Serena and I didn't have a fuck ounce of guilt over it. "It wasn't a crisis. We finalized the tracks last night *and Serena agreed*. It's not my fault that she changed her mind *again* and flipped out *again*. Besides, I asked for this morning off. Bianca cleared it."

"Just the morning. You were supposed to be back hours ago. Serena shouldn't be calling me because she can't reach you."

"Just how long do I have to be her bitch?" I snapped.

"If you're too good for this job," Dad said, voice chilly. "Just let me know. I've got plenty that are happy to do it."

I swallowed a furious retort. Pissing him off wouldn't do me any favors.

"That's not what I'm saying," I said after a tense pause. "I get even less sleep than Bianca. I almost missed seeing Adam off to school, and Val's face this morning..." I let out a long breath. "I'm never home, Dad. It's starting to hurt our relationship. I took the day off to be with her."

Levi's tone softened. "Fuck if I don't know how much of our time Interstellar takes. I had to bring your scrawny tail to work with me or I never would have seen you either." He sighed. "Look, we can work something out. Gwen will pick up the slack with Beyond Berlin. I can even hire another assistant. Bianca could use more time off herself."

I shook my head though he couldn't see. "Bianca could for sure use time off, but another assistant won't help me. Neither can Gwen. Serena refuses to work with anyone else. She tells Gwen to fuck off and get me whenever she opens her mouth."

"I'll take care of it."

Dad hung up. Gushy goodbyes weren't his thing but this particular sign-off was a lot better. Serena could push pretty much everyone around. But not Dad.

"Jaxson?" The sorority sisters flooded out of the dining room. Val hooked her arm through mine and dropped her head on my shoulder. Her sweet, strawberry flavor enveloped me.

Nope. I gave zero fucks about ignoring Serena.

"Ready to go?" she asked.

"Yes."

We said goodbye to Sofia, Hudson, and her friends. Then we made for the car.

"In the mood for anything special for dinner?"

She hummed. "Maybe... something delicious, but easy enough to make with Adam. It's been a while since the three of us cooked together. I know he'd love it."

"We'll make quesadillas again. Just the three of us." I pulled Val closer. We walked a noisy path through Greek Row, passing students lazing about on the front lawn, and shouting at each other across the street. "And then afterward, it's just the two of us."

"Before I forget, there's something I have to tell you."

"What's up?"

Val flashed me a sheepish smile. "I'm running for president of Zeta Rho Sigma."

Chapter Three

Valentina

"I don't understand how you went from dropping out of the sorority to becoming its freaking president."

"Jaxson," I whispered. I cut eyes to Adam over his shoulder.

The five-year-old happily stirred the quesadilla filling, oblivious to our conversation.

"I explained this to you in the car." I took his hand and moved us to the other side of the island. "This is my chance to learn more about the Sallys, Leighton, and how she dug up all that dirt on us. From what I've heard, they've been doing their little cult initiation to the new sisters for years. The president finds out all their secrets somehow, and if I'm president, I can discover who passes it on." I peeked at Adam, lowering my voice. "It might be the people Leighton called that night. Her *friends*."

Jaxson grasped my chin and gently turned me to face him. "Your plan is to take the head psycho's place, so the mysterious people who covered up a murder for her will seek you out. Baby, if this Leighton girl is still alive, don't you think she'd warn them about you and your possible ulterior motives?"

My jaw worked. *That's a good point.*

"It's still a win if she does," I settled on. "I'm *not* doing that initiation to pledges and if no one comes to me and reveals the supposed secrets of Zeta Rho, the girls can have a safe, normal year. It's worth it to protect my friends."

"How will you have time for any of that, Val?"

I pressed my cheek to his chest, listening to his heart beat beneath my ear. "I'll make time."

"Mommy, I'm finished."

When I faced my son, my smile was firmly in place. "Perfect, baby. Now Jaxson will melt the cheese and make us some yumminess."

The Sallys, Sams, and implications for the coming year haunted us like a specter, demanding we finish our argument. We ignored it and focused our night on reclaiming weeks of quality time for the three of us.

Jaxson danced in front of the stove, throwing cheese, beans, tomato, and corn in the pan like a magician performing a trick. Adam sat on the countertop, laughing his head off while I rested my chin on his shoulder, not holding back my chuckles as well.

We wanted it to be the three of us, but at some point, Ryder, Maverick, and Ezra strolled in, enjoying the show. Ezra whipped up a salad, Maverick poured drinks, and Ryder set the table for four, not six.

"Good night, Adam." I dropped a kiss on his forehead. "Be good for your daddies, and go to bed on time."

"Nite, Mommy."

Jaxson picked up our food in one hand and held mine with the other. We walked upstairs, drifting closer with every step.

"It's not the most romantic meal," he said. "But I promise the rest of the night will be."

I nipped his shoulder. "What are you talking about? The food is perfect. Making it together was perfect. The entire day has been perfect."

"You should expect more of me, Valentina," he whispered. "Because you deserve more. You deserve the world."

Stopping in front of our bedroom, I rose on tiptoe and brushed my lips on his scruffy jawline. The rough, prickling sensation the opposite of my smooth gentle touch. That's what Jaxson and I were: opposites.

He was passion, spontaneity, living in the moment, and worrying about consequences later. I was planning, caution, and thinking about every step before I made it. I shouldn't have fallen for the brash, arrogant jerk who claimed me his the second he met me, but here we were.

"I don't want the world, Jaxson Van Zandt. I want you."

Jaxson moved, pressing me back into our bedroom. Eagerness hummed through my veins, making my knees shake. I lost count of how many times we'd been together, and yet nerves still fluttered in my stomach every time.

He led me to the bed, gifted me a teasing kiss, and then went to work setting up our dinner.

The staff put a small table for two in our bedroom due to his crazy schedule. Easier to bring up a tray for him to get to when he could than to hope he'd make it to the dining room. I thought of that as he set the table and lit candles.

"Is it okay that you took the day off?"

"Define okay," he said with a chuckle. "I'm a grunt working a simple position in A and R but I'm gone one day and they act like the place will collapse without me." He stopped to look at me. "But I'd rather be with you."

I lay on my back, peering at him through my lashes. "Is it your boss having a meltdown... or Serena Blackwood?"

He sighed. "It's my job to get Beyond Berlin's new album recorded, no matter how much abuse I take in the process. Serena believes everyone at the label is there to serve her and I'm chief servant."

I didn't say anything. I never met the woman, but over the last few months, each text Jaxson sent me saying he'd be home late, or he had to cancel plans, included her name.

"But let's not talk about her." Sweeping out his hands, Jaxson bowed. "Dinner is served, my lady."

It was quesadillas, fizzy soda, and candles in our bedroom, but I loved it more than if he took me to a five-star restaurant.

"No clothes at the dinner table."

Especially because that wouldn't fly in a five-star restaurant.

We stripped each other in the heat of whispered nothings and giggles. Jaxson set me on his lap and buried his face between my breasts.

"I'm home," came his muffled voice.

I laughed. "I thought there was another part of me you called your home."

"There is and we're going to get *thoroughly* reacquainted tonight." He raised his head to treat me to waggling eyebrows. "Three weeks. We have a lot of time to make up for."

"I don't think we can cram three weeks of sex into one night," I said, smiling. "But if you really want to try..."

I shrieked as he flipped me back, dangling me off his lap. "That's the spirit, baby." Jaxson attacked me with nipping, growling kisses on my breasts and stomach. I squealed as my ticklishness battled my arousal. He was the master of making me laugh and turning me on at the same time.

I rolled off, a short-lived escape, and hopped on his lap, straddling him. I fed him bites of gooey, cheesy quesadilla and then tasted it on his lips.

Jaxson's fingers dug into my waist. He rocked me back and forth on him, grinding on his length. Pressed against that bundle of nerves, shudders rippled through me with every rock, pulling breathy cries out of me.

Definitely couldn't do this at a restaurant.

"Shit, Val," he breathed. His grip tightened. There'd be delicious reminders of our night marking my body in the morning. "We can finish this later, can't we?"

"Yes, we— Ah!"

Jaxson raced us to the bed. He threw me down and then flung himself on top of me. Looking down at me, our gaze connected in a spark of electricity that kicked my pulse into gear. Jaxson gazed at me like he was capturing the curves of my lips, lines of my cheekbones, and the fine hairs of my lashes to memory.

"You're so beautiful," he whispered. "I love you."

"I love you too."

Wrapping my arms around his neck, I drew him down. Jaxson caught my lip between his teeth, pulling me to meet him. Our mouths met in a rough fiery clash, tinged with the sweet, tangy flavor of imported green apple soda made with real sugar. I swore I tasted that sugar on his tongue. I wanted more. I wanted the far reaches of my body filled with the sugary sweetness of Jaxson.

He smiled. "Any requests?"

"Ohh," I replied. "How about something with a beat?"

"Coming right up."

He rolled off and reached for the remote on the nightstand. The room was soon filled with the heart-pounding melodies of Vibes Taranto. Jaxson and I had quite a few things that were just ours. One of them was playing music while we made love.

"How's th—"

I shoved him on the pillows and climbed on top of him. I was very glad we took care of the undressing earlier. Running my hands up his torso, I delighted in the hard muscle beneath my fingers.

And he's all mine.

My favorite Vibes song, *Dancehall Daze,* came on next. I could never resist dancing to this song and this time was no different. I gyrated, hair whipping across my face.

"Mmm," I moaned. "I love this song, baby. Want to dance with me?"

A wicked grin stole over his face. "You know I like to give my girl what she wants, but you're not on top tonight."

The bedpost whirled as he changed our positions. He swallowed my yelp of surprise with a kiss and then my second cry as he slipped a finger inside of me.

He broke away, dropping soft kisses down my jaw to my throat. Jaxson found his favorite sensitive spot and sucked. Goose bumps rippled over my heated skin. The music, his peppery expensive scent covering the sheets, and the fingers plunging in and out of me. I was transported to a world where nothing else existed but Jaxson.

He continued his journey to my breasts. "Hello, ladies. I'm back."

Amusement and arousal clouded my mind. I couldn't choose between a chuckle or a moan, so I went with both. Arching my back, my nipples rose to meet him and he greeted them in kind. A soft hiss escaped as his mouth closed over me.

Jaxson played with the helpless little nubs, swirling his tongue around them until I almost bit through my lip. My lower belly coiled in mounting pleasure. But I wasn't there yet. He wasn't hitting the spot I needed him to hit. Or rubbing the place that drove me wild. Most nights I wanted to drag out every tantalizing act. This wasn't one of them.

"Jaxson," I cried. "Please."

His response was to move over to the other breast. I nearly screamed in dizzying frustration.

"P-please," I gasped.

"Please what?"

"Make love to me."

Raising his head, I was gifted that smirk. "I've also got three weeks of foreplay to make up for."

I grabbed a pillow and smacked him square in the face.

"Ow," he cried. Jaxson pounced on me, wrestling me into the sheets.

Giggling, I flailed like I wasn't enjoying every minute and hit him again.

Jaxson tugged the pillow from me, flinging it across the room. "You're so damn bossy," he growled. Strong arms snaked around my waist and we both flew up. "But fuck, is it sexy."

He pressed me to his slick chest. We were both hot. Sweaty. Facing each other on bended knees.

I slid down his body, gazing into those darkened sapphire eyes, as I pushed down, down, down until he was as deep inside of me as he could be.

Nails digging into his back, his curved lips blurred. My eyes crossed, preventing me from seeing him, but I felt him. In and all around me. Filling my pores. Occupying my mind. Penetrating my soul.

"Did you say something about dancing?" I heard. His hands moved up my arms, gently pulled them away, and then laced our fingers. "Dance with me, Val."

A new song came on. One I didn't know, but the bass reverberated in my bones. I moved as I normally would to a Vibes song, wining my hips, and pleasure wracked me to the tune of our fevered cries.

Jaxson met my dips with his thrusts. I said once I'd never been so in sync with a dance partner than the first night Jaxson and I danced.

That's what he was. My partner. My love. My Jaxson.

Pressure mounting in my core, I squeezed his hands tighter. He twisted them behind my back and drew me closer still.

"First one of the night." His breath ghosted over my cheek. "I want to taste it."

I bounced on the balls of my feet, moving faster, and our lips met in a kiss that was surprisingly gentle.

Connected mind, body, and soul, the sensations thrilling my body reached the pinnacle. I hit my absolute limit and then he pushed me farther, he struck that spot again and we came together, crashing down to the final melody of our new favorite song.

I collapsed onto the comforter, bringing him with me. Jaxson nestled between my breasts, looking enormously pleased with life. I brushed his damp locks from his forehead, delighting in the feel of him on my skin.

"Do you think it was that good because we waited so long?"

"Yes," he said. Jaxson darted up and landed a kiss on my fingertips. "But we're never doing it again."

"No arguments here. I'm ready for round two, three, and four whenever you are."

"Oh, that's coming soon at a bed near you. But first"—Jaxson held out his hand—"come with me."

"Where are we going?"

"Not far."

We slipped off the bed and padded across the room. Jaxson eased open the door to the balcony.

Our balcony didn't have a lot going on. It looked out over the expanse of the lawn and then on into the forest. A quiet, peaceful space that we didn't take advantage of by putting out chairs to enjoy the sunset.

Jaxson raised his hand and I noticed the remote for the first time. Suddenly, Vibes was gone and a slow, soft melody floated out into the night.

We didn't have much on our balcony, which made it perfect as a dance floor.

"One more dance?" he asked.

My arms slipped under his, resting on his back, as I buried my face in his neck. Nothing could have made this moment more incredible.

Jaxson placed one hand on the small of my back and the other cupped my head. A playful, teasing wind cooled the sweat on our bodies, but it wasn't a cold night. I felt warm and comfortable just for being in his arms.

Back and forth we swayed on the bare granite. I smiled into his neck.

"You never told me you slow danced," I whispered. "You've been holding out on me."

I felt his chuckle on my lips. "I can't give away all my secrets."

Jaxson brushed my hair away and pressed his mouth to my ear. Softly he sang to me—loving, beautiful lyrics about being with the one you love until the world ended and after.

I was wrong. This night could be more incredible.

JAXSON

"What time should I get you?"

"My modern dance class gets out at three," said Val. "I'll head over to the Sally house to do some campaigning and you can pick me up there."

"Sounds good, baby. I'll take you around the department and show off the broom closet I work in."

She laughed. "Will I get to meet anyone? Your boss? Gwen?"

"You can meet them all. I'll even introduce you to whoever's recording today."

"Really? That would be amazing."

The excitement in her voice made me out-of-control happy, and a little smug.

"You can't listen to them sing a word, but there's no rules against saying hi."

Her squeal pierced my ear. "Forget campaigning. Pick me up after my class gets out. I love you. Bye."

"Love you too."

I hung up and shoved the phone into my pocket. Gwen looked at me over the rim of her hot cocoa.

The two of us were at the café picking up Bianca's, Dad's, and Daniel's orders. Gwen came along to make sure I didn't *forget* anything. We stopped to indulge in a treat of our own.

"Want half of my burrito?" I offered. For some reason, I was craving Mexican.

"Don't mind if I do." Gwen helped herself. "So who do you have to get?"

I reclined in my seat, basking in a rare chill minute. "Val. She's stopping by the label today."

"Ah yes, Valentina Moon," she said wistfully. "A lady oft spoken about but never seen."

Chuckling, I tossed my napkin at her. It bounced off her left cheek. She retaliated by whapping me under the table. We busted up.

I liked Gwen. If I thought about it, I might have said I liked her a lot. She was cool, fun, and into music. All the makings of someone I could call friend if that was something I did easily.

I made friends years ago. Real ones. The kind that died for you. The kind that killed for you. Stacked up against that, other relationships seemed a cheap waste of time. But not Gwen. Maybe.

"The legends and stories are true," I said. "The great and beautiful Valentina Moon does exist and will grace us all with her presence this afternoon."

"I can't wait to meet her." A grin stole over her face. "I'm sure Serena will love her too."

I groaned. "We're keeping those two far apart. Matter of fact, I'm recruiting you for interference. Val doesn't mess around. I may have to endure being Serena's bitch in silence, but Val won't watch that shit quietly."

Gwen scrunched up her face. "Serena might behave herself. She's an interview type. She knows when to put on a show."

"But just in case, you have my back?" I put up my hand.

"I have your back, J."

We shook like spies walking into a potentially fatal mission.

"While we're talking about the great and beautiful Valentina Moon," Gwen began. "Can I ask how it... you know... works with the five of you? Devastatingly, you insist you're not with the boys too—"

"Dammit, Gwen." I yanked on my collar, pointing at a spot on my neck. "See that? That right there? That's the rash I get whenever I sense you fantasizing about me and my boys. They're basically my brothers. It's all kinds of wrong."

Gwen laughed so hard, cocoa dribbled down her chin. "That's a hickey, perv," she retorted. "And fine. I'm sorry. But that gives me more questions. You and your brothers are cool with dating the same girl?"

I shrugged. "We didn't grow up thinking we'd be living and making babies with the same woman. Nah. But a lot of stuff went down between us in high school and it kind of worked out this way. I've got regrets but not about where Val and I ended up."

Dropping her eyes, Gwen gazed into the depths of her chocolatey drink. "Still... don't you ever wish it could just be the two of you? Building a life and future that's yours." She twirled her stirrer with her fingertip, eyes growing unfocused. "I could never share Maxie. My love for him consumes me. It's like that feeling when you're hiding a good secret. It's all you can think about, and you're bursting to share it with everyone. And randomly throughout the day, you smile thinking of it— of him." She met my eyes. "You know what I mean?"

I found myself nodding. "Yeah, mama. I know that one."

"It's the best fucking feeling in the world," she breathed. "One I could only feel for him. And it'd kill me if he didn't feel the same. I want to be the only secret he carries."

"And you are," I said lightly. "You and Max have something solid."

Red stained her cheeks. "Don't you want that too? Don't you deserve it?"

I was quiet for so long, Gwen went back to her drink.

"I deserve a lot of things," I finally replied. "Valentina isn't one of them. It's hard for people to understand, but I'm happy exactly how things are. I've got a beautiful girl, great kid, and good friends. I don't need much more than that."

She cracked a smile. "Except for a new Ferrari and the biggest record label in the country."

"Except for that."

We laughed, breaking the tension.

"Sorry if I overstepped," said Gwen.

I waved that away. "Nah. You were nice about it. You should have heard my dad."

Gwen hissed. "I can imagine."

"He just had *a lot* of questions. It's a good thing Val's studying to be a therapist. We're going to be working through that conversation for a long time."

Gwen and I wrapped it up and returned to the studio with the food. Bianca cried real tears seeing me stroll in with coffee in hand. I used the rest of the workday listening to demos, handling little tasks for her, and reviewing Serena's new lyrics.

I was technically done for the day when I rolled up on campus to pick up Valentina.

Sliding inside, she leaned over to kiss me.

"I'm so excited," she said. "Will your dad be there too?"

"Why is it the first thing you do is ask for my dad?"

She shoved my shoulder. "The first thing I did was kiss you, silly. I just want to say hi."

"Then, yes. He's up in his tower, basking in his greatness. We'll run up there and then I'll take you to Bianca."

"Can't wait. I've got to meet the second most important woman in your life."

I laughed. "I wouldn't call Bianca that."

"I meant Serena Blackwood."

My laughter died a fiery death. Valentina's calm tone gave nothing away, which was reason enough to worry.

Clearing my throat, I replied, "Serena is not the second, third, or fiftieth most important woman in my life. She's talent I'm managing to prove to Dad I can handle this job. Nothing more. Besides, she won't be around today."

"If she is, I'd like to meet her," she said, tone light.

"All right," I said aloud.

Nope, no, and hell no. I want to spend another fun day with my girl and no Beyond Berlin in sight.

I'm lucky I've got Gwen on deck. She'll be needed big-time.

VALENTINA

Levi rose from his desk, arms open. "There she is. Get over here, baby girl."

I dropped Jaxson's hand and ran into his hug. After spending more than five minutes with him, I learned where Jaxson picked up the "baby" thing.

"How's my college girl?"

"Good." I was cheesing harder than necessary but I couldn't help it. This man had met more music legends in person that I had seen on television. Being in his air was almost like being in theirs. "I started my dance minor this year, and this semester I'm taking a dance therapy class. I had so much fun today. I finally feel like a normal college student."

"Good to hear. You had a rough one last year."

Hands gripped my waist and tugged me free of Levi.

"How are you?" I asked. "Jaxson says you have a new girlfriend."

A rich, full laugh rolled out of his chest. "Jaxson's all messed up over you, he's got everyone paired off. Eve is just a friend."

"I found your friend's panties stuck in the sofa last week," Jaxson said.

A smirk so like Jaxson's curled his lips that I had a vision of my love at his age. Tall, smooth, distinguished. Devilishly handsome.

"A very good friend," corrected Levi. "But to answer your question, I can't complain. The label's going strong and it's looking like when the time comes, I'll be able to leave it in good hands." Levi ruffled Jaxson's hair. He hated that but didn't stop him.

I was proud of Jaxson. He wanted this and he was working hard for it when many in his situation would be content to sit back and have it handed to them.

"I'm taking Val to the broom closet you stuck me in," he said. "Showing her my deplorable working conditions, and calculating how much we'll get out of your ass when we sue."

Levi laughed out loud. "Sic that lawyer on me, J. I look like I'm shaking? You ain't leaving that closet anytime soon."

I watched their exchange in amused silence. Mom and I had an odd relationship but we didn't come close to these two. I kept waiting for Jaxson to admit Levi was his fun, kooky uncle, not his dad. Then I remembered a raging Levi dragging Jaxson out by the ear and the dad instincts showed themselves.

Levi turned a charming smile on me. "Glad to see you, Val. You two have fun with the rest of your day."

"We will." I stepped toward him, arms out, and was swiftly intercepted by Jaxson.

"That's enough hugging." He wrapped my arms around him instead and led me out. "Papa VZ, look after my future empire. I'll catch you later."

In the elevator, I snuggled into his side. "Does your broom closet at least have a lock?"

"Oh ho," he crowed. "Just what are you thinking?"

I snuck my hand under his shirt, stroking just above the band of his jeans. "You know what I'm thinking."

"Shit. You can meet Bianca later."

The elevator dinged and Jaxson was out and running before the doors were all the way open. Holding back my laugh, I ran after him, passing the glinting wall of records for Jaxson's private space.

Years ago, he brought me here on our first date and I took the first true step in letting someone into my heart. I would have had sex with him that night. Given myself to him completely. I loved that all this time, after drama, danger, living together, and falling even deeper for him than I knew possible, we were finishing what we started that night.

Jaxson and I rounded a corner and skidded to a stop.

A red-haired beauty stood in front of the only door in the tight corner. Nose wrinkling, she planted her hands on her hips.

"There you are," she snapped. "You were supposed to go over my new lyrics and tell me what you thought."

Jaxson drew me behind him. A protective gesture that I wondered if he registered.

"Yes, Serena, and I said I'd let you know *tomorrow*."

Serena.

I peeked over Jaxson's shoulder. Well, I wanted to meet her. Didn't know it would be this soon.

She scoffed. "How long does it take to read five pieces of paper? I'm sick of waiting, J. I revised the bridge and changed the chorus of *Epik*. I want those songs on the album."

"The revisions were great," he said. "But we'll get into it tomorrow 'cause I'm not really here. I just came by to introduce my girl to the people I work with." Jaxson put his arm around my waist and stepped to the side. Emerald eyes honed in on me. "Serena, this is Val. Val, this is Serena."

"Nice to meet you," I said.

The ticked-off expression vanished so quickly I might have imagined it. Serena lit up. "Oh my gosh. You're Val? Hi!" She bypassed my hand and went in for the full hug. Her hair and a cloud of Chanel perfume smacked me in the face.

"You're even prettier than J described," she said.

"Thank you."

"I can't believe he waited this long to bring you around," she said, dropping her arms. "We were starting to think he made you up."

I smiled. "I'm very real."

Serena placed her hand on Jaxson's arm. "J, have you brought her to meet Bianca yet? Oh, Bianca's the head of the department," she explained to me.

"I know who she is. We're on our way to meet her." I gave Jaxson a little tug and he fell out of her reach. "Good seeing you, Serena."

We turned back the way we came, our closet/office romp on hold.

"Ooh, I'll come with you."

Jaxson bumped into me with the force of the sudden addition on his arm.

"My band's in the studio," she said. Serena grinned at me across his chest. "You can meet the other members while I try to get this mysterious boyfriend of yours to tell me what's going on in his head." She playfully knocked on his forehead. "I know you liked *Epik*. We stayed up all night thinking up that song together."

My hold on him constricted.

"I'm off the clock." He slipped his arm out of hers. "And Val and I are chilling together. Alone. We'll figure the album out tomorrow, mama."

"Isn't it adorable how he calls his favorite women 'mama.'" She cocked her head at me. "Does he call you that, Val?"

I bristled. *What the fuck is this girl's problem?*

I opened my mouth to ask her directly. "What the—"

"I've got many nicknames for my lady," said Jaxson smoothly. "A few of them not meant for innocent ears."

"I'm hardly innocent," she replied, smiling away. She grabbed his hand. "Come on. Everyone's in studio four."

She ran off, trying to drag him along, but he shook her loose again. "We'll catch up."

Shrugging, she kept going and finally left us alone.

"So that's Serena Blackwood," I said lightly.

"I know. She's a lot."

Irritation battered my good mood. I didn't consider myself a jealous person. Why should I be when I trusted my guys absolutely? All the same, watching another girl paw their boyfriend would stretch anyone to the limit.

"Does she always hang off you like that?"

Jaxson pulled up short. "What? No." He took my face in his hands. "She was just playing nice, interview-type style. Trust me, baby. The woman yelling at me for not living according to her schedule is the real Serena Blackwood."

"Alright," I said. "Let's enjoy the rest of our time. I believe you were going to show me your office...?"

Jaxson spun us around and ran back the way we came.

His office truly was tiny, but we made good use of the chair, floor, and the top of the fridge. A delicious afternoon treat and then we lazily strolled through the department, greeting friendly faces on the way.

"This is Bianca's office," he said. "She's usually in there answering calls and grabbing a quick bite at this time."

"Then we shouldn't disturb her," I replied, slowing down.

"Nah. It's cool." Jaxson flung open the door.

Two women looked up from their seats. The older, tough-looking lady behind the desk I pegged as Bianca. The slight blonde woman tickled my memory.

"Gwen," Jaxson said.

Oh, that's Gwen. Jaxson talks about her all the time.

"Hey, Bianca. This is Val."

"Val." Bianca got up to hug me. She whistled. "You're a damn knockout, girl. How'd this guy manage to score you?"

"You kidding?" asked Jaxson. He strutted across the room, hips swaying, and finished with a spin. "She couldn't resist this."

I laughed. "As bad as it is to encourage him, it's true. I couldn't."

Jaxson flashed them an insufferably smug smile. "See."

"Stop feeling yourself and finish introductions," said Bianca.

"Right. My bad." Jaxson gestured at the blonde vision in jeans and a purple tank top. "This is my girl, Gwen. She does all the work I don't want to do."

"Nice to meet you," said Gwen. "But don't believe him. Your boyfriend works hard. Did you just get here? I'll come with you around the place. You have to see the art department."

"We're going there next. Val's never seen it. But we've been in A and R for a while, and already ran into a few people."

Gwen winced. For some reason, she mouthed "sorry" to Jaxson. "I was stuck in legal," she told him. "Mr. Meyer needed me to help his secretary reorganize the files."

"No worries."

"Before you head down, take these," said Bianca. She shoved a stack of demos on Gwen. "Now, get going. I'm sneaking in a couch nap before my conference call."

We followed Gwen out, ready for the next part of the tour.

"I'm so glad you're here, baby," he whispered in my ear. "I missed you."

I leaned against his shoulder. "I missed you too."

THE NEXT DAY, THE END of my final class saw me in the Sally house. Mai, Keily, Palmer, and I made ourselves at home in Sofia's room. Mai, Keily, and Sofia lay lengthways on Sofia's bed. Palmer sat on top of her dresser, riffling through the drawers.

Palmer tossed me a mini chocolate bar from Sofia's stash. "So why should we vote for you, Val?"

"Palmer," Mai scolded. "Of course, we're voting for Val."

"Well, duh, but she's got to have her spiel ready for when the other sisters ask," she replied. "Val's going up against Blair, a legacy, and Heather, Crista, and Eliana, all juniors. She needs to wow them."

"I don't know how I'll manage wow," I said from Sofia's window seat. "All I can do is tell them the truth. If I become president, we'll be living the easy life. No more early morning death marches. An end to boot camps. No twisted cult initiation."

"By that she means no more exercising or obstacle courses," said Sofia. "The last one I don't have to translate."

The girls glanced away.

"I'd vote for that," whispered Palmer. "I wish I knew how Leighton found out those things. She said she got it from me but that's bullshit. Unless she tapped my phone or something."

Sofia and I shared a look.

"We have no idea how she dug up that information," I said. "Private family stuff to corporate secrets. It shouldn't be possible which makes me think less than legal methods were used. One thing I can promise is I'll never put the pledges or anyone else through it. They called it a test of loyalty but it was cruel plain and simple.

"Sororities are supposed to be fun. A group of women sharing memories, building friendships, being there for each other, and carving out a community on this big campus. If I become president, that's what the Sallys will be about again."

Palmer grinned. "Now that's wow."

"You'll win over a lot of sisters," agreed Mai. "But what if you run into a few who want to stick with *tradition*? They all had to go through the initiation. They might be happy to let it keep going in the name of proving trust and loyalty."

I shrugged. "Then they'll have to vote for someone else. I won't do it."

"Knock, knock," a voice rang out. We looked toward the door as Blair walked in. "What's going on in here?"

"Val's telling us why she wants to be president," said Mai.

"Then I should be here too." Blair hopped on Mai's and Keily's backs, making them laugh. She could be fun when she was ready. "What do you got, Val?"

"My platform is fun, light sisterhood bonding," I teased. "The sisters in this sorority work hard and play hard—which is great. But it's possible to take it too far. If I become president, I'll turn it down a few notches."

"Meaning what?" she asked. "Leighton didn't just go around making things up to suit her. She followed the charter like she was supposed to."

"Bonding activities, maintaining our grades, and putting up with the Nu Alpha Thetas is in our charter," I replied. "Our little initiation ceremony isn't."

Blair pressed her lips together. None of us had spoken to her about that night and what was revealed. Blair didn't even speak up to deny it. Discovering she'd been carrying on an affair with her friend's father as far back to it being illegal wasn't something you brought up at the Sally movie night. We may have liked each other better now, but Blair and I weren't close.

"Certainly a surprise," she said tightly. "My mother could have warned me, but didn't. She said it's a test of a sister's mettle and one we must face unprepared. It's awful, but everyone goes through it. The older sisters might not go for someone coming in and changing everything the Sallys are built on."

"The sisters will vote for whoever they're going to vote for," I said. "If they don't want me or my changes, it's their choice." I put up my hands and Sofia tossed me a blanket. I snuggled in, getting comfortable. "What about you, Blair? Why do you want to be president?"

"My mother was president of the Sallys."

"No kidding?" asked Palmer. "I didn't know that."

"She was." Blair bunched up between Mai and Keily, facing me like the other girls. "Mom told me they were the best years of her life. She made a difference in her sisters' lives and they made one in hers. I believe I can do good for the Sallys. Get us back to where we were."

"Would you put the pledges through the test of loyalty if you were president?" Sofia asked bluntly.

Blair's expression remained neutral. "I don't think it's up to us, to be honest."

Keily spoke up. "What does that mean?"

"You guys were there the other day with Mrs. Kessler. We answer to people above us."

I nodded. *She might be right about that.*

"The initiation aside," said Sofia. "What else would you do?"

"Exercising and promoting healthy living is in the charter, but I wouldn't confine it to running and jumping jacks," replied Blair. "We could do yoga or Pilates. We could host cooking nights where we pick a healthy recipe and learn to make it together. Zeta Rho Sigma is about us growing together. That's how my mom described it. It's how I want it to be again."

"Sounds great, Blair," I said. "Really. Seems like either one of us would make a great president."

"But do either one of you honestly think you have a chance?" asked Palmer. "We're still newbies. One of the older sisters are locked to win."

"That's what we'll play on," I replied. "The older sisters will keep Zeta Rho the same. But Blair and I will make changes that benefit everyone. We're giving the Sallys a makeover. Right, Blair?"

Blair appeared hesitant for a moment, like she was looking for the trick in my words, then she smiled. "Yes, exactly. The upperclassmen are the old. Valentina and I are the new. I'm sure more sisters will go for it than you think."

Mai raised her hand. "You've already got me. So what does a sorority presidential campaign involve?"

Sofia was quick to answer. "It involves a six-hour Netflix binge and then Val and Blair making dinner for the sisters to get them all in one room and share why they're best for the house."

"Hmm. That's a good idea, Sof," I said. "But did part of you come up with it because you don't feel like making dinner tonight?"

"You're just a better cook than me, Val. I've accepted it and I'm happy to let you take over feeding me."

The girls cracked up.

"I want that chicken thing you made last time. With the peppers," Mai threw in.

"Yeah, yeah," I muttered. "I heard something about a Netflix binge."

We messed around for the rest of the day, and then Sofia sent me off to the kitchen to win some votes. As always, the smell of my cooking lured my sisters in like bees to the hive.

The Sallys encouraged a healthy diet by keeping the kitchen stocked with organic veggies, leafy greens, beans, lean meats, and fruits. Whenever we were low, the sister charged with the task bought more with money from the treasury.

It was all our food since our dues paid for it, but it didn't come with a chef and a fair amount of the girls didn't cook. Coming in and filling their hungry bellies with home-cooked deliciousness was sure to win me some love.

"Val, can you pass me the salt?" asked Blair.

Me and Blair, I corrected. What does this mean? Are we working together or against each other? *I like her ideas and actually think she'd make a good president. But I have to win if I'm going to find out what's going on around here.*

"Sure, Blair."

Hannah, one of the juniors, pulled up a stool at the island. She rubbed her hands together. "What are you making us tonight, Val?"

"I've got a request for chicken parm stuffed peppers."

"I'll have an order of that."

I laughed. "In exchange, hear our spiel for why we're best for Sally house?"

"The least I can do."

I couldn't say how well it was going, but at one point, the other candidates wandered in and non-subtly threw themselves in the ring. It started off a real discussion about what the Sallys wanted Zeta Rho Sigma to be going forward.

"Don't get me wrong," said Faith, a sophomore. "Leighton was a great president and she made sure we had a lot of fun too. It's just sometimes I felt like I was on a drill team."

"It's one of the duties as president," said Heather, one of the other candidates. We were all in the dining room, munching on my creations and sipping lemonade. "We have to implement an exercise routine for the sisters." She cut eyes to me. "Anyone who promises otherwise is saying they'll go against the charter."

"But three-mile runs, backyard drills, and weight-lifting?" I replied. "Plus, a military-style obstacle course for a spring break trip when a friendly game of basketball would have been just as good." I nudged Blair. "Tell them your ideas."

Blaire didn't hesitate. "We could do yoga or play sports like Val said. We can run, jog, and walk. There are fun workout classes held in the gym that we could take together. We're not talking about throwing away the charter," said Blair, gesturing at both of us. "Just getting creative with it."

"We can't get creative."

"Why?" This was asked by me, Blair, and half a dozen other girls.

Heather sank back in her seat, forehead wrinkling. "Because..."

Eliana jumped in when she trailed off. "Because the Sallys who came before us put up with weight-lifting and obstacle courses and came out just fine. Are we saying we can't handle it?"

"We're asking why we have to," Sofia cut in. "Of course we can do the extra volunteer hours, maintain the minimum grade point average, and train like army recruits, but we have to ask ourselves what the Sallys are about and how these things are getting us where we want to be. If the goal is promoting healthy habits or education, there are plenty of ways we can do that *and* have fun. Isn't there a middle option between the path of most resistance and the least?"

It was a strong, lively debate. We went back and forth until the plates were clean and every last drop was drunk. By the time we called it quits, there were two distinct camps, one for the old and one for the new, but each side was willing to say the other made good points.

"Night, Sof." I kissed her cheek at the bottom of the stairs. "See you tomorrow. Let's grab lunch before my modern dance class."

She nodded. "Night."

I made it out of the door and down the porch before I heard someone call my name.

"Val." Blair jogged out of the house. "Hold up."

"What's up?"

"I wanted to say thanks for in there. Backing me up and supporting my ideas. You didn't have to do that. And I didn't have to act like a bitch when you first said you wanted to run." Her lips quirked in a half smile. "It's kind of my default setting."

"I know that by now," I teased.

She chuckled. "But it's not yours. You've always been a good friend to me, Val, even when I didn't deserve it. And I was thinking..."

"Yeah?"

"No one is running for vice president. If you or I win, we could be each other's. I think we'd make a good team."

I hummed, considering it. Blair was Blair but she did care about the house and our ideas for the house were mostly aligned. This actually wasn't the worst idea.

Also, if I don't become president, then being close to the president is the next best thing.

"All right," I said. "I'd love to."

"Perfect."

We said goodbye and I continued home.

It was late, creeping close to ten. The mansion was dark and quiet. I padded upstairs in the direction of Adam's room. The rare times I wasn't there to put him to bed, Adam charmed one of the guys or Caroline to stay with him until he fell asleep. They all claimed they tried the "you're a big boy now, you can sleep by yourself" argument, but Adam's powers of persuasion were disturbingly strong for his age.

I poked my head inside and had to stifle a laugh. My son still had full command of his gift as Jaxson had been chosen as his pillow that night. He rested contentedly on his chest, out like a light. As

I stepped closer, Jaxson shifted and his blue eyes blinked at me through the dark.

"Hey," he whispered.

"Hi." I eased onto the bed.

"I'm trapped," he explained. "The little man threatens to wake up every time I move, and I can't go to sleep without an alarm."

"You are trapped."

His eyes got huge. "Help me."

I covered my mouth, holding in a giggle. "How? If we wake him up, he'll just follow us to our bedroom. I'm afraid you're sleeping on Superman sheets tonight." I gave him a soft peck. "But I'll wake you up tomorrow so you won't be late."

I drew back and he caught my wrist. "I'll have a few more of those first."

Snuggling in, we shared sweet kisses. We had more responsibilities than ever hanging over our heads, not to mention dangers we didn't understand. Still, lying in that bed with Jaxson and my son after a day dancing, learning, and working to better the Sallys, I felt a peace deep within me.

Everything is going to be okay. I'm looking forward to this year, the good I'll do for Zeta Rho, and the memories we'll make as a family.

Chapter Four

J*axson*

"Wake up, man."

Something hit me in the face.

"Get your slacker ass to work."

I peeled my eyes open. Standing over me, holding one of Adam's toy soldiers, was Ezra. "What the hell?" I griped.

"It's almost six. Get up."

Glancing down, I noticed I was kid-free. At some point in the night, Adam rolled into Val's arms. The two of them didn't stir.

"I'm up," I whispered. "Thanks."

"No problem. I figured you'd need someone else to be your alarm."

I rolled out of bed and trudged out. "Coffee," I said to no one in particular. "Lots of coffee."

Dad was ready and waiting for his breakfast when I walked into his office an hour later.

I set the bags and coffee carrier in front of him. He reached for the biggest cup.

"That's mine," I said, passing him the other one. "I need every drop."

"You look beat to shit, J. Did Bianca have you scouting last night?"

I shook my head. "I was on bedtime duty for Adam."

"Ah. I remember those days. At least you five can share it around. It was only me lying on your Ninja Turtle sheets—which you showered with piss almost every night."

"We don't need to trip down memory lane," I mumbled. "Val and I stayed up till past two. I'm running on less than four hours of sleep."

"Get that coffee in you. Beyond Berlin has an interview in Marchant today to talk about the upcoming album."

I straightened. "I didn't hear about an interview."

"Morning Melody had a last-minute cancellation and a buddy of mine is the producer. He rang me up to see if I had a band that would like the spot."

"Are they in the studio today?"

"Nah. You'll have to round them up."

Getting to my feet, I saluted him with my coffee cup. "It'll be done. You just keep mucking around up here while I do all the work."

Laughing, he put his hands behind his head and reclined. "That's the plan, J."

I took my food and carried it down to my space. Walking into pitch darkness, I flicked on the lights and illuminated the small, wrapped box sitting on my table. I put my food down and picked it up.

"Jaxson?"

"Yeah, mama."

"Are you busy tonight?" asked Gwen. "I— What's that?"

"Don't know. Haven't opened it yet." I tugged the ribbon off.

"Who is giving you presents and not me?"

Flicking off the lid, I tipped the box over and a silver keychain plopped in my hand. "It's a Bob Marley keychain," I said. "Must be from Dad. He's our favorite."

"Aw. That's sweet. You two can be cute," she said. "Anyway, back to what I was saying. Mr. Meyer needs me to help out in legal again but today is my anniversary. Maxie is taking me out to dinner."

My fist curled around the metal. "I can't. Beyond Berlin has an interview."

"I know but you'll definitely be back in time." Her eyes got all googly. "Please, please, please. Maxie and I are both so busy we barely see each other. And tonight's our anniversary. This is in the name of love."

"You'd owe me a serious favor," I warned.

A smile split her cheeks. "Anything. I promise. You're the best, Jaxson. Thank you." She ran out, no doubt to get away before I changed my mind.

Grumbling to myself, I put the new chain on my borrowed keys. What could be better after a night of no sleep than spending another with Daniel Meyer?

I finished up my breakfast, dropped in on Bianca, and then got in Ezra's car and drove out.

Rylan lived in Cottonwood with his girlfriend. They had a small, but swanky apartment that he was waiting outside of when I pulled up. As for Serena, Ty, and Chandler, they moved to Evergreen the day after their first big checks came through. They couldn't quite afford the neighborhood Ezra, Ryder, Maverick, and I grew up in, but between the three of them, they were splitting rent on a pretty decent mini-mansion.

"This is our first time being interviewed on TV," said Rylan. The guy was bouncing in his seat like a little kid. "Any tips? Advice?"

I turned into the driveway as I spoke. "Try not to laugh too much. People do that when they're nervous and it gives away that you're nervous. Take a breath and think about your answer before you give it. Make sure everything you say is something you want attached to you for the rest of your career."

"Good advice," he said. "But do you think I'll get to do much talking or will they ask Serena all the questions?"

"The hosts will have questions for all of you." I killed the engine. "Home, family, relationships, and what it's like being in a band. Think of what you'll say."

"Okay."

I left him mumbling to himself in the car.

Serena, Ty, and Chandler's rented home was a part of a recently developed complex built to attract new money that wanted to rub elbows with the old. Only one of the ways this white, modern place suited them.

The fountain in the front lawn was littered around with red plastic cups and beer bottles. Inside, posters of great bands were posted in every room, and one of the bedrooms was converted to a studio/stage for entertaining guests. It was what you imagined of a home for young rockers on the edge of all their dreams coming true.

I stepped onto the front porch and halted. The front door was cracked open.

Frowning, I edged closer, placed my hand on the door and pushed. It swung open and snagged on something. A t-shirt.

"Hello?" I stepped over the clothes strewn in the hall. "Chandler? Ty?"

I rounded the corner. "Sere—"

Wow. Living the life of young rockers is right.

The living room was a disaster area. Cigarette butts, bongs, traces of white powder covered the table. The white rug was stained with brown beer stains and ground-in chips.

The entire room reeked of sex and I put it down to the occupants. Ty and Chandler conked out on the couch, sandwiched between a naked guy and three naked girls, one of them Serena.

I cleared my throat. "Do you guys always leave the door wide open?"

Chandler tossed his head, face scrunched up.

"It's a pretty safe neighborhood but you shouldn't go tempting thieves."

"Wha...?" Chandler blinked blearily at me. The lipstick smears on his five o'clock shadow warped with his frown. All of a sudden, his eyes bugged out. "Jaxson!"

"Get dressed and be outside in twenty minutes," I said calmly. "You have a television interview."

"We do? But— But—" Chandler shot up and knocked one of the women to the floor.

Serena wasn't happy.

"What the fuck, Chandler?" She smacked his leg. "What's your problem?"

"Serena, we have to get dressed," he cried. "Ty! Wake up."

I stepped back just as she caught sight of me. She faced me, not bothering to cover up her attributes. "Jaxson," she said, lips curving into a grin. "You missed a fun party last night. You should join us next time."

"Serena!" Chandler hissed. He tripped over his feet trying to get his pants on.

"Nope," I replied. "But thanks for the offer. Twenty minutes or Rylan does the interview on his own."

"Interview?" she repeated.

I walked out.

Rylan was still in the car mumbling to himself. I left him to it and relaxed in the seat to wait. The other guys stumbled out of the house with three minutes to spare. Impressively, they didn't wear the activities of the night before. Chandler was fresh and clean-cut. Serena was effortlessly gorgeous in a sheer lace dress and black boots. They slid inside and swamped the space with cologne and perfume.

Chandler stuck his head between me and Rylan. "Jaxson, we're sorry."

"Don't apologize," Serena snapped. "We're adults. Fucking older than him. We can do what we want."

"We were just blowing off steam," he went on, ignoring her. "I promise we take this seriously. If we knew about the interview, we would have been ready."

"Dad snagged it for you last minute," I said. "You'll be on the Morning Melody show in forty-five minutes if we make it on time."

"Are you serious? Fucking fantastic."

"Let's go over what you're going to say on the drive." I was skating right past what I walked in on. Serena was right, it was none of my business and I didn't care anyway. The only thing that mattered was them smashing the interview and building buzz for the new album.

They clearly agreed because their attention shifted fully to the interview.

"What do you think they'll ask?"

"Why us?"

"Are we going to make it? Drive, Jaxson. Drive!" This was from Serena, of course, but this time I was fine to comply with her orders.

I pulled out onto the road, riding the high of their excitement. Times like this I remembered why I put up with the early mornings, late nights, and abuse. I was a part of something most people watched from the sidelines.

Partway through, I turned on one of their tracks and we belted out the lyrics.

"Is it obnoxious singing to your own music?" Rylan asked, laughing.

"Yeah," I said, "but I won't tell if you don't."

We cracked up and sang even louder.

VALENTINA

"So that's our new house mother," Sofia said out of the corner of her mouth. "She's not what I expected."

I had to agree. The two of us peeked on her through the living room's gossamer curtains. Jade Ortega was not the rosy-cheeked, beaming older woman with a twinkle in her eye that I pictured. The real Jade Ortega was a willowy, young thirty-something with shoulder-length dusky waves and cheekbones you could cut yourself on.

She and Mrs. Kessler were deep in conversation on the front lawn. Today was the day she moved in and we picked the new president of Zeta Rho Sigma.

"Ready for today?" she asked.

I sighed. "As ready as I can be. A good number of sisters agree with me and the changes I want to make, but even more are being cagey. I don't know how this'll go."

"Heather and Crista won't commit on if they'll end the *loyalty* initiation and Eliana flat-out said she won't. That puts you and Blair in the lead right there. I was talking to the girls last night and a lot of them agreed we can find another way to test a new sister's dedication. They don't like it either."

"Which makes all of this more complicated," I said softly, gazing out at Kessler and Ortega.

"What do you mean?"

"If most of the sisters agree with us, then they can't be involved in whatever Leighton, Reagan, and Patricia were. If this isn't a Zeta Rho Sigma plot... what is it?"

"We can't say it isn't yet. Those three did a great impression of normal people for months," she reminded. "More sisters could be putting on a show. And they might be willing to make changes because runs and obstacle races aren't important to what they're doing."

"Making people disappear," I whispered.

A grave look passed between us. There wasn't much more to be said.

We went to the dining room, joining the other girls to wait for the voting to begin. Kessler and Ana didn't keep us in suspense for long.

"Good afternoon, ladies," said Kessler. "Before we begin, let me introduce Miss Ortega. Your new house mother."

Miss Ortega smiled at our clapping. "Wonderful to finally meet all of you. I sent you an email explaining most of my story, so I won't bore you with the details again. I just want to say I'm excited to be here supporting you however I can. Please don't think of me as a spy or a chaperone. This is still your home and my aim is to ensure it remains a safe and comfortable one."

"Well said," praised Mrs. Kessler. "Candidates, if you would also say a few words. This is your final chance to tell your sisters why you're the best choice for Zeta Rho."

I blinked. I didn't know we'd be making a speech.

"Who'd like to go first?"

Heather stood. "Thank you, Mrs. Kessler. There are a few things I'd like to say. The first is this: The Sally house is the best sorority on campus and it's because of each of you. You're the smartest, most talented, hard-working women and just your being here proves you're not afraid of a challenge. There's been a lot of talk about easing up, being more like the other Greeks, and taking the pressure off."

Heather looked directly at me. "And while, of course, we want to enjoy college and get a little stereotypical every now and then, I'm going to be honest with you in that I believe it's a mistake to change our path.

"The Sallys go on to start companies, smash world records, form nonprofits, and a bunch of other amazing accomplishments because of what they did right here in this house. The studying seems intense, the exercising tedious, the challenges against the Sams pointless. The initiation of new sisters feels harsh."

My eyes flicked to Mrs. Kessler. Heather's last statement garnered no reaction.

The Sally house was in its early years by the time she was a college student. Were they doing the test of loyalty then?

Whether or not she went through it herself, she must know about it now. Does she approve of these methods?

"But they aren't pointless or tedious," Heather continued. "They're meant to push the Sallys to their greatest heights. You have limitless potential, girls. Don't sell yourself short, because if I'm chosen as your president, I promise you I won't."

Heather sat down to a round of whoops and applause.

I had to give it to her. It was a good speech and she did tap-dance on the part of me that hates to be seen as a slacker.

Wonder if she appealed to that in the others too?

The other juniors delivered their speeches in the same vein of continuing the Sallys' legacy of greatness and not backing down from challenges. Looking around at the other girls, it was hard to tell which way they were leaning. They talked a good game in the kitchen while they ate my chicken parm peppers, but they were cheering and clapping pretty hard for the junior girls for me to believe they were just being polite.

"Thank you, Eliana," said Mrs. Kessler. She slid past me and gestured to Blair. "Miss Davenport."

Clearing her throat, Blair rose to her feet, smoothing down her sailor dress and flashing that rare, but all-together stunning smile. "Ladies, you all know me. We eat, study, play, and party together. You've heard me talk about my dreams for the Sallys. You know I've had them long before I set foot on this campus.

"My mother was president of this sorority. She is an amazing woman and she's raised me on stories of the amazing women she shared this house with. You know that when I say I have the greatest respect for the people that came before us, I mean it. That the Sallys and their traditions have molded strong leaders is something I've known my whole life, and if I'm chosen as your president, these are the same principles that I'll maintain.

"There's been a lot of talk this week about changing the way we do things and naturally that worried a few of you. Why change what we know works?" Blair swept her gaze around the table. "And I say, we shouldn't. Let's not change the way we do things. Let's improve them. There are more options, opportunities, and methods available to us than when the charter was put into place. Let's take advantage of that. The Sallys became what we are by being strong, innovative, and willing to challenge themselves," she said. "Growing is a challenge. It takes work and commitment, and I believe we can do it together."

Blair sat down to raucous applause and her smirk wasn't put away. She patted my hand under the table, passing on support.

"Miss Moon," Kessler prompted.

I took a deep breath, imagined I was sitting on my porch wrapped up with Jaxson while watching Adam play, and stood before my entire sorority.

"I'm no good at giving speeches," I began. "I want to say all of this in the best possible way, using all the right words. Reduce you to tears. Inspire you to vote me in as president of this sorority and the country."

The girls chuckled.

"I'd like this speech to be perfect, but perfect is a tall order, so I'll just go with honest. I didn't want to join Sally house."

The smiles I earned were wiped away under confusion.

"I didn't," I repeated. "It was my first year of university and I already had so much on my plate. Pledging, exercising, and bonding activities sounded daunting. But then I joined and all of that exercising saw me completing that obstacle course when a year ago I would've taken one look at it and fallen on my face. I joined and I made friends for life and memories that I'll one day tell my kids—and some that I won't."

Laughing, the sisters' grins returned.

"The Sallys will be a key part of the person I become, and I know that because in my short time here, it's already had an impact on me." I motioned out of the room. "I want every sister who walks through that door to leave a stronger, brighter woman, and that happens by creating a safe, inclusive space for all of us."

I looked to Kessler. "I'll be blunt. If I'm chosen as president, the initiation ceremony is gone. Girls will show their loyalty by showing up and kicking ass every day. They'll give their trust if we earn it. Some of you might be thinking that if you went through it, the future sisters should too." I shook my head. "We don't have to be constrained by that thinking because constraining it is. Believing we have to continue doing things because it's the way we've always done them, will only hold us back.

"Running, jumping jacks, and bench presses aren't the only way to shape our bodies, so why not explore other ways? Healthy eating doesn't end with loading a fridge with veggies, so why not take it further and learn how to cook those bad boys together? An obstacle course isn't the only way to whip the boys' asses, so let's get creative.

"All I'm saying," I continued over their laughter, "is I want to make the Sallys more than their past. I want us to be the sorority girls can't help but join for every year to come."

The girls cheered and clapped me down. It wasn't the fanciest of speeches and I didn't know the rules on sneaking "asses" into it. But it was honest.

I wanted to be president if it meant protecting the sisters and finding out what was going on in this house and next door. However, I had no plans to lie about the kind of president I would be.

Kessler dipped her head to the candidates. "Thank you, ladies. Wonderful speeches. Before we begin, does anyone have questions for one or more of the candidates?"

The ladies looked around but didn't offer up a hand. We'd been talking, campaigning, and deliberating over this for a week. We made up our minds on who we wanted. No point in delaying it.

"Alright then," said Kessler. "Let's start the voting. The way we'll do this is I'll hand you each a sheet with the names of the candidates. You'll check the box next to the one you choose. Since no one opted to run for the vice president, I'll give the runner-up the option to take the position. Of course, you can refuse. Any questions?"

We shook our heads.

"All right." Kessler reached in her handbag and pulled out the ballots. "When you're done, turn your sheet over and I'll collect it. Miss Ortega and I will count the votes and announce your new president."

Simple and straightforward was right. I got my paper, ticked my name, and flipped it over. All the other girls did the same. Everyone's paper was wrong side up in two minutes. Like I said, we knew who we wanted.

Kessler collected them and then sent us out. Sofia and I gathered at the door to the living room. "What's the first thing you'll do, Madam President?"

I chuckled. "If I win, the first thing I'd do is organize something for the house. Maybe another barbecue by the pool."

"Oooh." She snapped her fingers. "I wish I voted for you now."

I shoved her away, both of us cracking up.

We fell into talk about our boyfriends while we waited for the tally. I snuck peeks at Blair—brimming with confidence—and the junior hopefuls—also secure in their victory.

I lingered on Heather. She steadfastly refused to consider making changes, and no doubt if she won, the chosen pledges would start their first day as sisters exposed before the entire sorority.

The real question is if she's fighting to keep tradition because it's what we've always done. Or if she knows the true purpose behind what the Sallys put the girls through and Heather's got a vested interest in seeing it continue.

I shook myself. *Come on, Moon,* my rational side voiced. *You're seeking kidnappers and plots everywhere. Heather isn't interested in change. Plenty of people feel the same.*

"All right, ladies." Kessler poked her head out. "Join us in the dining room."

"That was quick," said Sofia.

The sisters retook their seats, waiting with hushed breath. I glanced at the other candidates and they looked back at me. I could tell what they were thinking because the same thoughts were running through my head.

"Zeta Rho Sigma," Kessler began, "please stand and clap for your new president... Valentina Moon."

"Woot!" Sofia shot up, clapping and hooting her head off. The other girls weren't much quieter.

I sat there stunned. *I won? I really won?*

Sofia hauled me to my feet, hugging me, jumping up and down, and rattling my bones. Her shouts in my ear deafened me, and still I stood there.

I won, my mind supplied, driving the thought home.

I was the president of the Sallys, and if all went to plan, I would find out what that truly meant.

MAVERICK LOOKED UP just in time to shove his laptop aside.

I jumped on his lap. Giggling, I straddled him, pushing him back onto the couch.

"Hmm." His hands traveled up my thighs. "If you're down to break the no-sex-on-the-couch rule, so am I."

I nipped his nose. "I'm down for all the sex you want—in our bedroom. Adam likes to pop up at the uncanniest times."

Maverick heaved a sigh like he wasn't getting it on the regular.

"Did you get on the robotics team?" I asked. I wiggled on his lap, getting comfortable.

"They let me on before I opened my mouth. Could just be me, but I'm thinking the last name had something to do with it."

I pulled him close, pecking his lips. "Your name may get you in the door but your genius does the rest. You never have to worry about if you've earned it. Talent drips from those naughty fingers."

Maverick paused in his attempt to unbutton my pants, smirking away. "Thanks."

"Want to hear my good news?"

He popped the button. "Always."

"Riding your lap is the new president of Zeta Rho Sigma."

Maverick dropped his hands. "What? Val, you seriously went through with that?"

"Of course I did. I told you I would run. But the actual winning came as a surprise."

"Val, this is dangerous." He lifted me off and placed me next to him. "We still don't know who ran you off the road, covered up Leighton's crime, or where the former president of that asylum is. People *disappear* from those houses and now you're going to be there every day."

"Maverick—"

"You don't know who is involved. What if they all are? They ambushed you with that twisted initiation. You could walk in one day to bake cookies and find them waiting in the kitchen with duct tape, rope, and a sack."

"That would be scary," I said mildly.

"And what do you think is going to happen?" Maverick was on a roll and wouldn't be stopped. "Someone is going to slide up to you one day and say 'this is the number you call when you need a body taken care of, and by the way, that Blair girl is getting on my nerves. Let's have the black van pick her up next.' That's not going to happen, Val."

"Does seem far-fetched."

Maverick cupped my face, drawing me in to the fear etched into the lines of his brow. My teasing dried up.

"I'll be fine, Maverick." I placed my hand over his. "We talked about this. Even if I don't find out what's going on, I'll be there to keep the girls safe. And with me close by, Aiden won't risk pulling something."

He shook his head. "You won't be there all the time, Val. If someone is snatched out of their bed while you're curled up with me, what are you supposed to do?"

"What I won't do is swallow bullshit explanations about parents picking them up in the middle of the night or family emergencies that stop them from saying goodbye to anyone before they go," I retorted. "I will stir up such a fuss that no one can ignore me or what happened. If the president of the sorority is saying something is wrong, people will listen a lot better than they did to a pledge."

"I don't like this."

"I know you don't." I pressed my forehead to his, eyes fluttering shut. "I don't like it either. I wish it didn't have to be this way but someone has to do something."

"Val—"

Covering his lips with my finger, I said, "Your girlfriend just became the president of the most popular sorority on campus as a sophomore. Congratulate me and then take me upstairs and finish what those wandering hands started."

Maverick gently pulled my hand away. "I won't congratulate you on putting yourself in danger."

My face fell.

"You're president now—fine. You did what you had to do." He got to his feet. "And now I'm doing what I have to do."

"What does that mean?" I snapped around as he walked off. "Maverick, you can't dig into these people. We don't know how they found you out the first time!"

"I didn't cover my tracks well enough," he tossed over his shoulder, rounding the corner into the hall. "I won't make that mistake again because it's you."

Because it's you.

Maverick would do whatever he had to do to protect me. I knew it at Evergreen Academy. I knew it the night he went after Logan. And I know nothing I say will stop him protecting me from the threats among the Sallys and Sams.

I dropped my head on the couch. *I will need help to find out what's going on. Like Maverick said, no one will volunteer their secrets.*

A beep sounded in my pocket. I fished out my phone and tapped on the message.

Jaxson: I'm outside. Come out for a surprise.

Me: Is it another car?

Jaxson: Would you be disappointed if it was?

Me: That would be incredibly ungrateful. But you're the one who needs a new car.

Jaxson: Who said it was a car? Not me. Get out here already.

I bounded up and raced out. I may not need all the gifts my guys gave me, but that didn't mean I didn't like receiving and then *thanking* them.

Jaxson's borrowed car idled in the driveway. He waved through the windshield, flashing that wicked smile through the glass. Jaxson threw open the door and caught me as I jumped in another lap. My gift took up the entire passenger seat.

"A snow cone machine?"

"Yeah." Jaxson brushed his lips on my neck. "I've been slacking on the dad duties. I was thinking you, me, and Adam could spend the day by the pool swimming, grilling, and making snow cones. Do you like it?"

"Oh, baby." I kissed his cheeks, lips, nose, and everything else. "I love it. This is ten times better than a car."

Jaxson gripped my hips, rocking me on his hardness. "*This* is ten times better than a car." The tugging on my buttons resumed. "Just so you know, I accept thanks in blow jobs and anal."

"Jaxson," I cried, cracking up. "Since when does snow cone machine equal anal sex?"

"Since always, baby." He slammed the door shut, keeping me right where I was. "That's why I was saving this up for a special day."

"Today is a special day." I watched him glide my zipper down, revealing the pink lace panties beneath. "I was voted president of the Sallys."

Jaxson froze partially cupping my middle.

I gave him a half smile. "Total mood killer?"

"Little bit."

"You're not going to tell me how dangerous it is, are you? And that there's nothing I can do, so I shouldn't try."

Sighing, Jaxson pulled out. He grabbed the lever by his side, reclining his seat and folding his hands behind his head as he gazed up at me. "No, I'm not going to do that."

"So what?"

"I'm going to ask what happens now. Two people have gone missing. The former president and her friends were psychopaths who vanished. One of them is supposedly dead. Someone covered up what Leighton did to Logan and they could literally be anyone. They could be living in the sorority right now. You can do just about anything, baby, I won't play like I don't know that. But I'm guessing you don't know where to go from here either."

I settled on his chest, resting my chin on my hands, and propping my feet on the steering wheel. "Do I have to be honest?"

He cracked a grin. "I believe we swore on our sex lives to tell the truth and nothing but the truth."

"Sacred," I murmured. "In that case, you're right. I don't know where to go from here. I can't go around questioning the sisters. The innocent ones will think I'm nuts. The guilty ones will lie their asses off. If only I knew more about Leighton and how she became... that."

"I'm more interested in how she dug up those secrets." He raised his head. "Did you promise to get rid of the initiation?"

"Of course."

"Val, if you let it happen— or if you let the house think you're going through with it, you might find out how she got her hands on the dirt."

"No." I wiggled up his chest, dropping a kiss on his chin. "I can't go back on my promise the day after it gets them to vote for me. The only thing I can do is pay attention, get close to the older sisters who knew Leighton better, and find out what I can from Mrs. Kessler. She's been here through the years. She's seen all the sisters come and go."

"She might be the reason a few of your sisters came and *went*."

"More reason to learn what she's about."

Jaxson caressed my cheek reaching to push my hair behind my ears. "Promise me something?"

"Anal sex on the front seat? Not in the driveway with Caroline's bedroom overlooking us, but pull into the garage and you have a deal."

Smiling at my joke, Jaxson skated over the bait. "Promise me you'll have your guards with you everywhere you go, in and out of that house. I would follow you if I could. If it can't be me, I like the idea of highly trained professionals with guns."

I walked my fingers up his chest. "To protect me from a bunch of sorority girls?"

"I've got a healthy fear of them after Leighton Lewis."

I shivered. "Me too."

Jaxson gripped my ass, pushing me up closer. "I'm waiting on that promise."

"I promise. I have no interest in being the next one to disappear. My boys need me."

"That's what I'm saying. We'd be a fucking mess in six seconds flat."

"Generous. I'd give you three."

Jaxson jerked like he'd been struck. "Oh. She's got jokes?" He squeezed his plump handful. "I know what to do about that."

"A good, hard fuck in the ass?"

Groaning, he said, "Dammit, woman. Marry me."

I placed my palms on either side of him, rising up and hissing at his nails scraping down my thighs. "Do it just right, baby, and..." My gaze drifted over his head. "You'll get me... to... agree to anything..."

"Fuck, yeah. What are we still doing here?"

I fell to the side as Jaxson shot up. I zeroed in on the bit of white poking out from the leather. Throat closing up, I tugged it out of the seat, losing my breath as I held it before me.

"Jaxson," I rasped. "What is this?"

"What's what?" he asked without turning around. "Sit behind me, so I can pull up."

"What's *this*?" Twisting, I thrust the lace thong between us. "Why was it stuffed between the seat?!"

Jaxson shifted, grinning that grin. It wiped away with one look. His eyes bugged, darting from me to the thong. "Stuffed between the—"

"The seat, Jaxson." I shook it. "Where— *Who* did this come from?"

"But— but— Isn't it yours?"

"No, it's not mine! I don't leave my underwear all over the place. Unlike this bitch!" I flung the disgusting thing away. "Who is she?!"

"She?! It's not— This isn't— I swear—" Face paling, Jaxson stammered out something that was meant to be an explanation. "There is no she!"

Blinded by tears, my throat was so tight that if I cried, I'd gasp for air I couldn't breathe. I lunged for the door. "I have to get out of h-here."

"No, Val!" Jaxson shot in front of me, grabbing me around the middle. "I swear I don't know where that came from. Look at it again, baby. It has to be yours!"

"It's not mine!" I shrieked. "Who was taking off her fucking underwear in your car, Jaxson?"

"No one!"

I smacked the wheel. The horn ripped through our shouts. "No one was in your car today?! Then how did this get here?!"

Jaxson threw up his hands. "The fuck I know! I didn't let—" He stopped. "Well, except for..."

"Except for who?"

"I... drove Beyond Berlin to Marchant—"

"Serena." I didn't recognize the hiss that came from my own throat. I balled my fist, nails piercing half-moons into my skin. "It was her."

"Whoa, hold on." He reached for me and my bared teeth returned his hands to his sides. "Whatever you're thinking, it's not what happened. *Nothing* happened. Baby." Jaxson leaned in, slowly sliding arms around my stiff body. "Val. I would never cheat on you. Never. I don't even picture other women when I jerk off. It's you," he whispered. "It's always been you. Tell me you believe me. Please."

"S-say—" My voice, and heart, cracked on a sob. "Say it again."

"It's you." Jaxson took my face in his hands, filling my senses with him and only him. "I love you, Valentina. I would never do this to you."

He repeated that to me over and over. Punctuating it with kisses. Rubbing my arms until my muscles unwound.

I sank into him, burying my face in his neck, wetting him with my tears and breathing them back in.

"We went to Marchant today," he said. "I picked the band up at their place and found out they're sleeping together. It's possible while I was grabbing lunch, Serena had the same idea for car sex. That's the only explanation because she wasn't in here with me."

"I'm not... accusing you," I began, finding my voice. "But that doesn't explain why it was left in here."

"She forgot it."

"Despite decades of manufactured movie drama, women don't just *forget* their underwear. If she had time to straighten up and get dressed without you knowing what they did in here, she had time to fish her damn thong out of the seat and put it on."

"You think she left it there on purpose? Why would she do that?"

I strangled his forearms tightening my hold. "I have to spell it out?"

"Val, I can't imagine how pissed she'd have to be with me to pull some shit like that. And she wasn't pissed. Not today. The whole band was buzzing for the interview."

"Who says she had to be angry?"

Jaxson drew back. "What do you mean?"

My eyes burned peering into him. "She was hanging all over you the other day. Making those slick-ass comments about your favorite women."

"She didn't do that because she's into me," Jaxson replied, picking up straight off what I was hinting at. "She acted up because she's a mean girl with a screaming need for attention. Like most tortured artists. When she doesn't have that attention, as in when we're alone, she's never shown the slightest bit of interest in me."

"Maybe she does and you don't see it."

"Maybe"—he pressed his nose to mine—"it doesn't matter because I love you."

I pointed at the bunched-up fabric lying on the floor. "It matters if she's pulling shit like this."

"Can't argue with that," he said under his breath. "How about this? The band members have their own cars and I'm not their chauffeur. They drive themselves from now on." He kissed me again and that time I was in a better mood to receive it. "Nothing like this will ever happen again."

"Okay," I croaked. "But watch out for her, Jaxson. It's a sneaky, cruel, manipulative person that would do something like this. And if she is after you, she won't have the conscience to stop."

"Hey." He lifted my chin to meet his eyes. "This stops right here. You'll never have reason to doubt me again. I promise."

I swallowed hard, wetness springing to my eyes. "I love you."

The car was soon filled with our soft kisses and moans.

"So," Jaxson said, nipping a path along my chin. "Is anal off the table?"

I glared fit to singe his eyebrows.

"Oops." He cringed. "Thought I'd go for a joke. I see that was a mistake."

"Just get rid of that thing."

"I will. Then how about we take this inside." He patted the snow cone machine. "Grab Adam and sit out by the pool."

I wiped my face with the back of my hand. "Okay. Let me clean up first. I don't want Adam seeing me like this."

"We'll take a bath and—"

I slipped out of his grasp. "Give me a minute, please. Set up the snow cones on the patio. I'll be out there in a little bit."

Jaxson looked like he wanted to say something. Say more. Kiss away my frown.

Instead, he grabbed the box, climbed out, and took the white lace thong with him.

I slumped on the seat, the equivalent of a marionette without strings. It's not that I didn't believe him. I did. I knew when Jaxson lied to me as surely as I knew that he never did. Jaxson Van Zandt was unfailingly honest with me from the moment we met. Even the times I wished he'd sugarcoat it, he told me the truth. Trusting him was easy for my heart. Forgiving Serena Blackwood, on the other hand...

I trembled, boiling with such rage it threatened to explode out of me and shatter the windshield. There was nothing innocent about these panties being left in his car. Jaxson said that show she put on for me was just that, but if she has no interest in him, why would she jump at the first chance to taunt me and make me jealous? There's a need for attention and then there's a need for a fist through the teeth.

The late nights. Constant calls. Refusing to work with anyone but Jaxson. Since my boyfriend walked into that bar, Serena's been on a crusade to monopolize his time and have him all to herself.

My gaze fell on the door he disappeared through.

This was no accident.

JAXSON

Valentina cuddled Adam in her lap, laughing as he tried to feed her his snow cone and mostly got the cold, sticky treat on her face. Looking at her, you'd never guess our entire relationship nearly fell apart an hour ago.

She was perfect. Puffy, red eyes clear and shining. Wild chestnut locks flat and combed. Thin, twisted lips full and smiling. She was my Valentina again, but for a brief moment as she held that thong up and I looked in her eyes, she was as far from mine as she could be.

How did it end up in my car? Serena wouldn't really do something like this, would she? She is a demanding diva who thinks she owns me, but as a personal assistant, not a boy toy.

I'm not an idiot and I don't live on the right side of modest.

I was rich. About to inherit an empire. I could walk onto any modeling shoot and they'd kick everyone out and turn their cameras on me. I know when girls are hitting on me because they do it all the fucking time. Serena never has.

Pushing myself up, I abandoned my patio chair for Valentina's, wedging myself between her and the cushion, and wrapping my arms around my family. I relaxed as she burrowed into me. There was a part of me that feared she'd pull away.

"Here you go, Jaxson." Adam thrust the cone in my mouth and half up my nose.

I sputtered to their giggles. "Thanks, little man. Want to make me another one? Green apple."

"Okay!" Adam hopped out of her lap and ran to the machine. His little face screwed up in concentration as he pulled the lever for the shaved ice, filling the cup.

"Adam," Val called. "Let's have your friends over this weekend to swim and make snow cones. How does that sound?"

The kid cheered, jumping up and down and spilling the ice on his shoes.

Val turned her eyes up to me. "This really was a great gift. Thank you."

"Everyone loves snow cones."

"Not the ice, Jaxson." She kissed my jaw. "You. This. The three of us. That's the gift." Val looked away. "That I even thought for a second that you could betray me, proves how disconnected we've been."

"I've been working too much. Missing a lot. All of that is going to change and I won't waste time saying it. I'll show you."

"And Serena?"

I wondered if Val noticed the biting edge when she said her name. "I don't know for sure that it was hers," I admitted.

"Who else could it be?"

"If we're talking band members getting it on in my car, there are two other guys who could've rewarded a groupie. But whether or not it was Serena, I'm setting some rules. When we're done for the day, we're done. I'm going home and turning off my phone. Her calling me at three in the morning because she changed the lyrics again and I have to listen to it now— That's over. Work is always going to be a little crazy, but it doesn't have to be like the last few months. Let me tell you right now, I will never go another three weeks without you."

She laughed. "Good to know. I need our private dance sessions."

Adam came back, handed me my cone, and climbed on Val's lap. He dropped his head on her shoulder and promptly closed his eyes.

"Seems it won't be a fight today," she said softly. "I'm taking him up. Wait for me in your room. We'll have another dance session."

I raised a brow. "Promises were made earlier."

"You'll have to convince me," she tossed over her shoulder. "But I did say you could talk me into just about anything."

Chapter Five

*J*axson

"I'm here for whatever you need and I support you guys one hundred percent." I gestured to Gwen. "So does my other half. Whenever I'm out, just call her up and she's got you."

"Why does it feel like you're breaking up with us?" Chandler joked.

The next morning, Gwen, Beyond Berlin, and I snagged one of the meeting rooms. It was strange being in here and surrounded by pictures of Dad, Dad, and Dad wailing into a mic and thrusting his hips at the camera. I would've taken it into my closet if I could fit more than two people in there.

Heaving a sigh, I clutched my heart, lowering my head. "I am, C. What we had was special. You were a sweet and tender lover. But I'm in love with someone else."

Chandler tipped out of the chair howling. The other guys busted up, though Serena's blank expression didn't twitch. She swiveled in her chair, side to side, grating my ears with faint squeaks.

"He's not kidding," Gwen piped up. "He is in love with someone else."

"And she, plus my kid, need me to cut down on the late nights and broken promises," I said. "This isn't really a breakup. Gwen and I are working out how to split tasks to make it easier on us both. Bianca likes me listening to demos and scouting out new talent, and Gwen's great with album details and managing in the studio."

Serena kicked her feet onto the table. "You're pretty much saying we're her problem now."

"No," I replied. "I'm saying that Gwen and I will both be here to help you out. I've got other stuff on my plate now, but that's not going to change. Call me up whenever. Just know that when I'm off the clock, I might not get you back until the next morning."

Serena scoffed. "Are you serious, Jaxson? Stars don't live or work by nine to five. Inspiration strikes in the middle of the night. Concerts go until one in the morning. Stupid fucking sound guys bust the speakers and suddenly you're doing an a cappella set. There is no schedule. There's no off-the-clock.

"Isn't the whole point of you being down here instead of in the penthouse with Daddy, to prove you can handle all aspects of this job?" She spread out her hands, *squeak, squeak, squeaking* in her chair. "If you're to the point of passing all the work to the assistant, I say you failed. You can't handle it."

I bore her speech in silence, Val's warning coming back to me.

"It's a sneaky, cruel, manipulative person that would do something like this. And if she is after you, she won't have the conscience to stop."

I still couldn't say the thong I dumped in the trash the day before was Serena's, but if all that shit she said wasn't an attempt to keep me at her beck and call, I didn't know what was. Playing on my desire to prove myself to Dad was hard-level manipulation. If she brought up crushing Daniel Meyer's hopes that I'll fail, she'll have hit expert.

"Serena," Rylan said. "Ease up. The guy's got a girlfriend and a kid. An actual five-year-old which we're not. Jaxson doesn't need to hold our hand through everything."

"He's not holding our hand," she snapped. "He's doing his job. Jaxson knows us. He knows our songs, our style, and our sound. We can't work with anyone else. It's Jaxson or no one at all."

Serena handed down her ruling like a deity commanding her mortals. Folding her arms, she narrowed her eyes on me, daring me to contradict her.

"We're equal partners. Me and Gwen." I gripped her shoulder. "I'd never leave her with all the work or dump you guys. I've got your backs, you know that. But if we're going to pull in more talent on your level, I've got to hit the streets." I laughed. "I'll be stuck under a pile of demos today and then hitting Crystal Pub tonight. Hit Gwen up if you need anything, or get at me tomorrow." I headed for the door.

"Jaxson, we have to practice interviewing today," Serena shouted at my back. "We were a hot mess yesterday."

"You did great," I replied without slowing down. "Although practicing couldn't hurt. We'll do that tomorrow after lunch."

"We can't do it tomorrow! Listen to the demos tomorrow. We have to practice now."

"Then Gwen's got you."

I slipped out, shutting the door on her demands for me to come back. I felt bad for leaving Gwen to deal with the aftermath, but if I kept giving in to Serena, I'd be her bitch until I died.

I made it around the corner and halfway down the hall before I noticed footsteps coming up on me fast. Twisting around, my eyes bugged.

Serena stomped through Artist Alley, steam pouring out of her ears or just about. "Jaxson!" She snagged my arm, pulling me up short.

"Holy shit, Serena. Just practice with Gwen." It was an effort not to shout.

"I'm *not* doing shit with that bitch. Levi said we're your responsibility, so fucking act like it! It makes no sense wasting time on bands you'll never sign and pushing your biggest talent to the side."

I stepped out of her grasp. "You took the old man too literally."

"No, I didn't," she growled. "I only agreed to sign with you because Bianca said *you* would manage us. This isn't just a job to you. Your priority is ensuring Interstellar Records succeeds which means you'll push us until we do. Beyond Berlin is my life. I've killed myself for years to get here and I won't settle for less than the best." Serena got in my face. "I deal with you and only you. If you think I'm playing, try me. I haven't even begun to show you difficult."

Shit. I'm straight up being threatened.

I studied her, my promise to Val floating in my head. "I hear you on wanting the best," I finally said. "You're wrong if you think Gwen doesn't want the same for you. She is as committed to Interstellar as me, Bianca, my dad, and everyone else here. There's nothing to be gained by holding Beyond Berlin back and this department knows that as well as I do.

"But if you want to work with me"—I swallowed the scant distance, flickering surprise on her face—"listen up, or you'll be shocked how often I 'lose your number' or 'don't get your texts.' When I drive out of the parking lot, you don't call me short of someone lighting you and the guys on fire.

"Second, don't ever dog me out in my own fucking building again. You're forgetting who is gonna be running this place, Serena. I don't have anything left to prove to the old man. Interstellar Records is mine and your contract will be mine. Think about that the next time you disrespect me."

Serena's pink glittering lips trembled even as her glare shot acid. She could suck it the hell up. Being with Valentina smoothed out most of my rough edges, but my picture still sat next to *Rich Prick* in the dictionary.

"And last..." I got even closer, bending her neck back. "I found a thong in my back seat yesterday. Did you put it there?"

Her face crumpled in a frown. "A thong? What the hell are you talking about?"

"Serena," I hissed.

"I don't know what you're talking about," she snapped. "I didn't leave a fucking thong in your car. What the hell do I look like?"

I studied every line of her face. If she was lying, I couldn't tell.

"Fine," I said, stepping back. "I'll let it go for now, but I will find out how it got in there."

She gave me a mocking smile. "And I care? Are we practicing or not?"

"Right, I lied about that being the last rule. The real one is when I say I'm busy, I'm fucking busy. I'm not sitting in my broom closet sucking down paninis and laughing about pissing you off. I've got work to do and the reason I'm late home most nights is I'm forced to let it pile up while I'm playing bitch for one band. Hint: yours."

She sniffed. If she was any less apologetic, she'd be laughing in my face.

"If you respect my time, I'll respect yours." I held out my hand. "Deal?"

Serena eyed it like I wiped my ass with it and refused to wash. "Fine."

We shook.

"That said," I continued, "I can run through some stuff with you now in between listening to the demos. Take it or wait until tomorrow."

"Take it."

Serena dropped my hand and set off, leading the way to my office. I held back, dropping my head and tempering a sigh. The weird thing was my chat with Serena actually turned out better than I anticipated.

VALENTINA

"You're kidding?"

"I wish I was kidding." I stuck the phone in the crook of my neck, switching my bills for coffee. I thanked the barista and got back with Sofia.

I had a full day ahead of me. Two classes, lunch with Jaxson, and then a meeting at the Sally house with our new house mother, vice president Blair, and our council. We had to plan the semester's activities in light of my promise to toss all the old ways out the window. In spite of everything I had going on, there was always room to vent with Sofia.

"Jaxson drove the band to Marchant yesterday and the car returned sporting a new thong. Maybe it's just me, but I'm betting the wind didn't blow it in."

"It was that Blackwood chick," she said automatically. "That is screwed up, Val. What was she trying to do— Forget that. I know what she was trying to do. How were you supposed to take it when you found that in his car? You would've taken his head off and then Little Miss Glitter Hair would have been there to stitch it on and take your place."

"Exactly," I said. "Thank you. I thought I was the crazy one."

"Absolutely not. With the way she blows him up whenever he's out of her sight, it's obvious she thinks she owns him. That she's playing these kinds of games does not shock me the way it should."

I left the café sipping on mocha and vindication. "Jaxson reminded me we didn't have proof it was her. The panties weren't labeled or anything. All the same, he promised to talk to her and set boundaries. Plus, the car rides are over."

"Good," she said. "What about you two? Are you okay?"

My first smile of the morning appeared on my lips. "We are. Jaxson's been making more of an effort even before all of this shit went down. Coming home early, spending time with Adam, crazy hot monkey sex on the balcony."

She laughed. "That's what I want to hear. You've been stressed and it'll only get more stressful, Madam President. A girl needs hot monkey sex to unwind."

I groaned. "Why did you have to remind me of my presidency?"

"You're regretting it already? It's day one."

"I was cool until Blair sent me the agenda. I'll be the one getting home late tonight. The girl wants us to plan the entire semester down to what we're doing every millisecond."

"Rough. But think of it this way, control freaks make excellent seconds-in-command. Every job you give her, she won't rest until she's got it perfect."

"True."

I peeled my shirt from my skin, fanning some breeze in there. The coffee was delicious, sweet, and spiking my temperature on an already warm day.

Summer in Evergreen was as beautiful as its fellow seasons. Beaming rays beat on swaying flower gardens while friends and cute couples lay on their blankets around them, soaking up the heat before autumn began to steal it away.

I peeked over my shoulder. "How ya doing, Juliet? Sure you don't want any coffee?"

My bodyguard shook her head. She hung back four steps as agreed. Her colleagues—my two other guards—blended so well in the background, I wasn't sure where they were.

"I have any more and I'll jitter out of my pants," she replied.

I laughed. Juliet was neat, slight, and a pretty that drew appreciative eyes as we went. Even better she had a sense of humor.

"Get ready for a long day," I said. "After the meeting, I'm cooking dinner for the sisters. You're welcome to join us."

"That's very kind of you, Miss Moon. I'm sure the girls will take you up on your offer too."

"Oh, you're cooking?" Sofia cried, picking up our conversation. "What are you making me?"

"Beef stir-fry with a crunchy salad and spring rolls. Miss Ortega is doing the prep, so all I have to do is walk in and start cooking. This house mother thing is growing on me."

"Me too. Hudson and I will be your first customers. Skip going out for dinner and head straight for the dessert."

"You two are seriously making up for the dry spell."

She laughed, warming my heart. "You have no idea. I'm doing things with this man that has his grumpy ass smiling for the rest of the day, and I'm the same. See you tonight."

"See ya."

I hung up and turned back to Juliet. "First stop, Social Psychology."

"After you."

My guards were my trailing shadows throughout the morning. I collected looks from my professors as they scanned the room for invisible threats and then fanned out around me, staring hard at anyone who looked my way.

I wasn't about to fight their presence. The person who ran me off the road was still out there, along with Leighton Lewis. I had too many enemies doing a good job of hiding from me. The day they reappeared, I wouldn't be caught defenseless.

On my way to the car, I stopped off at the sushi place and grabbed two packaged rolls and two iced teas. Jaxson's favorite on-the-go lunch. I was done with being disconnected from him. He was making the effort to put us first and I'd do the same.

Walking out with my prize, I dialed Jaxson on the way to the car. "Hey, baby. Still free for lunch?"

JAXSON

"Of course. Love you."

I ended the call with Val and shifted to Serena, smiling wide. "Where do you get your inspiration?"

She sat up straight. "A song can come to me from anywhere. A line on the radio or—"

"Stop," I said, dropping the smile. "Important but little-known tip: mimic the interviewer."

"What does that mean?"

"If they smile, you smile. If they laugh, you laugh. Don't force it or be obvious, but it's human nature to respond to people who respond to you. Everything you were about to say, if you said it while returning my smile, I'd naturally like you more. You want to vibe with the hosts. That's what makes them go on to give sound bites about how sweet and charismatic you are."

"Right. Okay." Serena scribbled on her borrowed notepad, adding to her notes.

I never questioned that she was serious about taking Beyond Berlin to the top. Still it was a nice change of pace to work *with* her, not against her.

"Did I do that yesterday?" she asked.

"You were good yesterday. You took the time to give real, honest answers, you made Steve laugh a few times, and you shared the floor with the guys. All of you killed it. Did you think you didn't?"

"I said 'um' like fifty times. I was taking my time to answer because I didn't know what to say. We didn't have any time to prepare. Can't have that happen again."

At least her insistence we practice now makes more sense.

"It didn't come off like you were nervous. Share the tips with the guys, but don't get in your head about them. Just remember why you're doing this and it'll come across."

She paused, glancing up. "Are we done?"

"Yep." I crossed to the door and held it open for her. "I have to finish these demos and then I've got a lunch date."

"But we should do a full mock interview," she protested.

"Don't make me say tomorrow again. Go, Serena. You have to look over the final album covers anyway."

"You have to be there too."

"I live down in the art department. I've seen them and the covers kill. You can't go wrong whichever one you pick." I swept my arm out the door. "See you tomorrow."

Huffing, Serena marched out with my notepad.

"That's gratitude for ya," I mumbled.

Reclaiming my seat, I worked through the tracks, sorting them into the reject pile and the pile I'd pass on to Bianca. I was on my last one when a knock broke into the melody.

"Come in."

The door swung open, revealing Levi Van Zandt in all of his glory.

"Damn. This is a closet."

"What brings you down here, Dad? Planning to take pity on your old son and upgrade his working conditions?"

He grinned. "Not a chance. I'm down here escorting this beautiful lady."

"Val." I got up as he stood aside, letting my girlfriend through. I lifted a brow at the both of them. "Why am I not surprised you stopped by my dad first?"

She shoved my shoulder. "I wasn't coming all this way and not saying hi. Love me for my manners."

"Say bye before you leave too." Dad kissed her cheek. "Later, baby girl."

She waved him off, closing the door behind him. "Did you talk to Serena?"

"Straight to the point." I plopped down and patted my lap. "Let's mess around first."

Val shook her head, grin playing at her lips. "Read the room, playboy."

I heaved a sigh. "I talked to her and she swore she had nothing to do with the present in the back seat."

"And you believed her?"

"I can't prove she's lying. Even if she is, the car rides are over and she knows I'm not playing with her anymore." I held out my hand and Val slipped her palm on mine. I tugged her onto my lap. "I've spoken to Bianca, Gwen, Serena and the band. Things are going to change."

I brushed her hair behind her ears. It always hung in her eyes. A crime I couldn't allow. The added bonus of touching her, tangling in her silken strands, caressing her rosy cheeks stoked a flame in me. I read the room... and we wanted the same thing.

"Remember all those years ago, you promised me sex in the supply closet?"

She pecked my nose. "I've delivered—free of charge—countless times over the years."

"True. But I'm down to go again."

"Want to eat sushi off me?"

"Yes," I said seriously. "I very much do."

Val crossed her arms, grabbing the hem of her shirt.

"Jaxson." Someone pounded on the door. "Jaxson?"

"I'm busy," I called.

"I'll help you with the"—Gwen threw the door open—"demos."

Valentina tipped off my lap, yanking her shirt down.

"Oops." Gwen cringed. "I'm sorry. We really need to work out a sock-on-the-door thing."

"Do you need something?" I hoped I sounded as impatient as I felt.

"Paunch brought this up for you." Gwen unveiled a small package behind her back. "Came with a note that said to open it right away."

I edged away. "Is it a bomb?"

She laughed. "It went through security."

"Thanks." I took it from her and she sat down instead of backing out.

"I'm curious too," she explained.

Val handed me her keys. I used it to cut the tape and break open the box. A round aluminum tin covered in a damask design lay inside. There was no writing to give away what was inside. Val and Gwen leaned in at the same time as I pulled off the lid.

We reared back—a tiny *eep* coming out of Gwen.

Smoke billowed out of the tin, filling the box and seeping over the sides, seeking us and dissipating into vapor before it reached.

"Dry ice?" Val asked.

"What is that?"

The smoke cleared on tiny, golden-brown nuggets nestled on wax paper. Confusion fled beneath my grin.

"They're chocolate pastries," I said. "Wow. They look like the same ones we got in Versailles. The restaurant served them with smoke too."

"We?" asked Val.

"Me and Dad."

"Oh, so your dad got this for you. That was nice." She bumped my shoulder. "See? He does care about you locked away in your closet."

"Want one?" I offered it to both of them. We popped them in our mouths, cool from their ride, but melting fast on our tongues into flaky chocolatiness.

This I do want to eat off Val.

"Gwen, don't you have work to be getting back to?"

She chuckled. "I can take a hint."

I turned on Val as the door shut. "Where were we?"

VALENTINA

Zipping my jacket, I glanced at Juliet to see if she noticed the chocolate stains on my shirt. She averted her eyes as she held open my door.

My lunchtime rendezvous with Jaxson was over. Time to accept my mantle as Madam President.

The Sally house loomed pristine and pretty as a picture. Grass clippings littered the sidewalk courtesy of the freshly mown lawn. Someone swept the porch and set out new furniture—wicker chairs and a small table to sit out and people-watch Greek Row.

A good bet it was the doing of our new house mother. Sofia said Miss Ortega hopped right in seconds after unpacking her last bag.

Juliet held the door open for me and—

"Surprise!"

I stumbled back, nearly tripping off the front steps.

The girls streamed out of the house, taking hold of me and practically carrying me inside.

"Congrats, Val."

"Loved your speech."

"I can't wait for this year," Keily gushed. "It'll be twenty times more amazing with you at the helm."

I might have gotten something out if I wasn't bowled over by our home's new décor. A banner hung over the staircase proclaiming, "Congratulations, President Valentina!"

Pink and green streamers strung overhead and ran up the banister. A heavenly smell wafted out of the living room, and the girls carried me inside, beaming proudly at their spread of cupcakes, soda, cheesecake, muffins, and every other sinfully delicious treat under the sun.

Sofia stood by the mantle, looking plenty pleased with herself for keeping the secret.

"I can't believe you guys did this." I went around collecting hugs. "This is so much better than a council meeting."

"Sorry, Valentina," Miss Ortega said as she hugged me. "This doesn't get you out of the meeting, but we would be remiss if we didn't celebrate. How about an hour of cake and fun and then we can get started? How does that sound?"

"Sounds great."

I descended on the chocolate hazelnut brownies like they had my name on them. One of the girls kicked up the music and the party started. Sofia took the tray of brownies and led me off into a corner with Mai and Blair.

"We had to pull this together quickly," said Mai. "But our lovely brunch ladies were happy to come through for you."

"I am going to spend so much money in that place this year," I said.

"Did Ortega tell you we're still having the meeting?" asked Blair. "I've written up the agenda and I have some suggestions we should talk about."

"That can wait," Sofia spoke up. "This party is for you too, Blair. Enjoy. Let that hair down. Dance on the table."

She laughed. "It's not that kind of party. But there is something I need to ask you," she said, addressing that last sentence to me. "Since you're not moving into the house, it's cool that I take Leighton's old room, right? I've started packing my stuff but Ortega said I have to clear it with you first."

"Fine with me," I replied. "No point in it sitting empty. Any plans for how to decorate? Leighton went wild on the place. Coolest room I've ever been in."

"Right?" she breathed. "I loved what she did with the closet. Instead of a book nook, I was thinking of a study space—quiet and tucked away. The fish tank headboard is a bit hardcore for me. Instead, I'm hiring someone to make a mural on that entire wall..."

Blair fell into her version of letting her hair down, gushing about her plans for her new room while we stuffed ourselves.

Miss Ortega floated in and out, checking on us in between setting up the dining room.

"Shouldn't we help her?" I spoke up. "She doesn't have to go real mama bear on us. We can handle refilling our drinks and printing handouts."

"She's here to make life easier for us," Sofia said. "In every way. This morning she set out breakfast for us and offered to sit down with anyone needing to process Leighton's death."

"And she put in a maintenance request to fix my leaky sink," Mai put in. "Full-service house mother right there."

"Who is trying to get our attention," said Blair. "It's time, Val. Take the chocolate cupcakes with you."

"I will," I said around my mouthful.

Ortega was indeed waving for our attention. We crossed the room, meeting her out in the hall.

"I'd like to say this meeting will go quickly, but we have a lot to cover," she began. "The prep is done for dinner tonight. If we go over time, I'll cook, so you six can keep working."

"Thank you. You don't have to—" I stopped, the final part of her sentence penetrating. "Wait. The six of us?"

"They're ready to begin when you are." Ortega stepped into the dining room and gestured at our guests.

My eyes flared—slightly—but the surprise came through clear enough to twist Aiden's lips.

"Hey, Val." He saluted. "Congrats on the win. I had my money on Heather. Impressive upset."

"Aiden," I forced out. "Why are you here? This meeting is for the Sally house."

"Those plans will inevitably link up with us. The Halloween party. The end-of-semester trip. And there's talk you're shaking things up. Gotta be in on that."

I clenched my teeth. *Why does this insufferable asshole look like he's enjoying himself?*

"By the way, how's Ezra doing? Recovering from a gunshot wound must be brutal."

For sure this guy is enjoying himself.

I stalked up to him, leaning over his vice president to get in his face. "Ezra's great. The gang that you used to blackmail him and the guy who shot him have been taken out. Care to share how you found out about the Sons of Slaughter in the first place?" I matched his smile. "I am president now. It's my job to collect all the secrets."

If anything, his smile widened. "In due time."

"Valentina," Ortega spoke up. "Is everything okay?"

"Everything's fine." I backed away, claiming my spot across the table from him. "Let's get started."

The Sallys' treasurer and recruitment chair were seated and apparently in the middle of chatting with Aiden and his vice when we walked in. They perked to attention as I settled.

Blair sat next to me and my guards took their place in opposite corners of the room. Everyone gave them curious looks, but it was Aiden who got a stare in return. I wonder if he read the warning in their eyes, because he shifted around, giving Juliet and Hadley his back. Of course, my guards knew about him and his part in Sawyer's nighttime ride.

In front of us were the agendas Blair wrote up. I scanned through it while she, Aiden, and Matthew exchanged less hostile greetings.

I glanced up as Ortega pulled out the chair at the head of the table. "I hope you don't mind if I sit in," she said to my questioning look. "Not to step on any toes, but Mrs. Kessler wanted to ensure you had all the support you need. It won't be easy juggling the Sally house with school while living off campus."

"So much can happen while you're away," Aiden said.

A shiver went up my spine. That he was up to his forehead in the disappearance was indisputable. As was his taunting.

"Let's get started." I kept my tone and expression even. I had to work with this guy if I was ever going to find Teagan and Sawyer. "We're holding off on pledging this semester, so we don't have to worry about that."

I crossed the first line off the list.

"Bonding activities," I read. "We can keep doing the game nights, movie nights, and joint house parties. I was also thinking we could start celebrating the sisters' birthdays. That would count as bonding and girls would love it."

"Great idea," praised Miss Ortega. "I could collect birth dates and make a chart for the living room. We'll know who we have to plan for that particular month."

"That would be perfect," Blair said. "Also, let's get more fun with the bonding activities. Have scavenger hunts or horror nights leading up to Halloween where we pig out in the living room in our pajamas, watching scary movies."

Aiden raised his hand. "The Sams are on board with the pajama party."

The others laughed. I didn't.

"I mentioned cooking nights in my speech," I said, skating past his comment. "I'd like to make it a weekly thing and the girls in the house who cook can volunteer to choose the recipe and teach every-one to make it. Using the ingredients from the pantry, so it doesn't sit in there going bad. This can double as a bonding and health activity for the week."

"You can't—"

"Actually—"

Aiden and Miss Ortega spoke at the same time.

"If I may," Jade continued. "The health requirement is meant to be filled by at least seventy-five minutes of strenuous exercise a week. Cooking nights will not count."

"It doesn't say that in the charter."

I knew what the damn thing said backward and forward. Memorizing the charter was another in a long list of pledge tests.

"Since when do we have to do strenuous exercise?" I asked.

"It's an addendum to the charter. I've printed out a copy of all the recent changes. It's beneath the agenda."

Forehead scrunched up, I took up the second packet, scanning the new info, and jaw dropping as I read.

"What the hell?" I breathed. "Strenuous activity is required to meet the exercise requirement. These activities are limited to running, jogging, swimming laps, uphill hiking, basketball, or cycling at more than eleven miles per hour," I read. "When were these changes made?"

"As I said, they are recent."

I looked her in the eye. "'In the last twenty-four hours' recent?"

Miss Ortega didn't reply.

Blair leaned forward. "We planned to introduce yoga and Pilates. Val even thought of doing dance lessons."

"Those are all great ideas for bonding activities," Ortega replied. "Unfortunately, they cannot count toward the health requirement."

The addendum crumpled in my fist. Kessler's stony-faced silence as I waxed on about changing the Sallys suddenly made sense. She was thinking up the ways she'd cut me off at the gate.

Why? Why is it so important that we exercise this way and only this way? Is she really that determined for the Sallys to remain the same?

"Fine," I said. "This list still gives us more choices than last year's backyard drills and two-mile runs. I'll let the sisters decide what they want to do."

"The reason your predecessors chose runs and drills is that all the girls did it together," Ortega replied. "Limiting it to those and making them pick designated group times ensures the sisters actually complete the weekly requirement."

I smiled. "Smart thinking on their part, but we're all grown women and we don't need babysitters. If a sister says she did her exercises, I'll believe her."

"Oh no," Ortega cried, clapping a hand over her chest. "Please, don't think of it as babysitting. Certainly I can appreciate the thought of observing morning and nightly runs, gym trips, and afternoon drills is daunting when you have a lot on your plate, Valentina. It would be easier to operate on an honor system, but I can assure you the girls will let things slip.

"It's only natural when you've got a big test to study for, your homework is piling up, and your friends want to go out that night, that the trip to the gym gets canceled. Signing up for mandatory sessions is the only way we can be sure the girls remain in good standing." Ortega matched me smile for smile. "If you'd like, I can set up and maintain the sessions. I'm here to make everything easier."

I studied her, eyes narrowing slightly. Jade emailed us all a bio detailing her work, travels, and fondness for everything dipped in caramel. One thing was left out.

"Miss Ortega, were you in a sorority in college?"

"Of course." She laughed. "This one right here. Zeta Rho Sigma."

Just like that, it all clicked into place.

"Cool," I said simply. "Thanks for the offer, but I don't want to put more on your plate either. It'll be too much coordinating mandatory runs, jogs, hikes, and basketball games. Since it's important to me that the sisters have a choice, what I'll do is put it up for a vote each week. The sisters will decide if they want to hit the court or swing by the gym."

"Love that," said Blair. "I'll handle collecting the votes and choosing times that work with everyone's schedule."

"That's why you're the number one VP."

"Excellent compromise," Ortega said.

I couldn't tell if she truly meant it. Her face read nothing but polite support.

"Next on the list: social calendar."

Our treasurer, London Morgan, broke in. "We'll have more money this semester since we're not hosting pledges. We can have more parties. Get creative with our bonding activities. Also, we don't have to do the obstacle course this semester. We can go somewhere fun on our end-of-year trip."

Blair and I gushed over her idea.

"Can't," Aiden said. "You won't have pledges but Nu Alpha Theta will. You're supposed to help me evaluate them on the course."

"They won't have anyone to compete against," I said.

"They'll compete against each other."

"You seriously need me there?"

He shrugged. "This is how it's done."

I blew out a breath. "Fine. But the other sisters don't have to go. They can have their trip."

"That's not fair," London cried. "Why should you be stuck at the camp?"

Lowering my head, I said, "A good president sacrifices for her subjects."

"I'm pretty sure they say that about queens," Blair said.

"I'm that too."

We laughed, breaking the tension. Aiden didn't join us.

"Back to the social calendar," he said. "Let's do a joint party in two weeks and a party on Halloween. Forget the 'close enough' thing. That was Leighton's idea and the other houses ripped us off quick."

"Fine. I'm not bothered either way."

"Oh, and that fun trip everyone is taking at the end of the year, the Sams want in." Aiden spread out his hands, leaning back in his chair. "We've got extra money in the budget too."

"Didn't we just talk about the boot camp trip?"

"Move yours to a different weekend and we'll all go."

I opened my mouth to shove his suggestion down his throat.

"A lot of the Sallys are dating the Sams," he continued. "When you put it to a vote, I bet they'll be on board."

"We don't need to vote," said Blair. "I hear them cheering about it now."

She penciled it into her notes.

I swallowed my tongue, pushing on with the meeting. "What else do you want to get on the calendar, ladies?"

The next four hours continued in the same vein. Aiden found a way to horn into our activities, events, and trips. He offered to join our basketball games and said we should host a few movie nights on their big screen. Ortega and the other girls jumped on it while I gritted my teeth and agreed.

This man was dangerous. My instincts said to lure him out into the woods and drop his ass in a deep, dark hole where he can't hurt anyone. I did not want him near my Sallys or the Sams. All the same, instinct was beaten down. I couldn't learn his endgame without getting close to him and he was giving me every opportunity. I had to take them.

It was pushing six by the time I trudged out of the dining room. A tad early for dinner.

I can get it cooking now and leave it in the warmer for the girls to grab and go. Getting home early, sneaking into Ryder's office, and fooling around on his desk is what I need to be doing in the next hour.

"Valentina." Ortega patted my shoulder. "Ready to make dinner? The salad is done. Why don't I tackle the spring rolls and you the stir-fry?"

"I've got it, Miss Ortega."

"Please, call me Jade."

"Jade," I corrected. "You've done all of the prep. I wouldn't expect you to do the cooking too. Chill out for the rest of the night. I'll bring a plate up to you."

She covered her grin, eyes shining like I told the funniest joke. "That'd be a nice end to the day—reclining in bed and getting waited on. Thank you, Valentina, but you don't have to lighten my load. I'm here to help you with whatever you need."

Jade set off into the kitchen.

I watched her go, keenly aware of the second reason for my weariness. Jade constantly piped up throughout the meeting offering to take over my duties, or chiming in with her addendum to shoot down anything that veered too far off course of Sally traditions.

I was no dummy. There was an addendum to her job description and it was to make sure the ship Leighton left behind kept sailing smoothly.

But again, why? Is she in on whatever is up with this house? I'm here to protect the girls. What is Jade Ortega here for?

Picking up my feet, I went to join her in the kitchen.

I wouldn't find out the answer to my question by standing out in the hall. She was another person I'd have to keep close.

JAXSON

"Thanks, Paunch."

I accepted the takeout bags and beat it for the special elevator taking me directly to the top floor.

Dad wanted Thai from the restaurant down the block that delivered, giving me a break from my nightly food run to finish up work for Bianca.

After I drop this off, I'm out of here.

I walked in on my father pouring drinks at the wet bar. He wasn't alone.

"Hello, Jaxson. Good to see you again."

Dad's new *friend*, Eve Gregson, spread out on the couch, legs crossed and arm draped over the back like she was posing. She was a stunningly beautiful woman but models tended to be. Her shiny, dark crown was styled in a pixie cut and hazel eyes twinkled when she smiled. I asked if they taught her to do that for her job and she laughed a soft, ethereal laugh.

"Hey, Eve. I'm guessing the green mango salad is for you? They threw in tofu free of charge but I told them to put it on the side just in case."

"Thank you, J." She grinned at my father. "Top-notch assistant you have here, Levi."

"I was thinking of keeping him around." Dad took the bags out of my hand and replaced it with a scotch. He was always lax on the not-yet-twenty-one thing. "Did you get something for yourself?" he asked. "Stay and have dinner with us."

"Can't. I'm getting home on time for once."

"Tomorrow," he said as he set the food on the table. "Dinner. You and me. We'll talk about how things are going and what's next."

"Legal."

He gave me a look though I only said one word. "The deal was every department, J. You have to go to legal eventually."

"I know," I said simply. The only thing I wanted more than a hundred feet between me and Daniel Meyer at all times—was this label. A few weeks in the legal department and Dad would have full faith in me. I'd take that trade-off.

"I'm heading out. Later, Pops." I tipped my head. "The lovely Miss Eve."

"Such a charmer," she said.

I handed back his scotch. "Oh. And thanks for the chocolate. They delivered on the presentation."

"What?" Dad plopped down next to Eve. "What are you talking about?"

"The chocolate pastries you sent me. I got them today. Tasted fresh from the kitchen."

He frowned. "I didn't send you any chocolates."

"Yes, you did. The same ones we got in France."

"Those were good," he agreed, "but I still didn't send them to you."

"Seriously?" I stopped. "Well, Val didn't send them either and Ryder, Rick, Ezra, and I don't give each other presents. Wonder who they're from?"

"No card?"

"Nope."

"Maybe it's from one of the bands you've worked with," Eve spoke up. "A thank-you for all you've done."

"Could be, but I would've sworn they were the same from that restaurant in France. I'm trying to think who I told about them."

"Just a coincidence," Dad said. "Chocolate is a common thank-you gift."

"Yeah. That's true." I closed over the doorknob. "Have a good night. See you tomorrow, old man."

"Sliding in that 'old man' dig because I didn't give you the damn chocolates."

Laughing, I left them to it. Dad and Eve had been spending quite a lot of time together. More than friends usually do and I say that as someone who lives with his boys.

I rode the elevator down and nodded to Paunch on my way through security. "Hey, do you know who dropped off my package today?"

"Wallace. The regular guy."

"All right. Thanks."

I let it go. I had my money on Eve being right. A gift from a band.

Climbing into Ezra's car, I couldn't help scanning the seats for presents of a different kind. I couldn't prove Serena did it but I'd never be caught out like that again.

The drive home was long. The sun beat me across the horizon and streetlamps and cyclists with reflector lights led me the rest of the way. I jammed out to a demo tape by *Fuel*. Not for work. Because they were kickass. This band had a great sound and a destiny in Bianca's check-them-out pile.

I rolled into Ryder's driveway with minutes until dinner. Multiple times Dad asked me to move back home, saying Val was welcome any time. I couldn't leave. Wherever Val was, that is where I had to be.

Speaking of which...

I bounded into the house in search of her. This close to dinner she was either in the kitchen cooking or the chef got there first and shooed her off to the dining room. The voices floating down the main hallway told me the answer.

Adam jumped up at the sight of me. "Jaxson!"

"Hey, little man." I ruffled his hair, picking him up and carrying him to the empty seat next to Val. We sat down and got a kiss for our troubles.

"You're just in time," she said. "I was just telling everyone about the house mother/spy who has been sent to stop me making big changes to the Sallys."

"A spy?"

Val told us what went down at her meeting that day.

"Am I missing something?" Ryder replied. "Blindsiding you with a rule change before you get the chance to make good on your promises. Why is it so important that you guys do weekly strenuous activities?"

"Excellent question, my love, and it's the same one I'm asking myself."

Ezra's knuckles paled, clutching his knife. "And I'm asking why Aiden wants in on everything you're doing. He even said you have to go on that pledge trip with him? You're not going out there with him alone. Why should you go out there at all? He can evaluate his pledges by himself."

"He claims I'm supposed to help and Jade backed him up," Valentina replied. "I can't say he's being off because he's not asking me to do anything he didn't do with Leighton. They planned parties and events together. They evaluated the pledges like they both had to approve a new Sally or Sam."

"The guy is off," said Ezra. "He's going to dress it up as innocent but don't let your guard down around him."

"My *guards* are all over him," Val replied. "I'll never be alone with him or end up in a situation where someone isn't watching my back. Even if the entire sorority does come at me with duct tape and rope, Juliet's not going to hold the van door open for them. It's not about keeping me safe. It's about everyone—Sallys and Sams—making it to the end of the year."

"You want to find out what happened to Teagan and Sawyer. Where will you start?" Ryder asked.

"Getting in touch with their family was a dead end. I have to find out more about them another way. Why were they kidnapped out of everyone? Why did Sawyer keep his mouth shut after his girlfriend was snatched? Who drove him off in that van? Who did Leighton call that night?"

"I've started looking into all of that," said Maverick.

"You can't," Val cried. "It's too dangerous."

"Mommy?" Adam reached for her. "What's wrong?"

She wiped away her frown. "Nothing's wrong, baby." She put him on her lap, kissing him all over until he giggled. "We'll talk about this later," she said to Maverick.

Chef arrived with our lamb chops like he planned his entrance. A heavy atmosphere hung over us as we ate. For Adam and Caroline, we stuck to small talk, rattling on about our day.

"My father is planning another visit," said Ezra. "He's bringing his family and mentioned hitting the water park while they're here. I was thinking of stealing Adam that weekend."

Val chuckled. "No stealing necessary. We can make it a family trip. I'd love to spend time with your dad."

After dinner, Val handed Adam to Ryder. He carried him up to get ready for bed while the rest of us took dessert into the living room.

Valentina started in before our butts hit the chair. "Maverick, what if they find out what you're doing?"

"I played it smarter this time." Maverick squeezed his bulk into the armchair, kicking his legs up on the footrest. "Dad and I coded an algorithm that— I'll get into the tech stuff later. The point is only the NSA could detect me in their computers. I'm already in Aiden's. Haven't gone through all of the files yet, but I started with his email. There were a lot of messages going back and forth between him and Leighton Lewis."

Val put down her cake. "Recent ones?"

He shook his head. "None dated after her supposed death. If she is alive, she's being more careful than that. From the little I read, they mostly speak about the brothers and sisters, and who their favorites are. Stuff like 'Patrick aced the test' and 'Zaya's the fastest runner.' I've only read a few, but so far there's nothing incriminating."

"I need to read those," Val said.

"Does that mean you don't want me to stop?"

"That means I want you to be careful," she retorted. "But if you are going to do this, I need to know what you find out. Buried somewhere in those emails could be the truth about what happened to Teagan and Sawyer."

"I saw it with my own eyes. Chased that van down the street, and still I can't comprehend what's going on in those houses," said Ezra.

"I will figure it out and find them if I still can," Val said. "President Valentina is ending this shit."

Chapter Six

President Valentina is having more trouble than she wants to admit. In the two weeks since I was elected, I got no closer to uncovering Zeta Rho Sigma's secrets. Maverick combed through every email between Aiden and Leighton—on top of every other email he sent or received. The two kept it strictly house business, and when Aiden met with me, he did the same. The week before, we gathered in the Sally dining room with Blair and his vice president planning the Sam back-to-school party without a problem.

Maverick also dug up the emails mentioning Sawyer and Teagan. It was too much to ask that they'd lay out the plans for their kidnapping. All those two had to say about them were how well they were doing keeping up with their requirements on top of school.

Maverick intended to dig deeper but this time he was going slow. Covering his tracks. He went for the subtle approach while I played to my strengths.

"Are you going to do the initiation to these poor guys?"

Aiden and I stood on the porch. Juliet and the others respected my request for distance and posted up on the other side of the pool where they could keep me in sight.

There wasn't much for them to observe. The two of us stood two feet apart, overseeing the potential Sams putting out the tiki lights for the parties.

Eager to please and puffed up to impress, I thought. *They have no idea what they're in for.*

"All brothers must prove their loyalty."

136

"Why, Aiden? What do you get out of guys side-eyeing you when you come in the room? Scared and on edge about what you know or will uncover next. That's not trust or loyalty. It's intimidation."

His gaze did not waver. "Only to the weak."

I bristled. "Why won't you tell me how you found those secrets out? I'm president now. I have to know."

"Do you? I heard you're ending the initiation on your side of the lawn."

Leaning on the porch post, I said, "That's the plan. I suspect a new addendum will get out ahead of me though."

Aiden chuckled but didn't deny it.

The last two weeks had been interesting and not only because of Aiden. Miss Ortega was everywhere and in everything. Always smiling. Always supportive. Always gently reminding me of what I could and couldn't do.

The sisters chose basketball as their exercise for the week before, and she *kindly* offered to tag along with a stopwatch, ensuring every girl played for at least seventy-five minutes. Her standing off to the side, eagle-eyed and bearing her clipboard, leeched a fair amount of fun from the friendly game.

When I wasn't around, Sofia assured me she didn't attempt to take over or undermine me. But her true duties in the house were obvious to me. Even if she had the others fooled with her banana pancakes.

"How'd you find all of that stuff out, Aiden?" I continued. "You're shadily dodging the question like you want me to keep believing you're a bad guy."

"I'm not a bad guy."

"You had Sawyer kidnapped." I preferred this. We had reached the point where we could speak freely. All pretense dropped.

Stuffing his hands in his pockets, he rocked back on his heels, turning his face to the sunlight breaking onto the porch. To anyone watching we were a couple of pals shooting the shit.

"You can't prove that."

"I have a witness."

"He can't prove it either."

"You couldn't resist gloating to him that Sawyer was in a better place."

He lifted his shoulders. "Maybe he is. Did you ever think he likes it where he is? Couldn't it be possible that the reason he hasn't come back is because he wants to stay?"

"Nope."

Aiden barked a laugh. "I can see why that'd be hard for you to accept, but the fact remains, accusations without proof are a waste of time. You want to come at me with something, you better have more than your boyfriend's word."

I didn't skip a beat. "I've got plenty of proof for what you boys get down to in your basement. You found out about the Sons of Slaughter and threatened to give Ezra's brother over to them. Blackmail is illegal in this part of the world, genius."

"Blackmail is such a harsh word." Aiden leaned on the other post, facing me. "I prefer... encouragement. I encouraged him to stay out of Nu Alpha Theta business and put his attention where it was really needed. It all worked out in the end, didn't it?"

"How did you know, Connelly?"

He heaved a sigh. "You're being all intense like you think the answer is mind reading or something. How does anyone find out anything? The right person lets the wrong thing slip. A door is left unlocked that shouldn't be. A password isn't well hidden. A conversation is overheard. Nothing is truly a secret, Valentina. You know that as well as I. You've got a talent for digging them up too."

"You and I also know that wasn't a real answer."

He pushed off. "Yes, but it's the only one you're going to get. See you tonight, Val." Aiden stepped off the porch. "Only some of your boyfriends are invited."

I clenched my teeth to stop myself shouting what I really thought of his evasive ass and broke the illusion that we were getting on well. Aiden had most people fooled and kicking up a fuss around him while he sat there grinning, would have the brothers and sisters thinking I was the problem. I couldn't have that.

But am I going to this party tonight and playing nice?

Sawyer disappeared from one of their parties. Was that reason enough to go and keep an eye on Aiden?

You can't watch everyone at the same time, a voice countered. *One guy gets up to go to the bathroom and is never seen again. What could I do about it?*

I went into the house, stepping through the back door and landing on the entrance to the basement.

This wasn't a movie. I doubted Aiden hid the bodies of his enemies down there buried under a pile of evidence. Still...

I tried the door.

Locked.

Like it always was each time I snuck the chance to jiggle the knob. Does Aiden truly keep the pledge scores down there? Or is he keeping information of another kind?

"I think you're the one with the mind powers."

I whirled around, heart jumping into my throat.

Aiden cocked his brow through the screen door. "You're staring at that knob like you can will it unlocked."

"I can't. So, why don't you open it for me?"

"There's nothing interesting down there. Ezra would've told you that."

"If that's true, why is it always locked?"

"Pledge points," we said at the same time.

I rewarded him a mirthless smile. "You said I was supposed to help you evaluate the brothers, right? Let me see the points. Which pledges are in the running?"

"It's only been two weeks. It's too soon to tell."

"If they don't have points, what are you hiding?"

"I'm not hiding anything."

"Then open the door."

Aiden locked eyes with me through the screen. The grin played at his lips, but I picked up on the tiniest bit of irritation in the tightness around his eyes. I tripped him up.

"All right. Maybe this will finally prove you've got me the wrong way around."

Aiden came through and produced a key from his pocket. He inserted it without hesitation and let the door swing open. "After you."

"You won't be offended if I say I'm not interested in walking into a darkened basement alone with you?"

"What do you think I'm going to do?" he asked with a laugh. "I hope you also don't take it the wrong way when I say it's either you and me or you can walk off right now. What's it going to be?"

I scoffed. "Let's just get this over with."

Everyone knew I was at the Sam house and Aiden Connelly couldn't take me anyway. I led the way down the steps.

The basement was as Ezra described. A cement box of recreation. Worn couches sat around an old television set. Near the back corner was a pool cabinet and a shelf bursting with games. Next to that was a large whiteboard.

I squinted, peering through the dim light at the collection of names, birth dates, scores, and information collected on every Nu Alpha Theta pledge. It all added up to a final column where the points were assigned. Early days accounted for why most of the guys didn't have a score yet.

"What are these scores based on?" I asked.

Aiden came to my side. "Everyone starts at zero. If they've gotten a bid, they're already top of their class and killing it at extracurriculars. It's not about what they've done outside of the house anymore. It's about what they accomplish here.

"I observe how they get along with the guys. The effort they put in." He pointed. "Wyatt and Josiah offered to set up for the party before I asked. That's a point right there. We also pay attention to the standard stuff. How are they handling the pledge activities?

"Failing the test knocks them down a few points. Skipping out on bonding activities won't do them any favors either. They get a grace period the first couple of weeks for the exercises, but after a month, if they still can't keep up, they lose points for that too."

I noticed he slipped "we" in there.

"Am I expected to judge the new sisters the same way?"

"How else would you do it? We do these things to test them. Why should they get in if they fail?"

"You have a point," I agreed. "My trouble is understanding why their place should hinge on an hour and fifteen minutes of basketball. We're the best and we take the best. I get that. But we won't lose our reputation if we value what's truly important."

Aiden snorted. "It all makes sense now. You're an idealist. That's why they voted for you over Heather."

"They voted for me because the girls want Sally house to change." I waved a hand at the board. "Getting along with the brothers. Stepping up. Meeting the challenges thrown at them. All of that is important. But what really matters is us coming together and being there for each other." I turned on him. "It matters that my sisters, and the guys on this side of the lawn, are safe. I won't let anyone hurt them. Not even you."

"I keep telling you, Valentina. You've got me all wrong."

That he repeated the statement with that smirk on his mouth lessened the sincerity.

"Have you seen enough?"

There was nothing down here. Just the pledge points like he swore.

It won't be easy to get the truth out of this guy. The single good thing about his act is since he's so determined to play the good guy, he'll be careful when I'm around.

"I'll see you at the party tonight. Early. Helping you keep an eye on things."

On cue, my phone blew up. Juliet's name flashed on the screen. Disappearing into basements with shady kidnappers tended to put your bodyguards on alert.

"Juliet," I answered.

"Miss Moon. Where are you?"

"Dipping into the basement to talk over some president stuff. I'm coming out now. You can meet me at the car."

"I will meet you on the front steps and escort you to the car."

"That works too."

Juliet was where she promised. We set off together down Greek Row, passing by homes in a much rougher state but the occupants weren't suffering for it. Music poured out of most of them, and through the windows, snapshots of beer pong, study groups, and laughing friends told the story of their Greek life.

"Your sorority is quite different from the others," Juliet mused.

"You have no idea."

She took out her phone, read the screen, and signaled for me to stop. "Hadley." As she listened, her brows inched closer and closer together.

"Did anyone see them?" she asked. "Have you secured the area? Okay. Bring the car." She hung up, flashing me a look that I did not like.

"What's wrong?"

"There is an issue with the car. Remain here and—"

"Issue with the car? What issue?"

"Hadley went to get hers," she replied. "We'll drive you home. Wait here for—"

Spinning on my heels, I took off.

"Miss M— Val," she cried. "Please! You shouldn't have to see that!"

See that? See what?

I parked Ryder's car on the main street. Reaching the end of the Row, I rounded the corner and stumbled. My jaw dropped, eyes widening at the scene that had my guard, Kennedy, shaking her head as she relayed it to the person on the other end of her phone. Most likely the police.

Spiderwebs of cracks splintered my windshield, blooming from one, two, three points of impact. It looked like someone took a bat to it and all of my windows—if the shattered glass littering the front and back seats was anything to go by. But none of that was what horrified me. Spray-painted on my hood in big, angry red letters was a single word.

Whore!

I DIDN'T MAKE IT TO the Nu Alpha Theta party that night.

I lay on Ryder's bed, silent as he barked into the phone, berating my security for letting this happen under their watch. I might've slowed him down if my mind wasn't running a mile a minute.

Who did this?

Was I the target? It wasn't my car, though it was the one I borrowed most often. Was there a chance—even a small one—that I wasn't once again the target of a hateful lurking shadow?

That's too much to hope for.

Anyone paying attention the last two weeks as I dropped by the Sally house day after day, parking in the same spot because there was never anywhere to park on the Row, would know whose car to target.

"—anything like this happens again, you're fired!" Ryder ended the call and flung his phone across the room, pinging it off the couch.

"Ryder, please." I patted the spot next to me. "It wasn't Juliet, Kennedy, or Hadley's fault. All three of them were guarding me like they're paid to do. We couldn't anticipate something like this would happen."

"Something like this is what I hired them to stop." Ryder climbed in, pulling me to his chest. "What the fuck is going on, Val? Busting out your windows, breaking the windshield, and tagging your car in broad daylight. They risked a lot just to tell you what they thought of you, and that's what concerns me."

"What do you mean?"

"A regular, standard-issue asshole is lazy. They'll inbox you nasty shit. Hiss at you in the hallway when fifty of their friends are backing them up. They might even key your car while pretending to tie their shoe. But this was bold, risky, and out in the open. They wanted to teach you a lesson and didn't care if they got caught doing it."

A ripple crept beneath my skin. "Ryder, this is freaking me out."

"It should, Val. I think this was the same person who ran you off the road. Unless you can think of someone else."

"No," I said. "Aiden was in my sight all afternoon. Seriously. Even if he wasn't, I wouldn't put this down as his style. I amuse Aiden Connelly. He doesn't take me or my questions seriously. But the one person we know for certain holds malicious hate toward me is the mystery person in the white car. If it is them, they know where I go to school and how I spend my time."

"I'm doubling your security."

"Ryder, wait. This is one crazy person against a team of trained guards. If they wanted to test their luck with them, they would have done it already."

"You don't know that. They could be biding their time until you and Juliet turn a blind corner with the other two lagging far behind. It's a college campus. You see a lot of random faces wandering around every day. How would you know who shouldn't be there? And then there's Leighton Lewis and the sorority she ran for years before you came along. She could have plenty of friends in that house willing to do her bidding beyond the grave. If it's not her in the first place."

I dropped my head back, expelling a tired breath. "All right. I get it. I'm not underestimating the danger. I just don't want more people following me around everywhere. Do you know what it's like feeling someone's eyes on you all the time? Watching you eat, cough, and scratch? It reminds me every second that my sense of safety is shattered."

"I know, Val." Ryder lifted my head, pressing our foreheads together. "They're looking for this guy. Soon we'll find him and you can go back to your life. I promise."

I tapped his nose. "I'm going to hold you to that promise."

"Do it. You know I'm good for them."

Snuggling into his neck, I breathed him in. "For what it's worth, I don't think this is Leighton."

"Why not?"

"Calling me a whore is pretty telling. Whoever did this must have a problem with me and my four boyfriends. Leighton didn't care at all. Actually, she was so strongly in support of better treatment for women and their right to choose their partners that she slit Logan Bilius's throat. She's not running around spray-painting 'whore' on anyone's car."

"The only thing you know about Leighton... is that you don't know her at all."

I inclined my head. "Fair enough. But we keep coming back to the fact that Leighton doesn't have a reason to hate me. I haven't told the world what she did."

"If not Leighton or Aiden, we're looking at everyone." He kissed me. "You have to be careful, Val. This person followed you to the beach house and didn't disappear like we assumed."

"Maybe their next message will tell me what they want from me."

"There won't be a next message." Ryder grasped my chin between two fingers. "I've got five cars. Take a different one every day and mix up where you park. Juliet and Hadley are by your sides at all times from now on. Kennedy hangs back."

"I can do that. If this person is going to keep coming after me this recklessly, it won't be long until they trip up."

"They will. And I'll be there with a bat to smash their heads in."

A smile tugged at my lips. "My sexy, violent hero."

"That's me."

I laughed. "There's something else you can do to make me feel better."

"Have the chef send up ice cream, put a movie on, and binge out with Adam?"

"Well... I was going to say sex, but that works too— Ah!"

Ryder leaped on top of me, smooshing my shrieking self into the pillows. So much for ice cream.

JAXSON

"What is it this time?"

"I have to open it to find out."

Bianca rose an inch, peeking over her desk.

Paunch intercepted me in the hallway with another delivery. After the fifth one in two weeks, I concluded my mystery gift-giver was not my dad or a grateful band. I didn't know who this person was.

I grabbed her scissors off the desk, slicing through the tape. Black tissue paper greeted me. I reached inside and pulled out a small, black box covered in gold embossing.

"Scotch-infused toothpicks." I shook them at her. "See what I'm saying? Scotch toothpicks to go with the custom vinyl record, leather wallet, recipe book, wireless headphones, a new watch, keychain, and the pastries. I can't help but think this stuff is going to the wrong Van Zandt."

She gave me a wry look. "I've seen you knock back a scotch, minor. Don't pretend you don't like it. On top of that, Levi Van Zandt is well known, and he's got his face plastered all over the building if anyone wants to forget. No one is mixing senior up with junior. These love gifts are for you."

"Don't call them that. I'm taken and my girl doesn't mess around. She'll fuck up me, Paunch, the delivery guy, and the person who picked up on my love of scotch but somehow missed that I've got a girlfriend."

"If you don't want them, pass them here." Bianca plucked it out of my hand. "Scotch toothpicks. What will they think of next?"

"What will you think of next, boss? What do you got for me?"

"Hmm." She blinked at me like she forgot what I was here for. "Oh, yes. Pack a bag, junior. You're going to New Orleans."

"Um... what?"

"You heard me. The international music festival kicks off in two days. Their headliner fell through and they asked for Beyond Berlin specifically. The band is home right now packing their bags. I suggest you do the same."

"Holy shit. Why me?" I asked. "Gwen's been trying to get herself on a tour bus for months. She should go."

"It's you because your first thought was to pass the opportunity on to someone else. I like that about you, Jaxson. You don't make this job about you and what you'll get out of it. You're about getting the work done. Which is why you won't get starstruck or weak-kneed about a trip to the big city. Your priority will be keeping the band focused."

She nodded. "They need that. Those kids got talent leaking from their pores but they're still kids for all that they're older than you. Your first big festival can go to your head quick. Watch out for them. Get them on that stage and back on the bus in one piece."

"I can do that," I said. "How will the bus arrangements work?"

"Kitchen, bathroom, six bunks, and a bedroom for the only lady, Serena. It's a two-day drive, but you'll be comfortable. Beyond Berlin's new manager is tagging along, so it won't all be on your shoulders."

"Sweet. How many days will we be gone?"

"A week."

I rose from my seat. "I'll start packing."

"Damn. If I had five of you, I'd get more sleep. Thanks for the gift."

"You can have them all," I tossed over my shoulder.

I hooked a right out of her office and headed for mine. My first tour. Sure it was only to one festival and I'd be sleeping in a rolling coffin, but this was exactly what I signed up for.

Now to get my girl on board.

"SOMEONE BUSTED THE fucking windows!?"

"Mmm hmm." Valentina was sitting on my lap, stopping me from jumping up and flipping the table.

I came home to find everyone tense as fuck. Ezra told me what happened with fists clenched to put a hole in the nearest wall.

I got Val out of Ryder's bed and carried her to mine, sitting us both out on the balcony, and soaking in the warm, quiet night as her description of the day struck me cold.

"I'm sorry I wasn't here, baby."

"No, Jaxson. It's not your fault. I didn't call you because I didn't want you to rush back here. I was shaken up but now I'm okay. This isn't the first sicko to come after me and do something wicked and hateful."

I squeezed her tighter. "Ezra said we're thinking it's the person who ran you off the road."

"Maybe. I didn't want to mention this to Ryder, but is it possible it's Logan's cousin or one of the guys who attacked me coming back for revenge?"

"No," I replied without having to think about it. "Those guys wouldn't dare come near you again, Val. I can promise you that."

"Okay." Val's trust in us was unshakable. "If it's not them, and I don't believe it's Leighton or Aiden, that leaves the only other enemy I have out there."

"They're out there and we don't know who or where they're hiding. I can't go away with this going on, Val. Bianca will understand."

"Go away?" She sat up. "Did I miss part of the conversation?"

"Beyond Berlin was invited to headline a music festival in New Orleans. I'd be gone a week."

"A week," she repeated. "Stuck in a cramped bus with Serena Blackwood?"

"I don't have to go."

She looked away, lips pressed tight. I studied each emotion as it crossed her face.

"Yes, you do," she finally said. "This is your job and you love it. More than that, you're working to show your father that you can handle every aspect of this business. Dropping everything for me doesn't send that message."

"Fuck what message it sends."

She cracked a smile. "I love you, and I'd never say no to you being with me all the time. But you don't have to. I trust you and I want you to go. I'll be safe here. The plan is to mix up cars and parking spaces. My new psycho friend will have to work harder to target me with their spray paint."

"Val, it's one festival. I can miss it. Gwen will go in my place."

"*I* would go in your place. A trip to New Orleans sounds perfect right now."

I seized on an idea. "Babe, come with us."

"What? I can't miss an entire week of classes. Plus, there's this little cutie. Maybe you've met him? His name is Adam Moon and he won't stand for me to be away from him that long."

Tapping my chin, I hummed. "That name does sound familiar..."

Her laugh set the world on its axis and called it to spin again.

"No chance you'll both squeeze in my bunk with me?"

"Adam would probably love that."

"Well, if that's not going to work," I said. "Why don't you fly in for the festival? Amelia's got a private jet. Come down Saturday morning. Check out the bands. Fool around with me on the tour bus. And be back Sunday night."

"That does sound tempting."

I bumped her nose with mine. "You've been on for weeks. School, home, Zeta Rho. Now this. Take a break, baby. You deserve it."

"A break would be amazing," she said, turning the idea over. "I've never been to a music festival. Munching on beignets and dancing with you to killer bands is the perfect end to what will be a miserable week."

"That sounds like a yes."

Val popped a kiss on my lips. "It's definitely a yes. I'll call Amelia in the morning." She rested her head on my shoulder, content to watch the night with me.

It amazed me her ability to compartmentalize. What happened that day was pushed aside to be dealt with later.

Right now is all about us.

My mystery gift-giver could send all the presents they wanted. She was all I needed.

"I'M SO JEALOUS."

Gwen threw herself on my chair, flopping like a ragdoll. The two of us were in my office the next day, talking tour.

"Bianca told them about the festival and it was out of Serena's mouth that she wanted you to go before I opened mine," said Gwen. "She *really* doesn't like me."

"What's that about?" I couldn't resist asking. "She'd rather wait for me to be free than go to you for anything."

Gwen threw up her hands. "You see it too! It's starting to feel personal, J. The other guys don't have a problem with me, but Serena stiffens when I enter the room. I'm wracking my brain for what I did to offend her."

"Honestly, it's likely my fault. She hates that I keep pushing her at you."

"This is our job. We're supposed to work it together. Levi, Bianca, you, and her own bandmates have told her she can't put you on a leash. Why is that so hard for her to accept?" She sighed. "In the meantime, I'm sitting here while you're partying in some of the most amazing cities in the world."

"There's an extra bunk. I'll see if I can persuade Bianca to let you come too."

"No, that's okay. Doesn't seem the smart move to confine myself in a small space with Serena Blackwood. Besides, someone has to be here to fetch the coffee."

I squeezed her knee. "You'll be on the next bus, mama. Count on it."

"Thanks."

Knuckles beat on the door.

"I can guess who that is," she mumbled.

"Is your money on Serena or Paunch?"

"Serena. Five bucks and the champagne cupcake you're hiding in the mini fridge?"

"Whoa. Not my cupcake. You're taking it too far. This is just a friendly bet."

She snorted.

"Hello? I know you're in there."

Serena, Gwen mouthed to me, smug as ever.

I opened the door without getting up. Serena blew inside. "Jaxson, did Bianca tell you?"

"Yep. I'm already packed."

Serena slid a look to Gwen. "You're not coming."

"Jaxson, I'll take my cupcake."

I handed it over along with her five bucks. She earned it for dealing with Serena.

Gwen grabbed her winnings and left us alone. Serena claimed her seat. "We have a million things to do to prepare."

"Your manager will make sure you're ready."

She waved that away. Dad came through hiring Brant Titus to manage the band and take Serena everywhere she wanted her career to go. For some reason, she was still determined to drag me along.

"How did they hear about us?" she asked, passing my comment by. "This is huge for the band. It's the start of more festivals, concerts, and tours."

"It is. Beyond Berlin will be huge. I knew that the moment I heard you sing."

A rare smile transformed her face. "Thanks, Jaxson." She slid her hand down my thigh and squeezed my knee. I stood, knocking her off.

"I've got a lot to do if we're leaving in the morning." I held the door open. "Brant was in the cafeteria last I saw him. Hit him with your questions."

"See you tomorrow."

My gaze trailed her around the corner.
She definitely hit on me that time.

THE NEXT MORNING, I was first on the bus, checking out the accommodations. Dad hooked us up Interstellar-style. The kitchen and front lounge were spotless and fitted with all the finishes. The bunks had privacy curtains, a television, personal outlets, lighting, air-conditioning, and—

I pressed on the mattress. *Memory foam. Unless one of the guys snores through my earplugs, I'll sleep decent on this.*

I tossed my bag on the top bunk and then pushed into Serena's temporary bedroom. Her space had everything mine did except it wasn't all on top of her. The television hung across from the full-sized bed—done up with brown satin sheets and covered in pillows. A door on the other end hinted at a private bathroom.

A sense of rightness filled me, grounding me to the spot as my eyes closed. I breathed deep, inhaling nothing but disinfectant, but in my mind, it was sweat, spilled beer, open chip bags, and history in the making. I was a little kid again. Running through Dad's legs on a bus filled with legends.

There is no better life than this.

"Don't even think about it, Jaxson." Serena bumped me, knocking me out of my reverie. Shrieking, she flung herself on the bed. "This is all mine. Go back to your bunk."

A whistle sounded behind me. "This is sweet. Does this mean we've made it?" Ty came in and flopped next to Serena. "You won't make me sleep in the bunk, will you?"

Grinning, she flipped onto her stomach, kicking her feet in the air. "I guess there's room for two. If you ask nicely."

Ty pushed her spaghetti strap down.

Time to go.

"Make sure you have everything, guys," I said. "We leave in twenty minutes."

They were tongue-deep before the door closed.

Chandler hefted his stuff up the stairs. "Where's Serena and Ty?"

"Breaking in the bed."

"Could've helped me with the equipment first," he mumbled under his breath.

"I'll help."

"Thanks, Jaxson. Brant is babysitting it."

Beyond Berlin's new manager was a stout man with more hair on his chin than on his head. His style didn't cross into business, but his jeans didn't have rips and his button-up shirts were pressed. Above all, Brant's most impressive feature was his vast knowledge of the music industry.

Together we loaded the stuff on the bus. I put away the drumsticks, came out for one last check, and spotted Dad striding over.

"What's this?" I threw at him. "Tearful goodbye?"

"You get that mouth from me. That doesn't mean you should always be running it." Dad gripped my neck, crushing me to his chest in his version of a hug. "Keep your head out there, kid. You're still underage. Plus, you've got a kid of your own." He jerked his chin at the bus. "Our job is to give them this life. Not be sucked into it."

"You don't have to worry about me. This job's been mine since I was in diapers. This is where I'm supposed to be, Dad. I won't mess it up."

He flashed a grin. "Well, I'll say this. You're definitely my son."

"Jaxson," Brant called from the door of the bus. "We're kicking off in five minutes. Ready to go?"

"I'm coming."

I put two fingers to my temple, backing toward the ride. "See you in a week, Papa. Take care of my legacy."

He returned the salute.

I bounded up the steps, throwing myself on the couch. The leather welcomed me like we hadn't just met.

Brant came up behind the driver, shaking his shoulder. "Ready when you are, my man."

Chandler and Rylan made themselves comfortable in their bunks. Rylan's mushy conversation with his girlfriend had no trouble seeping through the privacy curtain. I left them to it and fell into conversation with Brant, talking about his old days as a roadie.

The town faded through the windows, becoming a hazy mass of gray buildings and trees, and then disappearing as we got onto the highway. Eventually, the guys dropped out of their bunks and suggested a game of poker. We were an hour deep when Serena and Ty emerged from the back room, damp from their showers, and spreading a cloud of minty steam.

"What are we playing?" Serena plopped down next to me, propping her chin on my shoulder.

"Ooh. I never learned how to play poker. Will you teach me?"

"Brant's got you. I have to call Val."

I slid the other way out of the booth, moving to my bunk. I didn't know what was up with her. Was this Serena being nice? Did she drape herself on all of her friends? Either way, I wasn't playing along. I strove to keep my relationship with Serena Blackwood professional from jump street. She'd get the hint quick.

I climbed onto my bed and drew the curtain. Val answered on the third ring.

"Hey, Jaxson. Are you guys on the road?"

"Just left. How are you? Everything normal?"

"So far. I parked in the east garage and my guards followed in front and behind to check there was no one on my tail. Juliet and Hadley are sticking to me like glue. We're safe."

"We?"

"Adam is tagging along for a trip to the Sally house. Isn't that right, baby? Isn't that right?"

Valentina dropped to cooing and Adam's excited babble came through the phone. I didn't share the excitement.

"It's the weekend, and after what you've been through, won't your friends give you a break? You don't need to be on campus."

"I organized this gourmet-popcorn-and-Meryl-Streep movie marathon. I'm excited about it. Whoever this person is they don't get to scare me out of living my life."

"I just can't stand you both being there while I'm getting farther away."

Her tone softened. "You won't be so far in a few days. I can't wait for us to hit that festival together. Amelia already said I can borrow the plane."

"Mama Melia always comes through."

The curtain flew open.

"Jaxson, why are you hiding in here?" Serena grabbed hold of my arm. "We're practicing intros. Come out and tell us which one you like best."

"Not now, Serena."

"Oh, is that Val?" She raised her voice. "Hi, Valentina. Don't worry, we're taking good care of him."

"I see you're busy," said Val. "I'll call you later. Say bye to Daddy, Adam."

"Bye!"

I barely got my goodbye out. Val hung up as Serena tugged me off the bunk.

"You're all ours now, Jaxson."

VALENTINA

Sofia pounced on Adam the minute I came through the door.

"There's my favorite godson." She had him out of my arms and on her hip in a blink. "We're making pizza bites, marshmallow treats, rainbow spritzers, and nachos to go with the gourmet popcorn. Want to help us, sweet boy?"

"Yeah!"

Adam's answer to everything was an enthusiastic yes. If Sofia asked if he wanted to hotwire the dean's car and take it for a spin, my son would be ride-or-dying in the passenger seat.

I laughed. "A few weeks of eating healthy and the girls had enough."

Her eyes glittered. "Basically."

"Okay, but don't let him eat too much sugar." I slid off his backpack. "I've got fruit and crackers in here for him."

Shaking her head, she tsked. "You know it's my godmotherly duty to sneak this kid all the treats he wants."

"Just like it was your godmotherly duty to buy Adam a horse?"

I wish I was kidding. There was a mare named Cinnamon enjoying her life in the Richards' stables as a little boy's birthday present.

"You're just making these up as you go along," I said.

She lifted her chin. "Rules are rules."

Sofia strode off with my son to make good on her promise to chock him full of sugar and then pass him back to me. I gave up the fight. I never formally named her his godmother but it was true all the same.

"Ladies, you can chill down in the living room. I'm going to find Miss Ortega."

"If it's all the same, we'd like to accompany you, sweep the room, and then, of course, we'll wait outside," said Juliet.

It was a fair request, so I agreed. Ryder wouldn't move on his threat to fire them if something else happened to me. I didn't have to make it harder for them to do their job.

I poked my head in the kitchen. Most of the house was in there. Some helping to make the food. More eating the ingredients and getting in the way. Adam kicked his little feet off the counter, beaming his missing-tooth grin as the girls showered him in attention. The only one who wasn't there was Miss Ortega.

I climbed the stairs and searched out her room on the top floor. Blair taking over the president's dorm gave her a choice between a room sandwiched between a couple of juniors or one at the top and at the end of the hallway. She chose the latter, and most nights when I said goodbye, I'd see her through the window, sitting in her rocking chair reading and looking out over Greek Row. Every time I'd ask myself what was truly going on in her head. Because in the weeks since I'd met her, I accepted I didn't truly know a thing about Jade Ortega.

Or what she wants, I thought as I stopped before her door. *The obvious objective of keeping me in line—I understand that. But the underlying reason of why Sally house must remain the same. That I don't know.*

What I did know is I had to find out more about the Sallys. And I had an idea to make that happen.

I knocked on her door.

"Yes? Who is it?"

"Valentina. Are you busy?"

"I'll be right there."

Footsteps sounded on the other side of the door, then it flew open. Jade filled the entrance in her floral sundress and matching sandals. I'd never seen the woman with a hair out of place. She was young, pretty, stylish, smart, and she knew how to act nice, at the very least. I overheard a few girls ask her why she took on a job babysitting a bunch of sorority girls and she repeated the same answer.

"It was time for a change."

"What can I do for you, Valentina?"

"I have the packet explaining my duties as president. It said I'd meet with Mrs. Kessler once a semester but her number wasn't in there. I was hoping you had it."

"Oh, I'm sorry. That was an oversight."

She backed into the room, giving me the full view. Jade transformed the space into a light, peaceful haven. Her yoga mat took up the middle of the room. The rocking chair I saw her in most nights rested next to an end table loaded down with books, and a queen-size bed with a purple spread was covered with more.

"I do have her number for you. Were you hoping to arrange that meeting now?"

"Yes," I replied. "Mrs. Kessler mentioned she organized the alumni events and I'd like to arrange one for this semester."

She paused reaching for her nightstand. "An alumni event?"

"I've heard so much about the great women who've graduated from the sorority. I'd love to meet them just as much as I'm sure the other girls would. I was thinking of doing a charity dinner and auction. Alumni and local businesses could donate to the auction, the proceeds go to a good cause, and the sisters get a chance to mingle with the amazing women who came before us."

"That's a wonderful idea, Valentina. I'm sure Mrs. Kessler will feel the same." Jade stepped up, phone in hand, and read out Kessler's number. I typed it in and hit dial immediately, waving goodbye as it rang.

"Hello. You've reached the office of Ophelia Kessler of Kessler's Kinder Toys. This is Mrs. Dove. How may I help you?"

"Hi, this is Valentina Moon, president of Zeta Rho. Is Mrs. Kessler available?" I headed for Sofia's room. "I'd like to speak to her about setting up a meeting."

"Yes, Miss Moon. I have your name here under her contacts," said Mrs. Dove. "I'm afraid Mrs. Kessler is unavailable, but I'd be happy to put that meeting on the books. She is available next week Tuesday, Thursday, or Friday at noon. Do either of those days work for you?"

"Thursday is perfect. Thank you."

We wrapped up the conversation. I went down to find my kid, freeing him from his adoring fans and carrying him into the living room to start on the popcorn and lay out cushions for movie-viewing.

I smiled as my little helper tossed the cushions every which way. My eyes watching him but my mind elsewhere.

I don't know enough about the Sallys to make a move. Time to change that.

Chapter Seven

J*axson*

"Jaxson! Check this out, man."

I put down the bowl of cereal and joined Chandler at the window. The guy was like a little kid at his first amusement park. But to be fair, the first sight of a city like New Orleans would thrill anyone.

The last two days on the bus had been an experience in and of itself. From the outside, Beyond Berlin was a tight-knit group. Apparently, close quarters can strain even the best of relationships. First there was the argument between Rylan and Serena and her refusal to let the guys use *her* bathroom. It quickly devolved into a shouting match that I was forced to break up.

We had two hours of peace, then Ty raided Chandler's food stash and ate his gluten-free cookies, and that kicked off when Chandler tipped out of his bunk and flung the last cookie at Ty's head, shouting that he was a selfish prick.

But the biggest fight was the night before and came on the heels of Serena refusing to end practice at three in the morning. Chandler reminded her that they needed to get some sleep and somehow that was taken as evidence he was less dedicated to the band.

Their raging penetrated our earplugs. Brant and I stumbled out of our bunks to shut them up and send the members to their separate corners.

Bianca's order to make sure they keep their heads makes a lot more sense now.

I didn't remember my tour bus times like this, but then I guess those hardened rockers were on their best behavior around the little blond kid.

No one is on their best behavior with me now.

"Amazing," a voice said from behind me. "I woke up this morning and I didn't know where I was. Then it hit me." An arm snaked through mine. "Being here still doesn't seem real."

"Told you about this, mama," I said mildly. "My lady doesn't take kindly to other women touching me."

"She's not here," Serena replied—though she dropped my hand.

"Actually, she is." I checked my watch. "Or she will be in an hour."

"Valentina's coming? Why? This isn't a vacation. You're working for us. Does your father know about this?"

I crooked a brow. Serena sounded a tad ticked off. "Why? You going to rat me out?"

"It'd be cool to meet your girlfriend," Chandler broke in. "We don't go on until tonight, so maybe we can all hang and listen to the bands until then."

"We're not on vacation either," Serena snapped. "We'll be practicing until we go on."

"Don't wear yourselves out before you perform," I said. "We're early. You have a couple of hours to stretch your legs, check out the city, and then be back at noon for a soundcheck. After that, you can chill on the bus or wander the festival, vibing with the audience and meeting the other bands. I'll call you when it's time for hair and makeup. After you're dressed, you'll warm up and then it's a countdown until you go live."

"In other words, we can have a little fun before we go on." Chandler pulled out his phone. "I looked up the best places for beignets and this says it's a place called Subodo's. Do you and Valentina want to meet us there before the soundcheck?"

"We can do that."

"If we have a soundcheck, we definitely need to practice," Serena said.

He walked off to the backroom.

"Chandler!" She trailed him, slamming the door.

I considered going after them to break up that fight and decided against it. They had a manager. He could work out with them when they should or shouldn't practice.

The manager in question emerged from the bathroom and made for the cereal I left on the table. "I heard you say your girl is coming," he spoke up. "Don't worry. I'll get these guys off the bus and out of your hair."

"That's why I love you, Brant."

He barked a laugh. "Save the sweet talk for your lady."

Brant handed over the cereal. We sat down to the city unveiling before us, alive with colors and boasting old-world charm that stretched as far back as the seventeen hundreds. There was nowhere on the earth quite like this city. Walking the streets, you tapped into the beauty that inspired the likes of Louis Armstrong, Fats Domino, and the Neville Brothers. Music pumped the lifeblood of New Orleans. It's where an artist could truly call home.

We made good time rolling onto the festival grounds. Fifteen minutes before Val's taxi brought her to the festival and plenty of time for me to kick the band off the bus.

"Run free, friends," I said. The band had their faces glued to the window, taking in the massive crowd. "It'd be a crime to come to New Orleans and not give her a proper visit. Chandler, text me the address to that place."

"For sure, Jaxson." He got up and grabbed his stuff, ignoring the daggers shot at him. "We're hitting Bourbon Street and then Jackson Square."

"I'm not going," said Serena. "I'm staying and running through our set list."

Brant stepped in. "Let's meet the organizers. If we're lucky, they'll let us check out the stage early. You can get a feel for where you need to be and how many lights will be in your face."

Serena's frown faded. "That's a good idea."

Brant winked at me over her head.

There was shuffling, searching for socks, locating Serena's purse, and Chandler coming back for a snack. Eventually, they filed out one by one and I was alone. My phone buzzed as I lost the back of Serena's head in the crowd.

Valentina: I'm here! Going through security now. Where are you?

Me: Lot D. The big bus with Interstellar Records on the side.

Dropping the phone on the couch, I dove under the sink, rescuing the trash bin. The bandmates were many things but tidy wasn't one of them. I swept the place like a whirlwind, sweeping crumbled chips into the bin, tossing discarded clothes on their bunks, throwing out fast-food wrappers, and spritzing cologne in the air.

A knock interrupted in the middle of tossing my cologne on the bed.

"Jaxson?"

"Coming!"

I ducked in the bathroom, winked at the sexy son of a bitch in the mirror, and then ran to throw open the door.

Valentina was perfection in the midst of chaos. Shrieks, laughter, and music sought us through the field of tour buses. The noise muted under her influence. In the short walk from the air-conditioned taxi to the lot, humidity stuck her hair to her forehead. She swept it from those lily-green pools, smiling into my eyes like it had been weeks instead of days.

She was ready for the festival. Black-and-white sneakers sank in the muddy grass and threadbare shorts reached as far as the middle of her thighs. Her backpack hung off one shoulder. I recognized the shirt she bunched up and tied at the end because it was mine. *The Undisturbed* scrawled proudly across her chest.

Grinning, I propped against the jamb. "We're gonna have to make this quick, mama. I'm waiting for my hot-ass girlfriend to arrive."

She swatted my thigh. "Let your hot-ass girlfriend in. It's boiling out here."

I scooped her up, crushing her to me as I slammed the door shut and pushed her against it, pulling out a gasp. I licked her lips, tasting that gasp, and then plunging inside. Val responded instantly, wrapping her legs around my waist and tangling in my hair.

"So that's why you wanted me to come," she purred. "You couldn't go an entire week without."

"Yep, and neither could you." I ground my hardness between her legs, cock twitching when she closed her eyes moaning. "That's why you got on the plane."

Her soft, breathy laugh shredded the last of my control. "True."

"I'm going to fuck you in front of that window. Hope you don't have any objections?"

"Why would I?"

Val slipped out of my grasp, racing up the stairs. I spun and was smacked in the face with my own shirt. She giggled, tossing her shorts after them.

Slowly, I pulled them down, feasting on the gorgeous pixie that had burrowed her way into my bed. My life. My head. My heart.

Val leaned against the table, clad only in her thong, balancing on the tips of her muddy sneakers.

"Never have I ever, Jaxson."

"Never have you what?"

She smirked. "Given a guy a blow job on a tour bus."

I whistled. "Missing out, baby. We should do something about that." I was on her in two leaps, startling a cry out of her as I lifted her up. "But me first. I've been dreaming about that pussy. Waking up swearing I could taste it on my tongue."

Val lay back, slipping through my hold and stretching out on the table. "I've been having the same dreams, except it's your cum"—her tongue skated over her glossy red lip gloss—"dripping from my lips."

"Lucky for you, I'm in the business of making dreams come true."

"Dirty dreams? Just what are you getting up to at work, Jaxson Van Zandt?"

I smacked her ass. She squealed, flipping over to play like she could get away. I trapped her and pulled her thong down in one smooth move.

"Never have I ever," she said. Val swayed her hips, side to side on my ridge. "Got it from the back in front of a window. Can anyone see us?"

"They tint the shit out of these buses. I can close the blinds to be sure."

"No. Leave them up."

I chuckled, laying myself on her and sinking my teeth into her shoulder. Val let out a low hiss as I scraped them down her back. "You want them watching while I have you begging on this table?"

She rocked back on me, impaling herself through my jeans. "I want you on your knees."

I dropped, helping her step out of her underwear but leaving the sneakers on. They were doing it for me. My clothes came off just as quickly.

Val sucked in a breath when I spread her legs. I was highly aware of everything she did. Every sound she made. Every moan from her lips. Some nights I counted all the different noises I could get her to make.

I licked a stripe from clit to ass, earning a soft squeak.

That's one.

"Turn over," I ordered.

Val flipped, scooting up, spreading her legs, and pressing her feet to the walls of the little breakfast nook. I curled my hand under her legs and went wild. I bobbed and shook my head, tasting each inch of her at once.

Crying out, Val fisted my hair, back arching and moving her clit in for the kill. I latched on and sucked until her cries reached a crescendo. Sound was my life, and the music Val made my addiction. Teasing that tiny bunch of nerves rewarded me broken, hoarse moans.

I spread her open, collecting her arousal on my fingers, and plunging in for the rest. My tongue thrust in and out, getting panted words out of her next.

"Yes, Jaxson. Ah, baby, yes. Just like that."

That's three.

I picked up speed and her groans matched the tune. Body coiling, she gripped fit to rip the hair out of my head and came so hard she spasmed on the table. I licked her from my lips and then my fingers for good measure.

"Taste even sweeter than my dreams."

"My turn," she sang.

Val held out her hand. I helped the lady off the table, anticipation humming in my veins, trailing her as she got onto the booth and on her knees. She bent down, ass in the air, sneakers on the pleather, and nails gripping the edge of the seat. "Like a lollipop, right?" she teased.

"Is there any other way?"

She was still chuckling as I pushed inside her mouth. The vibrations up her throat stiffened my impossibly hard cock. One suck and I'd probably blow.

Val's plump red lips swallowed me to the hilt. She looked me in the eyes, withdrawing to the tip, and tongue darting out to lick its treat. "Fuck, Val," I grunted.

I swore Val played the game too. But hers was to find all the ways to reduce me to a gibbering, sex-addled idiot.

She bobbed her head, her eyes sucking me in and drowning me in an emerald lake of lust.

"Shit!"

That was all the warning I gave her. Exploding in her mouth, I knuckled the seat, nearly buckling as my girl swallowed every drop.

Val jumped up as I fell on the booth, catching and pulling me to her chest. I caught her in turn, lifting her onto the table, and spreading her beneath me. Val's nipples were beacons on two supple mounds, luring me in. I sucked one, then the other. Flicking the hardened pebbles until I got my *oh, oh, ohs.*

That's four.

I didn't give her a chance to catch her breath. I drew back, gripping her calves, and pushed inside. Her lips formed a small "o," eyes rolling up and disappearing completely as I started pumping.

Bodies slick with sweat, she slid up and down the surface, anchoring on the window and meeting me thrust for thrust.

Not to be a total guy, but the sounds coming from Val as I fucked her bare, heard no matter how loudly we played our sex soundtracks—those sounds were my favorite.

Our grunts, moans, and cries filled the luxury bus. A melody of our own making.

I wasn't about to last long with the memory of that blow job playing on repeat and Val coming apart beneath me, squeezing as she reached the end of her rope.

We came at the same time, shaking the table and drowning out the music festival with cries that broke the sound barrier.

I collapsed on top, dropping my slick forehead on hers.

Val came down. Eyes glassy. Smirk on her lips.

"Never have I ever."

A laugh escaped me. "How do you have any firsts left? I thought we took care of all of those."

"I've got one or two more," she said. "Want to help me with that? I've never been fucked in a tour bus bunk. Is it like doing it in a space pod?"

Just like that, my boy was semi-hard and ready to go again. "We'll find out."

VALENTINA

The television played on low, adding to our soft murmuring. We shared a pillow, fingers trailing each other's bodies, legs tangled beneath the sheets, and breaths mingling while we talked about the little that happened in our time apart.

"I'm meeting with Kessler on Thursday. If it works out the way I want, she'll let me organize the event and hand over the contacts for the alumni."

"Why do you need it?"

"It's just a guess that the disappearances have happened before. Ezra's brother mentioned guys washing out of Nu Alpha Theta who dropped out of school altogether. I still say that's an overreaction and there must be more to the story. Administration isn't about to hand over a list of dropouts, but I can get a list from the other brothers and sisters who were in the house at the same time. They'll tell me the names of the people who left and I will see if they ever turned up again."

"That's smart, baby. Really smart."

I grinned. "Thank you. I thought so too."

He kissed the tip of my nose. "What will you do if she says no? Organizing these events is her gig. She might say it's not in your job description."

"You know how persuasive I can be."

"Also true. It's a rare individual who can say no to you."

I snuggled tighter—so happy to be in his arms I could bust. "What about you? You texted that close quarters was driving everyone crazy. Was it that bad?"

"I broke up a few fights, but no, it wasn't that bad." Jaxson rested his chin on my crown. "I love this, Val. Kicking back watching cities go by. Listening to the next hit track before it breaks the airwaves."

"Being a part of something that will last long after we're gone," I murmured. "We still hear the voices of the legends who walked these streets. How many of us wished we could be there? Listen to Louis Armstrong live. Play jazz with the greats."

"Damn, baby. Why do you get me so well?"

I smiled into his shoulder. "I believe that's because I'm your soul mate, Jaxson Van Zandt. We understand each other inside and out."

"Don't fly out tomorrow, Val." Sounded like the wild idea just occurred to him. "Ride back with me. Be a part of it too."

"I can't," I said, though I wished I didn't have to. "I have the meeting, remember."

His sigh tickled my strands. "Right, of course. Next time."

"Next time. If you're allowed to bring your girlfriend along for the ride."

"Mama, I own everything you see around us. I bring you wherever I want."

"Oh?" I leaned back, cocking a brow at him. "Is that why you're stuck as top bunk to the bassist?"

"Just have to rub that in, don't you? I didn't hear you complaining about my bunk. Matter of fact, those are your toeprints on the ceiling."

"Oh no, I like the bunk. I was thinking we should break it in one more time."

"Great i—"

The door banged open.

We froze, staring wide-eyed at each other.

"Yes, Mom. Huge stage. Brant says I should move around, interact with the audience, and pump the hype. Suddenly, I'm forgetting how to walk and sing at the same time." Serena Blackwood laughed at her own joke. "I wish you could be here too. Watch me live, Mom, I'll wave to you. Bye."

I poked Jaxson, mouthing about our clothes.

"What?"

"Jaxson," said a dry voice that sounded quite close. "Valentina. I'm guessing you're both in there since your clothes are all over the place."

"Something I can do for you, Serena?" asked Jaxson.

"I'm done checking out the stage and other bands. The guys called from the square. They're heading to the restaurant if you still want to join us."

Jaxson glanced at me.

I rubbed my stomach, pulling a face. I was hungry.

"Sure," he said. "We'll catch up to you."

"Why? Brant's calling a cab. We'll wait for you to get dressed and go together."

Another glance at me and I nodded.

"Give us ten minutes."

We heard the click and roused ourselves, climbing out and picking our clothes up off the floor, booth, and stove.

Serena and Brant waited at the entrance to the festival, standing by an idling cab. We hopped in and rode through the twisty, historic streets for a trendy restaurant sandwiched between a bookstore and a hostel.

The host greeted us like old friends, praising my shirt and taste in music. They led us to the table in the back with the others.

"How'd the sightseeing go?" I asked the guys.

Rylan held up two bags of souvenirs. "My girlfriend is going to love these. She's always wanted to visit New Orleans. I'll bring her back one day."

"When you do, stay at a cute little hotel called the Imperial. So romantic. They have claw-foot tubs. A balcony attached to every room. And a special service for couples including wine, cheese, and chocolate-covered strawberries brought up with your meals. Also, rose-petal turndown service." I smiled up at Jaxson. "That's the hotel I booked for us, J."

"Can't wait."

"Sounds perfect," Rylan agreed. "Thanks for the rec. That should make up for me getting here first."

"You're moving to a hotel?" Serena asked.

"Just for the night," Jaxson replied.

"You can't."

"Why can't I?"

"We go on early tomorrow morning. You have to be there."

"I will be there."

For some reason, her frown lines deepened. Jaxson's face was smooth, but I knew him and his tension read in the taut line of his shoulders.

"What part of this 'isn't a vacation' don't you get?"

I stiffened. *What is her problem? It's just one night.*

"Serena, if I don't follow through or let you guys down, come for me. I'll deserve it. But don't get on me for not leaving my girlfriend by herself in a new city. I'll be on time tomorrow. That's all you need to worry about."

Serena opened her mouth.

"I'm stuck between the shrimp beignets and the sweet potato," Brant spoke up. "What's everyone else having?"

The bomb defused and we shifted into awkward silence, and eventually, small talk when Chandler asked me how school was going. Soon we relaxed and focused on the sweet and savory beignets—ordering almost every beignet on the menu and splitting them.

Throughout the meal, Serena didn't say or do anything that could be construed as unkind, but I picked up on her habit of steering the conversation toward the band, recording in the studio, and getting ready for the set. Effectively boxing me out of the conversation.

I'm being paranoid, I thought. *I get the feeling the band is on her mind twenty-four seven. I shouldn't read into it. Besides, Jaxson would let me know if I had something to worry about.*

We wrapped up our food and headed out. Beyond Berlin had a soundcheck.

Jaxson and I stood to the side waiting for the cab.

"So, that talk with Serena," I began, "about boundaries and remembering she doesn't own you. Looks like it didn't take."

Jaxson gazed across at the willowy redhead. "Honestly, Val, I don't think that's it. She's been getting handsy lately. Touching my leg. Hugging me from behind. Falling against me when she laughs. And somehow, she's not hearing me say back up."

I dropped his arm, eyes flaring. "Excuse me?"

I said Jaxson would tell me if I had something to worry about... and he just did.

"What the fuck does she think she's doing?" I gritted out.

"Barking up the wrong tree." Jaxson stroked my cheek. "I'd never lie to you, baby. Ever. Serena's been stepping over the line, but I'll push her ass back. You have nothing to worry about."

I took a deep breath and let it go. "I know. I trust you completely." I grasped his cheek in turn, smiling wide. "But if her ass doesn't get back over the line today, I'll push her myself."

"Understood."

Jaxson opted for a second cab. We dropped him at the festival first to get ready and I continued on to the hotel to check in and shower.

The room was even better than the photographs. Rose petals decorated the pillows and candles floating in crystal clear water waited for us to light. It was rare these days that the boys and I indulged in a romantic getaway. Between school, work, and Adam, we always had a strong reason to stay home. I had one night in New Orleans with Jaxson and, his work aside, we would make the most of it.

I cleaned up and grabbed another ride out to the festival. Jaxson asked me to meet him at stage 3R and hooked me up with passes to let me run free.

Stepping on the grounds again, I melded into the throng of head-bobbing music lovers. They streamed through the place munching on food truck treats and consulting their maps on where to go next. I found stage 3R easily. The biggest stage positioned near the entrance. No one could miss it. This was one festival in one city, but I'd say a spot like this was proof Beyond Berlin was on their way up.

Official people holding clipboards and sporting earpieces wandered up and down the stage. My Jaxson was one of them. He stood off to the side speaking to the band, pointing and gesturing and looking all sexy as he commanded his job.

Serena nodded along. She pointed above her and then to the back of the stage. Jaxson moved to her side, looking where she gestured. As I watched, Serena rested her hand on his shoulder and moved in closer still. Jaxson nodded, said something in response, and then stepped back, consulting someone through his earpiece.

Jaxson spotted me and waved, gesturing for me to come up. I rounded the stage, finding the back stairs, and security waved me on. Jaxson met me at the top, taking my hand.

"We're all set here," he said. "But I wanted you to see what it's like."

We raced to the edge, looking out over the festival. In a blink I was there. Millions of cheering fans were at my feet, jumping, dancing, and living as a single organism that thrived on one thing: the music.

I draped his arm over my shoulder, resting my head on him. "You never wanted this, Jaxson? You could have it. I've heard you sing."

"Nah. I'm made for the old man's desk. You can be the legend or the legend maker, and lucky for me, I'll always be both."

"Will you?" I asked. "What makes you a legend?"

He patted his package. "This right here."

I flung my head back groaning. "Jaxson! You're such a mess. I'll forgive you because I love you."

"You'll forgive me because you know it's true."

Rolling my eyes, I hid a grin and tugged him off. "Come on. There's cotton candy next to stage 4F. Kimber and the Nightingales go on in ten minutes. Sofia turned me on to them a couple weeks ago, and don't think she's not jealous that I'm seeing them live."

"After them, there's a jazz set in the bar across the entrance. They're a part of the festival too."

"And then after that"—I grinned over my shoulder—"we go back to the hotel and break the bed."

Jaxson stopped dead. "You know, Kimber and her birds can wait."

I laughed. "Uh-uh. Easy, legend. We'll get there."

Jaxson and I ran off the stage like kids set loose on the playground. We stood in line for the cotton candy, moaning about the heat. Partway through, he left and returned with ice cream, feeding me the cone with little better accuracy than Adam, and us cracking up as he licked the treat from my chin.

Loaded down with food, we headed over to the Kimber stage, stretched out on the grass, and ate while the band crooned about love, heartbreak, and revolution. I recorded their whole set with plans to send it to Sofia.

As they wrapped up, we got out ahead of the crowd and made for the entrance. The little jazz bar that scored the indoor venue spot was smaller and cozier than I anticipated. Booths took up every wall except for the one sharing the bar and stage. In the middle were intimate two-person tables and couples holding hands around the votive candles.

Jaxson and I found a booth near the stage and relaxed. The humid, sticky day cooled on our bodies and beneath the table we used the obscurity to let our hands roam.

The lights dimmed and the band of young hopefuls came on. I didn't know as much about jazz as Jaxson did but I enjoyed their light steady sound and how it lulled me to sleep on his shoulder. An early morning flight followed by a vigorous welcome from Jaxson, and then running around the festival. I was exhausted.

Tonight, after our activities, I'll be out like a light. Indulging a full, deep sleep that I know not to take for granted.

Jaxson woke me with kisses on my forehead. "Hate jazz that much?"

Chuckling, I rose up and stretched, arching my back. "Put that down to how tired I am, not the quality of the band. They were amazing."

Concern flicked across his face. "Want me to take you back to the hotel? Get some rest. When I'm done, I'll pick you up for dinner and we'll have the night to ourselves."

"When you're done? What else do you have to do. You said Beyond Berlin was all set on stage."

"They've still got hair, makeup, final practices, and then I've got to stay for the show. When they finish the set, I'm leaving the breakdown to the roadies and"—he kissed my nose—"taking my girl out for crawfish jambalaya. I know this place that serves the best you've ever had or will ever have."

"Can't wait," I murmured.

Jaxson checked his watch. "We've got a couple of hours until I'm back to work. Want to see some more bands or chill at the hotel together?"

"I'll stay. There are more bands on my list." I slid my hand down his arm and laced our fingers together. "And I want to see them with you." We kissed. "But I'm fine to leave when Beyond Berlin goes on. I'll catch a nap, freshen up, and then we'll go out."

"Sounds good."

We rejoined the crowd and made good on our threat to see every band we could in three hours. A few weren't for us. Some we loved. And a couple became our new obsession.

"How did we allow London Panic to sign with anyone other than us?" Jaxson cried. "They're fucking incredible."

"Baby, that guitar solo changed my life."

We stumbled through the crowd laughing and gushing over the mind-blowing experience witnessed by all at stage 2K. Jaxson's nonstop vibrating phone warned him that our time was up and he had to return for Beyond Berlin's final warm-up.

"I've never heard of London Panic before today, and now I'll never forget their name."

"That song they sang about Sadie." Jaxson shook his head. "Wow."

"I'll head to the entrance and call a ride," I said. "You work your Interstellar magic on the stage."

"I'll walk you."

Hand in hand, we exited the grounds and said goodbye at the taxi stand.

The sun began to set, bathing the city in its artwork of colors. We zipped through the streets for the old Imperial Hotel. Pulling in under the awning, the bellhop opened the door and escorted me inside. I went straight up to the front desk and requested cheese and a substitute for the wine sent up to my room.

An hour later I was bubbling in the tub, munching on cheese and catching up with home.

"How's Adam?"

"He asks where you are about every five minutes," said Ezra. "Caroline is distracting him with baking cookies."

"Aw, my poor baby."

"Sounds like your separation anxiety is just as bad."

"Leave me alone." I laughed. "I spent so much time away from him while I was at Evergreen. Now I get hives whenever we're apart for more than a few hours."

"And what do you get when you're away from me?"

I smirked. "An ache between my legs where you should be."

His voice dropped. "I can be in New Orleans in two hours."

"Very tempting, Lennox, but Jaxson and I have the night planned. I'll be back early tomorrow and we can do all of the things you're thinking of. Yes," I teased, "even that."

A beep sounded in my ear.

"You sure? Because the *that* I'm thinking of is meeting you at the hangar and bending you over in a private plane."

"I just said yes, didn't I?"

"I'll be there," he said. "What's up?"

I heard Maverick's deep voice on the other end.

"Your phone stop working? Fine." Ezra got back with me. "Love you, Val. See you tomorrow."

"Bye, lover. Kiss our son a thousand times for me."

"Yes, ma'am."

There was some shuffling and words exchanged. Maverick came on the phone.

"Hey, Val, I want to hear about your trip," he said over my greeting. "But I found something on Aiden's computer and you need to know."

I bolted up, splashing water over the rim. "Did you find out what happened to Teagan and Sawyer? Where Leighton is?"

"No, but now I know why," he said. "There's a hidden file on his drive, Val."

"What?"

"Hidden and very well. It's taken me this long to find it and it explains why he ruthlessly cut off Ezra when he discovered we were digging into him. People who have nothing to find don't have hidden encrypted files buried in their computer."

"Can you get in?"

"No." I could practically see him shaking his head. "I mean, yes. I could find a way in eventually, but now that I know who I'm dealing with, it'd be stupid to believe he doesn't have a failsafe in place."

"Maverick, we're so close. You've proven he's hiding something. Now we have to see what. In that file could be the proof we need to send to the police. Is there any way you could get in without him finding out?"

"I... can try. I'll talk to my dad. See what he says. Until then, I'm glad you're in New Orleans and far away from this guy."

"I'm not afraid of Aiden Connelly. He should be afraid of us. We're putting his smirking ass in a jail cell where it belongs."

Another beep chimed in my ear, alerting me to the text.

"Tell me about you now. How's the festival?"

"It's incredible. I've added like five new bands to my favorites list. I wish you all could be here."

"We don't take enough vacations. Why don't we make it a tradition to go to this or another music festival every year?"

"I would love that. Even if it's not a festival and we just get away and spend time together. Away from the craziness that's become synonymous with our lives."

"I'm all for another ski trip. We'll finally do it right."

"Cocoa by the fire. Snowball fights. Racing the slopes."

"Yeah, we can do that stuff in between."

"I swear." I reclined, pushing the suds around with my toes. "One-track mind. All four of you."

"Five of us. You're thinking the same."

"True. We can get to that other stuff if we ever leave the room."

"We won't," he growled. "I'll book us a cabin tonight. Hope you didn't have other plans for winter break."

I dropped my smile. "Oh, wait. There is one thing. I have to sell Mrs. Kessler on a charity dinner during the break. I won't schedule it too close to Christmas, so you're good to whisk me away around then."

"Okay."

We talked a little more about my day. As the water cooled, I glanced at the screen for the time and lit on Jaxson's name.

"I have to go. Jaxson will be here soon."

"All right, bye. I love you."

"Love you too."

I ended the call and tapped open on Jaxson.

Jaxson: Baby, this isn't easy for me to tell you. I've been thinking a lot about our relationship and I can't do this anymore. I never wanted to share. I only agreed because it was the only way I could be with you, but deep down I thought you'd one day choose me. I can't wait for that day anymore, mama. It's over, Val. I've found someone else. You should just go home.

The cell nearly slipped from my fingers and plunged into the bath. I read that text once, twice, a dozen times and each read splintered my heart deeper.

I found someone else.

"Jaxson's breaking up with me?" I rasped.

Why would he do this? We had so much fun. He seemed happy. Said he loved me so many times I lost count. Why?!

"No." My mind rebelled. This didn't make sense. I've been with Jaxson since I was sixteen years old. I know him better than I do myself. Sharing me with the boys never bothered him, and if it did, I would have seen it.

"This can't be real." I shot out of the tub, dripping water everywhere, rushing to my backpack. I dialed Jaxson as I shoved my clothes on.

It rang and rang. Voicemail picked up.

"Jaxson, baby, call me as soon as you get this."

It was almost seven thirty. Beyond Berlin should be wrapping it up, but I couldn't wait for Jaxson to get to the hotel. Some twisted piece of shit had his phone because it wasn't possible my Jaxson would leave me—let alone end a four-year relationship over text while I waited for him surrounded by bubbles and rose petals.

When I find the shit who wrote this, I'm drowning them in these bubbles.

Jamming on my shoes, I burst into the hall still damp from my bath. My clothes stuck to my body and the phone stuck to my ear. Ringing and ringing.

"You've reached Jaxson. I obviously can't get to the phone right now. Leave a message and I'll hit you up."

I took the stairs two at a time, jabbing redial.

The concierge jumped when I half fell on his desk. "Ma'am? Is there a problem?"

"I need you to call a cab, please. To the NOLA music festival."

"Certainly, ma'am. If you'd like to wait in the lounge, I'll let you know when it arrives."

"You've reached Jaxson. I—"

I hung up and dialed again. "Thank you," I threw at the man.

"You've reached Jaxson. I obviously can't—"

I tried Jaxson over and over again on the car ride through the city. He wasn't picking up which solidified that someone else had his phone. The real Jaxson wouldn't ghost me like this. He'd own the text like he owned everything he said and did.

The cab rolled to a stop before the entrance and I was out in the middle of his goodbye. I passed off a wad of cash through the window and took off, pushing through a crowd surging in the opposite direction. The festival was wrapping up. The headliners making for their buses and hotels. And Jaxson meant to be coming back to me.

Where are you?

Stage 3R loomed in the distance. The lights were on but the music wasn't. The set was over.

People jostled me on all sides as I pushed through to the stage. I reached the front where Jaxson and I stood, looking out over the festival. I strained to find him, scanning the men on stage breaking down the equipment and cleaning up.

Brant walked up the side steps. He was speaking into his phone.

Brant! He'll know where Jaxson is.

I raced around the stage, heading for the stairs. A couple of beefy guards held up their hands as I barreled toward them. I jerked up my pass and ran past.

"Jaxson!"

I skidded to a stop at the bottom of the stairs and grabbed the railing. Something flashed out of the corner of my eye. I lifted my foot off the step, backed up, and there he was.

"Jaxson."

Jaxson stood behind the stage, clearly speaking to someone if his moving lips and raised hands were anything to go by. A metal pillar blocked my view of the person until they helpfully stepped out, keeping distance with him. I couldn't mistake that glittery red hair.

"Look out, ma'am."

"Jax—!"

Serena launched forward, falling into his arms, and kissed him.

I jerked like I'd been slapped, and then I took a real knock, stumbling back.

"Sorry about that." The roadies clambered down the steps carrying the drum set and obscuring the sight of Jaxson and Serena. "Excuse us."

Darting around them, I landed on Serena... and just her. Jaxson was nowhere to be seen.

"Jaxson!? Jaxson!"

Serena spun at my shout. I stomped up to her.

"Where's Jaxson?" I demanded.

Up close, Serena was damp from her set. Makeup ran a bit under her eyes and beads of sweat collected above her lip. Hair plastered to her forehead and she brushed it away with a wipe of her hand, scoffing. "What do I look like? His secretary?"

"No," I hissed. "You look like the girl who's about to be dangled off that stage. I saw you kiss my boyfriend!"

Her eyes widened, and just as quickly, narrowed in confusion. "You're mad? Seriously?"

"Tell me what I fucking look like." It was an effort not to scream. "Do I look mad?"

Serena's frown deepened. "I don't get it. Why would you be mad about Jaxson kissing someone else? Don't you have, like, five other boyfriends?"

I moved in, closing the distance. "What was that? It didn't sound like an apology."

"Because it's not and you won't get one. Everyone at Interstellar knows about you, Jaxson, and your little arrangement." She tossed her head. "You're telling me you can fuck other guys but freak when Jaxson kisses another girl? How fucking backward is that?"

"Jaxson didn't kiss another girl," I forced through gritted teeth. "*You* kissed him and"—I made a show of looking around—"he pushed you off and left quick."

She smirked. "So what? He's hung up on us working together, but he'll get over it and so should you. You're not monogamous. Why should Jaxson be? Chandler, Ty, and I are together but I sleep with other guys and they sleep with other girls."

"I don't give a fuck what you and your band do. It has nothing to do with my relationship which you know is not like yours. Because it was you, wasn't it?" I flung. "You sent me that text. And you stuffed your thong in his car. Why are you trying so hard to break us up if you truly believe you've got a free shot?"

"Are we on that stupid thong again? And what text?" she cried. "I don't know what you're talking about and I don't care. If Jaxson wants to be with me, your selfish ass can either get over it or crawl back to your stable of boyfriends. I'm sure you won't miss one."

Red blotted my vision. *Is this girl for real?*

"You're not hearing me. Stay away from Jaxson!"

Serena shoved me. Hard. "Make me, bitch!"

I staggered back, nearly falling to the ground, and came back charging, fist in the air. I punched her dead in the face, sending the rock princess flying.

Chapter Eight

*J*axson

"I'm done, Dad. Serena just fucking kissed me."

"She what?"

"Mauled me behind the stage, and don't get me started on how many times I had to get her hands off me the last few days." I paced before the door to our bus. "I don't have time for this shit. If she can't be professional, she can be someone else's problem."

Dad cursed under his breath. "No arguments from me. That kind of bullshit doesn't go down with my employees—let alone my son. Gwen works with Beyond Berlin. I'll hire another assistant to help Bianca, and you'll make the switch to legal."

I never thought I'd be happy at the prospect of working with Daniel Meyer.

"Fine with me. I'm not riding back with them. Valentina flew down on Amelia's plane. We both come back in the morning."

"Alright. Brant's got it from here. That's why I hired him. You chill with Val, forget about this whole thing."

"That's exactly what I'm going to do."

We talked a little more and then ended the call. I ducked into the tour bus and found Rylan where I left him, sitting with his laptop at the table. "Thanks for letting me use your phone," I said. "I have to make one more call. Check in with Val."

He waved me on. "Go for it."

I called Valentina and got her voicemail. "Sorry I'm late, baby. I lost my phone and then there was another issue. I'll tell you about it when I see you. Leaving now. Love you."

Rylan accepted his phone, sliding it into his pocket. "Any idea what happened to yours? I saw you with it before we went on."

"No clue. I did have it on the stage, and then after the set, it was gone. But I don't have time to look, Val's waiting for me. I'll have that one shut off and grab another one when I get home. Speaking of which," I said as I moved to my bunk. "I'm flying back with Val in the morning."

"Can't blame you." He laughed. "I'd take a private plane with my girlfriend over Chandler snoring in the next bunk."

"Nah. I liked hanging with you guys." That I meant the masculine form of "guys" went unsaid. "And for our last ride together, I'm glad I got to see you kill at the festival. There's nowhere else but up for Beyond Berlin. I promise you that."

"Our last ride?"

"My time in A and R is up." I shoved the last of my things into my bag and popped into the bathroom to grab my toothbrush. "I'm transferring to legal."

I came out and Rylan was there, holding out his hand. "It's been great working with you, Jaxson. Son of the owner, but you put up with all of our bullshit. Came through for us every day. We won't forget it."

We shook, pounding each other on the back. Rylan was good people. Chill. Hard-working. Drama-free.

"I'll see you around the building, man."

I shouldered my stuff and headed for the door. It flew open as I reached for the knob. Chandler climbed out of the mud, hair wild and looking harassed.

"Jaxson. Is Serena in there?"

"No."

"Have you seen her?"

"Last saw her behind the stage." I stepped down to leave. "Good job today. See you at the studio."

"Wait. If she's not here, I need your help to look for her. London Panic invited us for drinks. Hang out. Sign any autographs that come our way. She was supposed to clean up and meet us at the stage."

"She probably got held up with fans on the way."

I tried again to leave. Chandler didn't budge.

"Serena wouldn't be late for this. We heard them play and their crowd was screaming just as loud as ours. Serena wanted us to take pics, post them on our pages, and get some cross-promotion. Please, Jaxson. Rylan, you too. We have to look for her. She's not answering my calls and I have a bad feeling," he said. "You know how fans can get. One guy grabbed her on the way out of a gig last year. Fucker pulled and yanked her so hard, he bruised her arm."

I bit back a sigh. There was more than friendship between Serena and Chandler. If Val was missing for five minutes, I'd expect him to help me find her. "All right," I agreed. "I'll alert security and check our stage. Rylan, mind if I borrow your phone again?"

He handed it over.

"Search near the entrance," I told him. "Chandler, call the London Panic guys and ask if they've seen her."

We got off the bus and went in three different directions. I wasn't convinced Serena was in trouble. More likely she was smarting from me pushing her away and swiping off her kiss like it burned. All the same, I called the number for security that came in the festival's information packet.

"What does she look like?"

"Short. Red hair. Wearing a silver top and black miniskirt. She's the lead singer, so we're concerned she got caught out by overzealous fans."

"Understood," the woman said. "I'll pull a few guys off clearing the park and start the search."

I made it to the stage. I looked on top, around, and behind it. I spoke to the guys packing up the stage. All of them shook their heads when I asked if they saw her.

Chandler ran up to me as I stepped off the stairs. "Is she here? Did you call security?"

"No and yes. They're searching the grounds now."

He blew out a breath. "I called Mark from London Panic. They're at the bar and Serena's not with them."

"We can't check this entire place," I said. "It's clearing out but there's still too many people. Let's head back to the bus. She might be there with a dead phone wondering where everyone went."

"Good idea."

We trekked back the way we came, passing two stages for the parking lot at the back.

"Did you try Brant?" I asked.

"He said he was taking your lead. Grabbing a hotel for the night, calling his family, and getting some real sleep. I figured he cut out first thing."

"Call him just in case. He was still hanging around when—" *When Serena pretended she needed to talk about something important and instead slung her shot.* "When I last saw Serena," I finished. "He might have seen which direction she went off."

"Okay." He fumbled fishing out his phone.

"Hey," I said, grabbing his shoulder. "We'll find her. Safe and sound."

Lampposts flickered overhead, casting long shadows through the lot. I grabbed my borrowed phone and called Valentina again. She might as well go to dinner without me. We'd have our romantic evening afterward.

I passed the final bus for ours and pressed *call*, holding the cell to my ear.

"What's that noise?" Chandler asked.

Slowing down, I cocked my head to listen. *Wait. Isn't that…?*

"Valentina?"

I kept going, passing the door, and walking around the front to the other side of our bus.

Valentina stood there. Cell chiming in her pocket. White sneakers brown from the mud. And red from the blood. Serena's body lay at her feet. Still and peaceful as if in sleep.

The phone slipped from my hand, ending the call and abruptly silencing the ringtone.

Val's head shot up, eyes huge. "Jaxson, I—"

"What the fuck did you do?!" Chandler shoved me out of the way racing to Serena. "Serena? Serena!?" The singer didn't stir at his shouts or shaking. "Hurry! Get help! Call the police!"

I had no chance to do either.

Security barreled onto the scene. I didn't understand how they'd gotten there so fast, but I blinked through my haze and we were surrounded.

"It was her!" Chandler cried, shaky finger leveled on my Valentina. "She did it!"

Her terrified, pale face disappeared behind a wall of bodies.

"I DIDN'T DO IT," VAL repeated.

The two of us were stuffed in the booth. I held her tight to my chest as though I was protecting her from the cops sitting across from us. And I was. I lost it when security tried to haul her away, simultaneously threatening to kick their heads in, fire, and sue them. It worked that they let her go and allowed me to get Val onto the tour bus where they stood vigilantly waiting for the police.

"Why don't you explain what happened, Miss Moon?" Officer Kinkirk asked.

She nodded. Val looked wretched. There was a bruise at the corner of her lip and my Undisturbed t-shirt was torn at the collar. Then there were her shoes. Sitting in an evidence bag on the table between us.

"I came to the festival to see Jaxson."

"Why?"

"I got this text." She woke up her phone and slid it across the table. "Supposedly from Jaxson, but I knew it couldn't be."

Kinkirk's partner, Nielson, was a heavyset man with bulging broken veins along his nose. He picked up the phone and squinted to read. "Baby, this isn't easy for me to tell you…"

My eyes bugged as Nielson repeated the entire thing word for word. "I-I never sent that!" I spun on Val. "I swear, I didn't write that. I lost my phone. I would never—"

"I know." She smiled, gently cupping my cheek. "I know you didn't, Jaxson. But that's why I came back," Val addressed the cops. "Someone clearly stole his phone and sent me that load of bullshit. I had to find out who and what was going on."

"And you suspected Miss Blackwood," Kinkirk filled in.

"I didn't… until I saw her kiss my boyfriend."

I tensed. The reaction that had on the police was visible too. They sat up straight in their seats, exchanging a look.

"What did you do then?" Kinkirk asked.

"Jaxson was gone. I went to confront her and we got into a fight." She gestured at her mouth and ripped shirt.

"And then, in a rage, you hit her over the head," Nielson said. "You didn't mean to. It all happened so fast."

Val glared. "Putting words in people's mouths and making up your own story. Does that usually work to get a confession?"

Nielson smirked. "You'd be surprised."

"That's enough," I said. "She's not saying any more without a lawyer."

"No, Jaxson." She put a soothing hand on my arm. "It's okay. I can end this right now."

"Is that so?" Nielson asked.

"Serena and I got into it and Brant Titus broke us up. She ran off before he could say anything to her, but he stayed to help me. *Both of us* went to the medical tent to get me checked out, and we walked back to the bus together. That's when we heard a noise and found Serena. Mr. Titus ran off to get help and I stayed with her. Chandler found us and got the wrong idea." She jerked her chin at the door. "Mr. Titus would tell you the same thing if you didn't have him standing outside."

The partners exchanged another look.

"You're claiming you were with Mr. Titus up to the point you discovered Miss Blackwood?" Nielson repeated.

"I'm not claiming it. It's what happened. You can ask the nurses at the medical tent too. They'll tell you we were together."

There wasn't much else to say after that. Brant confirmed everything Valentina said and the police were forced to stop wasting our time and focus on the thousands of other suspects scattering throughout the city.

Our big romantic night was shot to hell. I got Val to the hotel, cleaned her up, and put her to bed. Only then did I sink into an armchair and allow the flood of shame free.

Serena was in a hospital bed. The rest of the band paced outside her hotel room. Her mother was on a plane to New Orleans and an attempted killer was on the loose. Bianca's orders ran on a loop through my mind, and the surety of my failure ran with it.

VALENTINA

"That's horrible, Val. Is she going to be okay?"

I glanced at Adam. He was absorbed with his Lego set, not paying us any mind.

Jaxson put me on the plane the morning after Serena's attack, refusing to let me stay with him. He couldn't go until he knew she was okay, but him being there when a crazed person was bashing people's heads in didn't set me at ease.

"Jaxson said she'll be fine. It was a nasty hit though. She'll be taking it easy for the next few weeks."

"Who would do this?" asked Sofia.

I shook my head. "Not that she deserved it, but Serena wasn't the nicest person. For all we know she drop-kicked a fan asking for her autograph and he came back swinging."

She took my hands. "At least you're okay. What if you were still arguing with Serena when this guy made their move?"

"If I was, she might not have gotten hurt."

"They will find the bastard. And now that Jaxson isn't working with the band anymore, the screwing with your relationship stops too. I agree that she doesn't deserve to be hit over the head, but still, Serena Blackwood was fucked up. Sending you that breakup text was cruel."

"She denied it—though sticking her tongue down his mouth gave her away."

"Did Jaxson find his phone?"

"No." I sighed. "It was such a perfect day that ended so terribly. I want to say things get better from here, but I've got my meeting with Mrs. Kessler tomorrow. Dealing with the other terrible things going on in our lives."

"Want some backup?"

"Love it," I admitted. "But I'm meeting her around lunch and you have Chem 102."

"So what?"

I cracked a smile. "I'll be fine. I'll convince her to go for the charity dinner."

"Really think she'll hand over contact info on the alumni?"

"I just need their phone numbers. They don't all have to talk to me. If a few people give it up that Mandy, Cindy, and Bella *dropped out* while they were there and we don't find proof they're safe and well with a nice career and three kids, that's enough to prove something has been going on and it's been going on for a while."

"But is it enough to get the police to act?" She reached for the teapot on the coffee table. "There's that saying: no body, no crime. If no one filed a missing persons report, the school says they dropped out, and their sorority backs it up, it doesn't add up to foul play."

"I'm not even worried about the police right now. I just need to know if Zeta Rho and Nu Alpha always had secrets in the closet, or if Aiden and Leighton put them there."

She nodded. "While you're talking with Kessler, get a straight answer for why we can't fudging do yoga," she cried. "That uphill hike you missed out on killed me twenty minutes in, and Jade made us do the whole seventy-five minutes."

I winced. "Ouch. Who voted for that?"

"No one. We've been picking basketball and jogging, so she said we should mix it up. She sweetened the deal promising we'd have a picnic at the top. It wasn't worth it, Val. It just wasn't worth it."

I stifled a laugh. "I'm back now. It'll all be okay."

Sofia drained her cup and stood. "I'm going home to have lunch with the folks. Mind if I take my favorite godson along? He can say hi to Cinnamon."

"What if he's afraid of horses?"

"You're afraid of horses for him, mama bear," she replied, grinning. "And swimming. And beds too high off the ground. Adam isn't afraid of anything. Are you, Adam?" she cooed. "Are you afraid of horses?"

"No, 'Fia."

She threw me a knowing look.

I huffed. "He's five. He'd say he wasn't afraid of scaling the Empire State Building with suction cups."

"True," she said, laughing. "If he does get scared, I've got his back." Sofia scooped my son up.

"Bye, Mommy," he called, waving over her shoulder.

"Love you." My son had his own social calendar and I just had to pencil myself in.

Now that I'm on the subject, I've got a few things on my calendar to deal with.

THE NEXT DAY, I SAT outside the office of Ophelia Kessler of Kessler's Kinder Toys. Evergreen was rolling hills and oversized mansions, and Cottonwood was where most of those mansion owners commuted to work.

The office of Kessler's Kinder Toys wasn't what I expected. A bland office building in a sea of bland office buildings. The sign blazoned on the front was a rainbow mix with teddy bears holding the letters. That's where the rainbow stopped.

The lobby was gray on gray. The inside of the elevator silver and gray. The receptionist that showed me, and my bodyguards, to Kessler's floor dressed in all black. And the waiting room I reviewed my notes in opted for a white décor. There wasn't a hint of color in this place.

White seats. White tile. White frames for Kessler's many credentials and achievements.

"Miss Moon."

I lifted my head.

"Mrs. Kessler is ready to see you," said the receptionist. "You can go right in."

"Thank you."

I didn't have expectations of a toy land after seeing the rest of her building, so it was no surprise that Kessler's office followed the same minimal design.

Minimal. But chic.

Paintings hung around the space, providing the only pops of color. Two white leather armchairs sat before a glass desk and sitting at that desk smiling at me was Mrs. Kessler.

"Hello, Valentina." We shook hands over her desk. "Please, sit. Get comfortable."

I set my stuff on one chair and sat on the other. In my head I ran through my speech. I couldn't leave this office unless I was holding a list of names and phone numbers.

"I hope you don't mind if we have a working lunch," she said. "I usually grab a bite at this time. Are you hungry?"

"I haven't eaten yet," I admitted. "I was going to grab something on campus after this."

She waved that away. "You came all this way to see me. The least I can do is treat you." Kessler tapped a button on her phone. "Mrs. Dove, I'll have a Cobb salad and green tea, please. Valentina, what would you like?"

"The same."

"Make that two, Mrs. Dove. Thank you."

Kessler took her finger off the intercom and folded her hands on the desk, giving me her full attention. "I hear you're planning a party, Miss Moon."

Didn't surprise me in the least that Jade told her.

"Yes, I'd like to do an alumni dinner and charity event. I know you usually handle those but I'd love to plan it this year."

She inclined her head. "We'll get to that. First, let's talk about you and the Sallys. How are you managing your first term as president?"

"It's going really well. The sisters seem happy with the way we've mixed the new with the traditional. I've had a few girls tell me that they like having more choice in the activities."

"That's wonderful. Any difficulties with running the house and living off campus?"

"No. Anything I can't be there for, Blair takes care of. Couldn't ask for a better vice president."

"I'm very happy to hear that," she replied. "I know you were cut off at the knees there with the addendums to the charter. It's a relief to hear you found your way despite that."

I blinked. Kessler came right out and said it.

If she's going to be frank, so am I.

"Why was I cut off at the knees?" I asked. "I support the commitment to healthy living and eating. I just don't understand why it has to be done in that way? Would it be so terrible if the girls did seventy-five minutes of Pilates?"

"I'm glad that you ask and that we now have a chance to discuss it." Kessler got up from behind her desk. I moved my bag to let her sit next to me. "In my mission to keep things as simple as possible, I swept in, told you all to choose a president, and swept out without giving a proper explanation of your duties.

"You're not the first group of sisters to seek changes at Sally house and you won't be the last. It's like you ladies said in your speeches, we have more opportunities. Better access to information. Better understanding," she said. "It's natural you wish to apply this to Zeta Rho and I'd never want it to be felt that we do not encourage innovation."

"Then why?"

"Zeta Rho and Nu Alpha were created for a single reason: honoring Sally Hollenbeck. She was brave. Intelligent. Hardworking. A fighter," she said. "The organization was tasked with defining those qualities and how they'd apply to the brothers and sisters. Specifically, what it means to be a strong, resilient fighter. In the beginning, they chose runs, jogs, drills, and the gym, and the following presidents did the same.

"Now that we're redefining how we view health and strength, the call to introduce alternatives proved that the charter needed to be revisited and expectations clarified. Strenuous exercise is what we decided builds strong men and women and I have no doubt you all can meet the challenge."

I bobbed my head, taking in her speech. "I understand what you're saying. But I guess my next question is why this emphasis on being like the real Sally? What she did was heroic and she deserves to be honored, but remembering her and what she sacrificed does that. Why take it further and model everything the brothers and sisters do after her?"

The silence stretched between us.

"Did that question make me sound like an insensitive ass?"

Kessler cracked a smile. "Not at all, Valentina. The truth is you're the first person to ask me that and it's a fair question. We model our country in the memory of the founders, but don't run around today with wooden teeth, enslaving people and forcing women into the kitchen. We can honor without emulating.

"In our case, we wanted the Zetas and Nus to have a purpose. Some sororities are known for their philanthropy and some fraternities are known for their legacy. From the beginning, we wished our men and women to be recognized for their effort, character, and willingness to take the hard road. To achieve that aim, we modeled our tenets on the woman who inspired them."

"Makes sense," I grudgingly admitted.

There I was thinking I'd have to whittle straight answers out of her and she was hitting me back with reasonable explanations for everything I swore couldn't have one.

But I'm not done yet.

"The initiation. How do we emulate Sally Hollenbeck by digging into people's lives and forcing them to spill their secrets for a place in the house?"

"If you ask me, we don't."

"Excuse me?"

Sighing, Kessler leaned back in her seat, eyes drifting over my head. "The initiation didn't exist when I was a Sally. A Nu Alpha Theta president started it in 2005 and both houses have done it ever since. Each new president continued the practice and didn't suggest stopping it until you."

"Why didn't the head organization stop it? The charter says no hazing."

"We tried several years ago. The councils made the argument it wasn't hazing since everyone had to share their truth. No one was singled out and what was revealed was never to be shared or used against the person. Incredibly, they were supported by the majority of the house. The members wanted it to continue, and unless we planned to monitor them twenty-four seven, we couldn't stop it."

I glanced away, turning over what she said. *They fought against banning the initiation? Wasn't expecting that.*

Heather and her supporters wanted to keep it too, a voice reminded. *Chock it up to one of those things you'll never truly understand.*

"Alright," I finally said. "Then, I guess I have one more question before we talk about the event?"

"And that would be?"

"The physical health requirement," I began. "Can we make some additions?"

Her brows snapped together. "What do you mean?"

"Sally knew martial arts, didn't she? What if along with runs and basketball, the girls also had the option to take self-defense or martial arts classes? Those require hard work, commitment, and strength training. If the girls choose that option, we could lower their strenuous exercise requirement. I think a lot of the girls would like it. The university has free classes and most people are on board with learning to defend themselves."

"Huh." Kessler leaned back, considering me. "Goodness me. That's a great idea, Valentina."

"Is it?" I didn't mean to sound so surprised, but she had expertly thrown out my other ideas.

"I'm asking myself why we didn't think of this before." She patted my knee. "This is why we have these meetings. Bright young minds push us forward."

"So... we can do it?"

"Absolutely," she said. "I have to check with the rest of the organization but I'm certain they'll agree. If the girls commit to one class a week, we can slash the strenuous requirement in half. If they do more, we can cut it down further."

"Great."

Wow. That was easier than I thought. Let's see if I can keep this up.

"About the charity—"

Mrs. Dove walked in with our salads and tea. Kessler balanced her food on her knee, picking up her fork, and gesturing for me to go on. "I'm listening."

I explained my idea for the event. Offering up the Evergreen Country Club. Telling her about the items we put up for auction and the charities we would sponsor.

"My boyfriends' companies are willing to put up a two-week tropical vacation, art pieces, the latest in MT tech, and a lunch with a celebrity artist of Interstellar Records as the big prizes," I said. "It'll be around Christmas, so we can do holiday-themed prizes too. All the proceeds will go to the local food bank and I'll arrange everything, Mrs. Kessler. You won't have to lift a finger."

"My, my," she said, sounding amused. "It's not often I get a proposal like this."

"What do you think?"

"I think it's a fabulous idea, Valentina."

My hope soared.

"But you don't have to organize it to get my approval. Send me your boyfriends' contact information as well as any other relevant contacts, and I'll begin the preparation."

I wouldn't fall down on the first volley.

"If it's all right, I'd like to plan the event," I said. "Zeta Rho Sigma is the only thing on my resume that falls under extracurricular. I can't join more clubs or groups, but I've been looking into ways I can take on more responsibility within the sorority. Pulling off an event like this would be huge."

She paused for the time it took to sip her tea. "Well, you've obviously done quite a bit of work on this already. I don't see the harm in letting you take the reins."

I pushed down a triumphant smile. "Great. I just need a list of your usual vendors and, oh yeah, the contact info of the alumni. I'm getting fancy, wintery invitations done up."

"Don't put yourself through too much trouble," she said. "E-vites will do."

Kessler moved around to her side of the desk, setting her food aside, and taking up her planner. "I will get the list of vendors and contact info to you this afternoon. Include me in every email you send out and loop me in on the final decisions. This is your show, but since we represent the Sams, Sallys, and my position as event coordinator, I have to ensure everything goes off without a hitch."

"Understood."

She wrote the final word with a flourish. "Very good. Thank you for meeting with me, Valentina. I will run your self-defense suggestion up the flagpole. You should hear back from me soon."

"Thank you."

I stood, shook her hand, and got out of there before she changed her mind.

I called Sofia in the elevator.

"She said yes," I told her by way of greeting. "She's emailing me the list this afternoon."

"Which means we're staying up late tonight. I'll get the takeout."

"This is why you're my best friend. I'll be there in an hour."

JAXSON

"Why do you have to move out of your office?" Gwen asked. "You'll be on another floor, not in another town."

"Meyer heard I took over the place and ordered me to clean it out." I lifted Gwen's feet off the table and pushed it out of the door. Bianca called dibs on it and my mini fridge and microwave. My loss was her gain like she said in her teasing goodbye. "I'll have a cubicle that will *more than suit my needs.*"

She cringed. "A cubicle? That's like a coffin for a guy like you. You should be out there. Scoping out bands. Going on tours—" Gwen dropped her eyes. "Sorry."

"Don't be." I held out my hand. She grabbed it and let me pull her off the chair. It was destined for the art department. "New Orleans was a shitshow and it was my fault. I've seen how fans can get and Chandler admitted Serena's been assaulted before. We should've had security."

"J, don't do that." She squeezed my forearm. "You can't beat yourself up. No one could've predicted what happened. A lot of singers have overzealous fans, but most don't have violent, psycho killer stalkers."

I blew out a breath. "It's a fucking mess. Serena is still in New Orleans and she can't identify the attacker. The album is on hold—which doesn't change anything for me since I'm out of A and R."

"Would it help if I kicked the good demos your way every now and then? Sneak your headphones in and jam out while you're filing."

"It would. I know this was the rotation I agreed to, but it still feels like I'm getting demoted."

Gwen helped me pack up the rest of my stuff and move it to their new locations. I helped Bianca put her food into the new mini fridge to delay the inevitable, then there was nothing left to stop me.

Suck it up. I zeroed in on the elevator numbers carrying me down to the pit of despairing, overworked, suited drones. *Serena was attacked but she still kissed me. Working with her after that was impossible. Might as well check off the last stop in my internship and move on to pushing Papa VZ out of his office.*

The elevator opened on Daniel Meyer. Arms folded. Straight-backed. Waiting for me.

"You're late."

"Good afternoon to you too," I said, grinning. "How is the wife? Kids? By the way, that's a badass suit. Where did you get it?"

The lines around his mouth deepened. "Bianca may have let you get away with whatever you wanted, but on my floor, you're going to work. I expect you on time and properly dressed."

"I was late packing up my office like you ordered me to. And what are you talking about properly dressed?" I glanced down at my low-slung jeans and band shirts. "I'm not an actual lawyer. You expect me to suit up for five weeks stuck in the file room?"

"This is my department. You will dress in appropriate attire or explain to your father why you failed this internship."

I put two fingers to my temple. "Cool. I'll run home and get changed." Spinning on my heels, I made for the elevator and my reprieve out of this place.

"Stop," he barked. "Tomorrow, Jaxson. You'll wear a suit and tie tomorrow. Today, I want you in the file room. We're changing the system from alphabetical to stored by year, band name, and then last names of the members. It'll take you a while and you're not leaving until it's done. Better get started."

A smile curled into my cheeks. "You've been waiting a long time for this, haven't you, Meyer?"

He remained expressionless. "I'm sure I don't know what you mean. You have two fifteen-minute breaks at ten and three. Lunch break at noon. Any questions?"

"Who do I report to?"

"Me."

Repeat that for a joke. I wouldn't come to you if my ass was on fire.

I glanced around at the silent workers tip-tapping on their keyboards. I'd find someone throwing me a less hostile look and go to them if I had questions.

"You know where the file room is," said Meyer. "Get to it."

I saved us more conversation and sidestepped him, passing through the cubicles for the hallway. At its end was the large, windowless room where I'd spend five entire weeks of my life.

Walking inside, I counted the five rows made up of four cabinets each, reaching as high as my head. And that was just in the middle of the room. Cabinets took up every inch of wall rounding out to thirty-eight cabinets and the hundreds of files each contained.

The door swung shut, enclosing me in silence—the complete opposite of the noise, music, and chatter on the A and R floor.

I opened the first drawer and pulled a stack out.

Like he said, I better get started.

VALENTINA

"How do you want to do this?" Sofia asked. "We can't just call a bunch of strangers and pelt them with questions on who dropped out of their year."

"We'll be subtler than that, Sof. Trust me."

The two of us were in her bedroom. The event details I planned to show Kessler covered her sheets and we sat in the middle of the chaos, scanning the list of names, numbers, and addresses Mrs. Dove emailed.

"Piper Davenport," Sofia read. "She must be Blair's mom. Blair told us she was president of the Sallys. Mrs. Davenport would know everyone who *left* under her reign."

"Let's save her for last. We know two presidents who are up to their necks in the shady stuff going down in the houses. No offense to Piper Davenport—who could be perfectly decent. We'll stick to the regular brothers and sisters for now."

She handed me her phone. "Show me how it's done."

"Will do." The list of alumni was sorted by the years they graduated. In the thirty-six years since the Sams and Sallys were founded, they racked up about two thousand graduates. I didn't need to talk to all of them. Just a few brothers and sisters dropping a few names, and we'd be off to a real start.

I chose Nora Holmes and dialed her number.

"Hello?" she answered.

"Hello, Mrs. Holmes. This is Valentina Moon, the current president of Zeta Rho Sigma."

"Oh, hi." Her hesitation fled under a cheerier greeting. "What can I do for you?"

"I apologize for cold-calling you like this. I'm planning an alumni charity event in December and I thought I'd see how much interest there is before sending out two thousand invitations."

She laughed with me. *Good.*

The first step is charming them if I've learned anything from Ezra.

"The event would be held in the Evergreen Country Club. It's a dinner and charity auction. We will bid on prizes, gift cards, and getaways sponsored by local businesses. All proceeds will be donated to the food bank."

"That sounds nice."

"If you'd like to sponsor a prize too, I'm giving all the alumni the option."

"My company makes organic jams and jellies," she offered. "I'd be happy to offer a basket."

"Awesome."

"What day is the party?" she asked.

"I'm shooting for December twelfth, Saturday. Not too close to Christmas, but close enough for plenty of eggnog."

She laughed again. "December twelfth works for me. I am definitely interested."

"Great. I will send the invitation this week. Along with the information for your donation."

"Thank you so much, Valentina."

"Before you go," I threw in, heading off her goodbye. "Would you happen to have the email address for Emma Johnson?"

"Who?"

"Emma Johnson," I repeated. "One of your sisters. She dropped out of the Sallys and the university while you were there."

"Dropped out of the— Oh! Do you mean Miriam Brown? She dropped out in our junior year. Family emergency. I'm pretty sure she was the only one."

"Yes, of course." I mouthed to Sofia, telling her to grab her pen. "Miriam Brown. Sorry, I read the wrong name."

"Why are you asking about Miriam?"

"I'm inviting all of the Sallys and Sams to the event," I explained. "I'm thinking of it like a networking opportunity, and also a reunion.

And even those who were forced to leave the house due to difficult circumstances should be invited. Once a sister, always a sister, right?"

"Absolutely. Poor Miriam's mother died in the middle of the year. She didn't leave a number or email for us to contact her. I'd love to see her again and find out how she's doing after all these years."

"Thank you, Mrs. Holmes. Have a nice evening."

She said the same and I ended the call, smirking at Sofia's clapping.

"Impressive," she said.

"That's how it's done. People love to correct you. Throw out a fake dropout and they'll be quick with the real one." I tapped her notebook. "Miriam Brown supposedly left because her mom passed away. We have the year she would've graduated and therefore how old she is. Hopefully that's enough for Maverick to dig up something on what truly happened to her."

"How many people are we going to call?"

"Focus on the alumni who graduated after 2006."

She nodded. Taking up her laptop, she moved to the bay window, so we couldn't talk over each other. For two straight hours, we called former Sallys and Sams alike, gushing about the upcoming party and asking after the random dropouts in their year. One after the other, they threw out names. Five people had nothing to tell me. Twelve alumni did.

"—thank you, Mr. Bellingham," I said. "I'll send out your invitation in a few days."

I wrote down Alexander Olsen.

A knock broke into Sofia's spiel.

"Yes?" she called.

"Is Valentina in there?" Blair asked. "There's a package for her downstairs."

"Package? For me? Are you sure?"

"Your name is on it."

I closed the notebook and stepped out, meeting Blair at the top of the stairs. The bodyguards who had been waiting outside the room fell in step with us.

"What are you two doing in there? I thought I heard Sofia say auction."

"We're checking on interest in the charity dinner," I replied. "Mrs. Kessler gave me the go-ahead and almost everyone we called said they'd attend and donate something for the auction. I'll have to book the country club's large ballroom."

"You're planning for the party? Why didn't you tell me? I should be doing this with you. I'm your vice president."

"You are doing this with me," I said as we climbed off the steps. "This week we'll send out the invitations, call the vendors, and put a deposit down for the country club. I'd get nowhere trying to do all of that without you."

That seemed to mollify her. "I'll draft up the invitation tonight. I also think I should keep track of the donations."

"The job is yours."

She jerked her chin toward the hall. "Your package is on the living room table."

I walked in on a study session. The girls didn't pay me any mind, huddled over the table, reciting from their textbooks. Waiting for me was a small, brown box. I picked it up, noting my name typed on the front and the Zeta Rho address beneath.

Must be president business.

Ripping open the box, a small blue notepad fell out. I picked it off the floor and read the front.

Flick Book.

A tiny arrow pointed to the bottom corner and two words above it urged me to flip.

I know what this is, I thought, smile appearing on my lips. *One of those books where you flip the pages fast and it looks like the drawings are moving.*

I balanced it on my wrist, letting the pages fly.

A small car puttered down the road, exhaust tooting from the tailpipe. A little white car appeared, rolling behind.

My grin faded as the white car drew closer and closer and finally rammed the bumper, sending the tiny car careening toward me. A dark-haired woman ejected through the windshield and splayed out on the hood, tongue lolling from her mouth and her eyes crossed out.

I screamed, startling the room, and flung the vile thing away.

"Valentina!" Juliet cried. She shot to my side, hand on her holster. "What's wrong?!"

My finger shook as I pointed.

Juliet and Hadley descended on the flipbook, hands still on their guns as they prodded it. The study group craned to see. Suddenly, economics wasn't as interesting.

Juliet took up the book and flipped through the pages. I observed the same consternation followed by horror lighting her eyes. "You can't have what's mine," she said. "What is that supposed to mean?"

"What?" I croaked.

My heart pounded like a jackhammer, beating wildly on my tight chest. I clutched my hands trying to stop their shaking.

"They added a message." Juliet brought me the notebook.

Written in huge block letters was a single phrase.

You can't have what's mine.

"YOU CAN'T HAVE WHAT'S mine?" Sofia repeated. "What are they talking about and why would they send you such an awful thing?"

I made to answer and got her hair in my mouth. Sofia was hugging me pretty tight with no sign of letting up.

My scream alerted half the house. Sofia came out running as my bodyguards hustled me off, holding the book and packaging out in front of them like they feared it had more terrible prizes to deliver.

Sofia came with us and thus I ended up in my living room, smothered by her while my boys and bodyguards hovered.

"What kind of sick, twisted fuck would send you that?" Ezra raged.

"Is it a warning?" I asked. "Are they saying next time they'll finish the job?"

"There won't be a next time," Sofia cried. If possible, she hugged me tighter.

"We've settled the argument on if this guy has been following you around," said Ryder. "They addressed it to you at the sorority."

"The return address is a PO box," Juliet said. "We'll track it down, but I have a feeling it won't turn up much."

"Are we still not admitting Leighton Lewis is behind this?" Maverick spoke up. "*Taking what's mine.* Valentina became president and took her sorority."

"I didn't take anything," I said. "She's the one who *died*. If she wants to be president so badly, she can come back to life and we'll vote all over again!"

I might have been a tad stressed. I'd dealt with a fair amount of warped, cruel individuals. The person who sent me that flipbook was worse than all of them. Sadistic on a level I couldn't comprehend.

"But that aside, whoever mailed me that hates me," I said. "Honestly, truly hates me and wants me dead. Leighton doesn't fit that description. Same for Patricia and Reagan."

"Enough with this argument," Ezra said. "It could be Leighton Lewis, or we could admit the five of us have collected dozens of enemies over the last few years. We won't know who's targeting Valentina until we catch the son of a bitch, or they give up why they're coming after her. What the fuck did she take that *belongs to them*?"

Sofia eased up a little. "If this is about the presidency, Valentina beat out a few girls who figured they were locked to win."

I shook my head. "Heather wouldn't run me off the road for becoming president months before I decided to run. This all started the day I went to the beach house. What was going on then that I managed to make someone want to kill me?"

"Sons of Slaughter." Ezra sat next to me, freeing me from Sofia and securing me in his arms instead. "Aiden Connelly."

"The guys who attacked you," Sofia added. "A lot went down last year."

"Who among those people would come after me like this, or believes I took something from them?"

No one. Not my bodyguards, boyfriends, and best friend had an answer.

I took a deep breath. "Whoever they are, they sent me that disgusting book because they couldn't think of another way to get to me. Juliet and her team keep them away. Changing cars throws them off. Unmarked mail isn't delivered here. They sent it to the Sally house because it was their last option, and if it happens again, I'm turning it over to the police. They can deal with this sicko. I'm done."

I stood free of my hug. "I'm tired of people like this turning my life upside down. I have enough going on trying to find Teagan and Sawyer." I turned on Juliet. "From now on, I don't run around opening up random packages and I leave finding this guy to you and the police."

"We will find him," she said without skipping a beat. "Until then, there won't be a repeat of today. I apologize for not vetting that package."

"Don't apologize. We haven't gotten to the point that I want my mail searched."

"We're at that point now," Ryder said.

We'll have that argument after everyone leaves.

"I also ask that you start carrying a weapon," Juliet continued. "You have to be able to defend yourself if anything happens to me, Hadley, or Kennedy. Whoever this person is, they mean business."

"What kind of weapon? I have a son. I won't have anything dangerous around him."

"Would you consider a taser?"

"We'll talk about it. Sof," I said, twisting to face her. "We left the list in your room. It's too late to call more people, but we can get started on the names we have already."

She blinked at me like she didn't know what I was talking about. "You want to do that right now?"

"What else are we going to do?"

Sofia didn't move.

"Please," I said. "It's important. Plus, it'll take my mind off what's going on."

"Okay." It sounded like a question. "I'll run back to campus and get it."

"Get what?" Maverick asked as she got up to leave.

"Mrs. Kessler said yes to the event," I told him. "She emailed me the list of alumni and I have the names of twelve people who suddenly dropped out of Zeta Rho and Nu Alpha. Sofia has more."

Maverick crossed the scant distance and kissed me. "Are you sure you're okay?" he whispered. "You can take a break, Val. One night off from saving the world."

The barest smile tugged at my lips. "Saving the world takes my mind off the rest. I'm okay. I promise."

He heaved a sigh. "In that case, I know what we're doing tonight."

An hour later, Sofia, Maverick, and I had taken up the available surfaces in his room. I spread my laptop and papers on his bed. Maverick sat at the desk. Sofia had the couch and coffee table, and at her feet, half-finished robots lay on the carpet.

"Miriam Brown," I said. "Lives in Tacoma with her husband and kids."

I crossed her name off the list.

"Same for Theodore Snyder," Sofia spoke. "Well, not the Tacoma-and-kids part. He lives with his husband in New York."

Social media made it scary easy to track a stranger down. Which is why it was suspect when we typed in a name that turned up absolutely nothing.

"No record of Ian Campos," I told Maverick.

"I've got five Melissa Beckers," Sofia threw in. "Can't say which one—if any of them—dropped out of Somerset."

"I'll track them down," Maverick replied. "Just keep the names coming."

Our task took us well into the night. Sofia ended up crashing in the guest bedroom. I passed out on my notepad, fully clothed, and above the sheets. The crick in my neck the next day revealed how my body felt about that.

I cracked my eyes open, finding Maverick standing above me holding a mug.

"Chamomile tea. Two spoons of honey, just like you like."

"Thank you, my love." I stretched, arching my back off the bed and hearing things pop and crack. "Sorry I fell asleep and left you with the work."

"You did all the work, Val. You got the list and convinced those people to give you the names. Now we can find out how many Teagans and Sawyers there have been over the years."

"What does it mean if this has happened before?" I sat up and accepted my tea. "We've started back as far as 2006. Aiden and Leighton were children then. They can't be responsible. If the disappearances stretch years, someone else has been snatching coeds and covering it up."

The bed dipped as Maverick sank down. "We can't forget what Ezra heard in the basement or who sent Sawyer to the van. Aiden didn't do anything to Melissa Becker, but he's involved. If this has happened before, the person has to be connected to the fraternity. Close enough to bring Aiden and his friends on board. Possibly close enough to trade Leighton Lewis a favor. *Help me cover up Teagan's disappearance and I'll clean up your crime scenes.*"

I shivered. "Who would trade a favor like that? How do you convince a normal college student to help you cover up the disappearance of their frat brother? Why would Aiden go along with that? And why is that smug bastard always walking around like he knows the bomb that's about to drop and he can't wait to see the look on our faces?" Letting out a breath, I dropped my head on his shoulder. "Sorry. I'm pelting you with questions when you're just as in the dark as I am."

"We'll figure this out, Val. The answers might be somewhere in that list of names. If they are, I'll find them."

Chapter Nine

*J*axson

"J? You in here?"

"Of course, I'm here." I poked my head over a stack of manila folders. "This is where I'll die. You'll file my corpse under J and then V, and then back to J when Meyer changes his mind."

Levi Van Zandt, the most famous music producer of our time, stepped into my lowly file room. "Suffering that much?"

"No," I said, getting to my feet. "I'm not complaining. Meyer's got his ear to the wall waiting for me to say I can't take it."

Dad looked me up and down. It had been week since and as ordered, I showed up in the legal department wearing a dress shirt, ironed pants, shined shoes, and a tie.

A fucking tie.

Meyer sought me out every morning to make sure I was properly dressed. And smirked at me to start my day off desperate to punch him.

"You look ridiculous," Dad deadpanned.

"It's your words of encouragement that get me through the tough times."

He laughed. "Like when you were a kid, sneaking into my closet and trying on my boots and hats. Just doesn't fit, J."

"No arguments here. So, what's up?"

"I thought you'd want to know Serena is back. Fully recovered but taking it easy at home. She's eager to finish the album but won't play another concert or festival until we upgrade her security. A fair demand."

"What are you going to do?"

"The police haven't found the person responsible, so the threat remains until we know for certain they won't try again. I'm arranging a security team for the band. Where they go, the bodyguards go."

"Good. Serena fucked with my relationship and got into it with Val, but I don't want crazed fans getting their hands on her."

"They won't. Not while she's under this label."

"Thanks for letting me know," I said. "Was that all?"

Dad didn't answer right away. He veered down a row, looking around at the open drawers and the stacks I had scattered all over the room. "This all he has you doing?"

"I also fetch coffee."

He nodded. "And you haven't complained or tried to pass off the job."

"No."

"Are you trying to prove something, J?"

I pulled a face. "To Meyer?"

"To me." Dad finally faced me. "Because you don't have to. I know you can do this job, son."

"I know I can too. But the point of this internship wasn't to prove it to me or you. It was to prove it to everyone else. I won't get far if my employees side-eye me, openly thinking this was handed to me. They had to see me work for it. Know that I understand what makes this label great and that I appreciate what they do. And now... Daniel Meyer has to see me punished for nearly destroying it."

Levi lifted his chin, peering at me over our shared nose. "I didn't raise you to be this perceptive. Must be Valentina's influence."

"I can back that up. A few years with her wiped away most of your parenting flaws."

Dad grabbed my neck, snapping my forehead to his chest. "You don't have flaws, J. I made a lot of mistakes. You weren't one of them."

"I know, Dad."

Clearing his throat, he let me go. "Finish up in here. I'm taking you out to lunch. Eve and I have something to talk to you about."

"Yes," I said. "You have my blessing. Also yes to being your best man."

"Slow down." Levi laughed. "We're just moving in together. Act like it's the first you're hearing of it at lunch. Eve wanted to tell you together."

I put two fingers to my temple. "Bet you're glad I didn't move back home now."

Dad smiled. "No."

He patted my shoulder and walked out. That's about as mushy as we got.

I bent to pick a folder off the stack and heard creaking hinges.

"Dad?"

"Jaxson."

My fist curled on the files. "Meyer."

"It's Mr. Meyer—as I've told you repeatedly."

"Need me to do another coffee run?" I skated past his correction.

He stopped in front of me. Hands folded behind his back. Shoulders square. Eyes glittering.

"You gave your father a nice speech. Do you truly believe you learned your lesson? That one year of doing actual work and at twenty years old, you know all you need to know to run the label we built?"

"Seems like I was right about you listening through the walls," I said, hiding a smirk at his purpling face. "I'm not taking over the top floor tomorrow. But yes. When Dad's ready to hand over the reins, I'll be ready to take them."

His lips curled. "Levi overindulges you. He always has. Swallowing your half-assed apologies and excusing your behavior because he wants to be your friend more than your father."

"Or maybe, just maybe, the man who raised me knows me better than you do."

Meyer stepped forward, getting in my face. "I know you, Jaxson. All too well. Let me make something clear," he hissed. "As long as I'm a partner in this label, you will never take over."

I held his gaze unflinchingly. "Take it down, Meyer. Choose your words carefully. Don't say something that you'll regret."

His eyes flared. "Are you threatening me?"

"Nope. I'm telling you that I *will* take over this label. I'll do right by my staff and my artists. You can accept that or not. We can work together or you can get yourself fired working against me. But there is no future where Jaxson Van Zandt isn't synonymous with Interstellar Records."

"We'll see about that." Meyer pushed past me, stalking to the other side of the room. "Empty this cabinet and refile it. Today. You don't leave until it's done."

He swept out, leaving me to imagine all the ways I could crush his head like a grape.

Drop one of these file cabinets on him. Speed bump over him with my new car.

The increasingly graphic fantasies cooled my temper. Daniel Meyer hated me for the precise reason that he knew he was stuck with me. He could mess around with most people in the building. He could even mess around with me. But he couldn't mess around with Levi Van Zandt.

I emptied out the cabinet, flipping through the files to see what the documents were about and where to file them. The band names were written on the tabs.

The Undisturbed. Cana's Dream. Controlled Chaos.

I slowed down, brows scrunching up. I took some of the documents out and gave it a closer look.

"A covenant not to sue," I read aloud.

Quickly, it dawned on me. I looked through the other files to be sure and they all held the same.

These were the bands I secretly recorded and their agreements not to sue the label after their hours of hard work leaked onto the internet.

I wanted to be mad at Meyer, but honestly, I was surprised he didn't order me to stumble on this weeks ago. I messed up and nearly put the label and these bands' careers in the shitter. I didn't deserve to act like it never happened.

I paused flipping through Controlled Chaos's file, picking out a name.

What? It can't be...

I read the name again, casting my mind back. I wasn't sure what this meant. Or what I should do in response.

I closed the file, stuffed it in the drawer, and walked out for lunch.

VALENTINA

"A buffet makes more sense."

Aiden tossed his head. "This is a big event. Alumni are showing up in their bow ties and ball gowns with pockets full of cash to throw down on the auction. You can't make them wait in line for their gravy."

"A sit-down dinner is more expensive," I argued. "The country club insists we use their servers and the fee for that would feed all of Evergreen for a week. This is a charity event—as in the money goes to those in need. Not to us."

"Treating the alumni to a nice night doesn't take away from what we're trying to do."

"We?" I couldn't resist saying. "I'm not sure what you mean by *we*."

Aiden and I had been arguing back and forth on party details since Mrs. Kessler insisted we work together two weeks before. I couldn't prove he called her up and got himself assigned to my event, but I bet it happened anyway.

Aiden leaned over the dining room table. "Moon, this matters just as much to me and the brothers as it does to you. We've got CEOs, judges, athletes, authors, and business owners on the guest list. The Nu Alphas are looking to make good impressions too."

"Think how much small talk they can make on the buffet line."

He blew out a breath, turning his head up to the ceiling as though beseeching help. "We've got extra money in our budget," he said. "I'll drop the end-of-semester trip with you guys and pay the fee for servers. Deal?"

I pressed my lips together.

"Come on, Moon. What are you saying no to now? It's coming out of my pocket."

"Fine. We'll do a sit-down dinner. Three courses only."

He sat down, smirking away. "Whatever you want."

"Great," Blair spoke up. I'd forgotten she was in the room. "We can finally move on to music."

Aiden and I spoke at the same time.

"Band."

"D.J."

"Here we go again," my treasurer mumbled.

"We're not going anywhere," I said. "The stage will be taken up by the items for auction. We don't have a place to put an entire band, so we can only do a deejay."

Aiden inclined his head. "Good point. Deejay it is."

My council perked up.

"Perfect," said Blair. "Now for the decorations. We're doing a Christmas theme, but I was thinking we go classy with white and gold instead of red and green. My mother's event planner put together a few centerpieces. What do you think?" She pulled photos out of her voluminous binder.

The truth was the event stopped being mine about two days after it got approved. Blair walked into Sofia's room armed with her binder and that was that.

I couldn't deny she had great ideas. And her mom's connections benefited us from all the way in New York. We were getting a discount on linens, the caterer and, apparently, the decorations.

"I love this centerpiece," I said, tapping the second photo she showed me. A tiny Christmas tree nestled in a bed of ornaments and frosted leaves.

"I love it too," Blair said. "I was thinking we could wrap the chairs in—"

Jade walked into the dining room. She noticed she caused an interruption and motioned to a chair. "Please, don't mind me. I'd like to sit in and—" She cut eyes to me. "Speak to you after the meeting, Valentina."

"Sure."

We made it through the next hour with only two more disagreements between me and Aiden. It was a relief to close my notebook and watch the backs of my council leave the room.

"What's going on, Jade?" I asked, turning to her. "Do you need me to take over for dinner?"

"No," she clipped. "I need you to explain why you're asking about Alexander Olsen, Melissa Becker, and Ian Campos."

I froze. "How did you know about that?"

"Peter Bellingham is a friend. We spoke the other day and he mentioned that he hoped your search for Alexander was going well. I had no idea what he was talking about." Jade moved around the table and I did too. Maintaining the distance between us. I'd never seen that expression on her face. It seemed the sunshine-and-giggles act was over.

"Peter explained that you were inviting all the brothers and sisters. Something about once a brother, always a brother. Imagine my surprise when I called a few of the other alumni and discovered you questioned them in the same way. It's interesting that you neglected to tell us the full extent of your guest list."

"Is that a problem? There's no rule that I can't invite—"

"Spare me, Valentina."

I blinked at the snap. Yep. She wasn't playing nice anymore.

"Do you think I'm unaware of the accusations your boyfriend leveled at Aiden Connelly last year? He believes there's something sinister behind Teagan Kainer's and Sawyer Burn's disappearance. Were you hoping to establish a pattern by tracking down our past dropouts?"

Got it in one, Jade.

"No," I said clearly. "How would I even do that? People change their names. People *share* a name with fifty others. They live their life off social media or they pack up and leave the country. I'd have no way of knowing if something happened to them unless someone reported it. I don't have ulterior motives, Jade. I asked for those names to put them on the guest list. Miriam Brown and Theodore Snyder are excited to see their old friends."

Jade visibly stiffened.

Likely at the confirmation that I've been tracking these names down.

"This is not how we do things, Valentina," she said. "The people on the alumni list were the only ones you were allowed to invite. You used me, Mrs. Kessler, Zeta Rho, and this event for your own purposes. That will not stand." Jade came around quick, suddenly in front of me. "Effective immediately, you're turning over this event to me. You will delete the alumni contact list while I watch and, in the future, any and all events will be run by Mrs. Kessler."

I nodded along, lips pursed. "This reaction has me thinking there was something to find among those names. Or I should say, nothing to find. What did happen to those people I couldn't track down, Jade?"

"How should I know? We don't keep tabs on our brothers or sisters after they walk out that door."

"Course not," I drew out. "But now that I'm thinking about it, it is a little strange that so many students left because of family emergencies, but I can't find those obituaries, sick sisters, or what became of the dads rushed to the hospital. I tried tracking down Teagan and Sawyer to send out their invitations, and still it's bounced emails and disconnected numbers. Isn't that strange?"

"No," she snapped. "It's not strange that students going through such a difficult time that they had to drop out of school, would then block harassing calls and emails. Whatever you or your boyfriend believe happened to Miss Kainer or Mr. Burn, I can promise you that you're wrong." She closed the scant distance between us. "I'm warning you, Valentina. Let this go. You could be a good president—possibly a great one. The doors the Sallys would open for you doesn't compare to any other organization or job. You're sabotaging your future over things you do not understand."

I raised a brow. "And you're here to what? Look out for me? Keep me on the right track? How sweet."

Red stained her cheeks. "I'm here to ensure you don't abuse your power. Which you have." She put out her hand. "Give me the binder, Valentina, and the laptop while you're at it. I want those contacts deleted."

I didn't move, locking in for a battle of wills I'd win either way. *Sofia has a copy of the contacts and Maverick's been digging for weeks. It's much too late.*

"The party is planned. The details are finalized. The invitations are sent out. The top prizes were secured by me. I'll delete the contacts but you taking over now doesn't make sense. It'll look weird to the sisters, and when they ask why, I'll tell them I'm being punished for inviting formers Sallys and Sams who left under difficult circumstances. I bet they'll question why that could possibly be wrong."

"I'd be happy to explain it to them," she replied, tone even. "Binder, please."

"Excuse me?"

We whipped our heads around.

Juliet eyed us with the same scrutiny we gave her. "Is there a problem, Valentina?"

"None." Just like that, I handed over the binder. "Jade was offering to take a few things off my plate. Super nice of her."

"If you're all done here, we should head out. The bell rings in twenty minutes."

I checked my watch and confirmed the time. Arguing with Aiden and ambushed by Jade nearly made me late to pick up Adam.

"Let's go." I stepped around Jade.

"Drop this, Valentina." The soft voice stopped me. "I won't say it again."

"Don't say it at all."

Juliet and Hadley waited in the hall with Sofia. She was coming with me to pick Adam up from school and then staying for dinner. Fortunate since we had a new topic for dinner conversation.

The four of us made our way through campus to the parking garage near the science building. I filled her in on my short conversation with Jade.

"Val, it sounds like she threatened you."

"Threatened or warned. It was hard to get a read off her other than pissed."

"She proves there's something going on," said Sofia. "I just wish I knew what. Every explanation I come up with is more horrible than the last, but how can there be a good explanation for almost a dozen people vanishing off the face of the earth?"

"There isn't one." We stepped off the sidewalk and climbed up the side stairs for level B. "But I won't stop until I find out the truth and put a stop to it. Jade's threat/warning guaranteed it."

My car was sandwiched between two Jeeps in the middle row of the garage. Juliet and Hadley walked us to the car and continued on to their own. We jumped inside, reaching for our buckles.

"Val, what's that?"

"What's what?" I asked without looking up.

"There's a present on your hood."

My head snapped up.

A small box wrapped in metallic blue paper and secured with a green bow lay innocently on the hood of the car. I cycled through the possibilities that it could indeed be innocent. A gift from my guys or a thank-you from a friend.

Every possibility turned up no.

"Sof, run out and grab Juliet and Hadley, please. My new friend finally figured out where to leave their gift."

She rushed out, calling for the guards. Carefully, I climbed out of the car and edged closer. My caution was warranted. This person made it clear they wanted me dead. That they hunted me down and found my car despite me constantly changing parking spaces shows they were highly motivated to get this to me.

"Valentina!"

I jumped.

"Step away from that, please," Juliet ordered.

The request was quickly followed by Hadley grabbing me by the forearms and dragging me away. She shoved me behind her as Juliet approached the gift.

Peering over her shoulder, Sofia and I held our breath, watching her inch the present closer, pause as though she was listening for ticking, and then begin to unwrap.

She revealed a white box. Juliet pried off the lid and looked inside.

"It's safe," she said, inviting us to breathe. "Val, you should look at this. Tell us what it means."

"What is it?"

She tipped the box over and something white fell out. I went up and laid eyes on the toy car decorating my hood. Looped through the bottom was a gold string attached to a note.

"You can't take a hint, so I'm spelling it out for you," I read. "Jaxson doesn't want you. Stay away from him, whore, or the next time we **run** into each other, I'll finish the job."

"The fuck?!" Sofia cried. "I'm calling the police."

"Next time we run into each other," I said. "Gotta love that wordplay."

"Miss Moon, are you alright?" asked Hadley.

"I'm fine. More than fine actually. I finally know who I'm dealing with."

JAXSON

"See you tomorrow, Jaxson."

I waved across the cubicles. Meyer was a jackass, but not everyone he employed was the same. I was fetching coffee for some pretty decent guys. A few even offered to help me file or grab the lunch orders when they noticed Meyer riding me.

"I'll sneak a chocolate chocolate chip muffin in with your coffee tomorrow."

"My wife's got me on a diet," he called back. "Therefore, bless you. Make it two."

I said my goodbyes, escaping into the hallway and rolling up to security.

"Night, Paunch."

"There's a package for you behind the security desk," he said. "I'm assuming it's another gift from your secret admirer."

I slid through the metal detector, not slowing down. "You can have it."

"Are you sure? Don't you want to see what it is?"

"Nope. It's all yours," I tossed over my shoulder. See you way too early tomorrow."

I crossed the parking lot, thoughts returning to evening plans with Val. I was going to surprise her with dinner on the balcony and dessert in the tub. Something about Valentina covered in suds got us both going. We'd be in there long after the water turned to ice.

My phone rang as I got in the car.

"Hello?"

"Hey, J. Something happened and I wanted you to hear it from me."

I froze, key hovering over the ignition. "What? Are you okay? Is Eve?"

"Eve and I are fine," he replied. "It's Daniel. He got into an accident on his way home from work. His wife called me from the hospital."

"Shit. How bad is it?"

"They rushed him into surgery. Fernanda's at the hospital alone. I'm going over there to support her and find out how he's doing. If I stay the night, I'll need you to bring me some stuff in the morning."

"No problem. Whatever you need, I've got you."

My problems with Daniel Meyer aside, he was my dad's best friend. I'd be the real asshole if I didn't let my shit go to support Dad..

"Thanks, son." A weary sigh expelled through the phone, asking me if that was a sound I'd ever heard my father make.

Once. It followed the first time I saw him cry.

"I'll keep you updated," he said. "Hold down the fort for me."

"Will do."

I let him go, continuing on home.

"You're not going to believe this shit, Jaxson."

Ezra accosted me as I got in the door, storming down the stairs with Val on his heels.

"They found Val's car and left her another present." Ezra shoved something in my hand. "The thong, the text, the flipbook, and the threats. All the same person."

"Whoa, slow up." I squinted to read the note. "Can't take a hint... Stay away from Jaxson? Who the hell is this?!"

"I thought Serena, but you didn't know her when I was run off the road," Val said. "There's someone else after you and they're... crazy."

"Who is it, J?" Ezra asked.

"I don't know!" The events of the last few months ran through my mind too fast for me to grab one and hold on to it.

Someone tried to kill Valentina... over me? They got into my car. Planted the underwear. Sent the flipbook and declared me theirs.

Did they also...

"Send the text?" I whispered. "Val, that breakup text... I don't think Serena did that either."

Her eyes widened with the same realization. "If they sent that text, they followed us to New Orleans, got close enough to steal your phone, and"—the blood drained from her face—"close enough to see Serena kiss you. Jaxson, Serena wasn't attacked by a fan."

I dropped. Hard. Falling on my ass. Keys skittering across the foyer.

"It was me," I rasped. "They put her in the hospital and almost killed you because of me." I punched the floor. "And I had no fucking clue!"

"Jaxson." Val knelt, taking my face in her hands. "You can't blame yourself. You didn't know—"

"I did know," I said. "Someone has been sending me gifts for weeks. I just ignored them and gave them away. Such an idiot! I should've realized it passed normal after the second, third, and *fifth* gift. They sent me another one today."

Ezra grasped my shoulder. "Someone sent you toothpicks. It's a big jump up from grateful bandmembers to homicidal stalker. You couldn't have known."

"Especially when we were convinced Serena was behind everything," Val added. "All that matters is we finally know why they're coming after me and we can figure out who it is."

"Has to be someone close to you," Ezra said. "They picked out gifts they knew you'd like. Found a way into your car. Knew where to find you in New Orleans."

A name detached itself from my memory, striking me through the chest. "I know who it is," I said. "And I know why."

I WAS UP BEFORE MY alarm the next morning.

Ezra and Val held me back, saying we had to go about it carefully if we were going to get the confession that led to serious jail time.

Fuck careful.

I shoved my pants on in the dark, highly aware of Val's still form beneath my sheets.

Val was almost killed. She's been harassed, taunted, and screwed with for weeks. This ends now.

Slipping out the door, I padded downstairs, got in the car, and pulled out of our drive.

My grip tightened the closer I got to Cottonwood. She'd be there bright and early. Playing the happy employee like she played me for a year.

I should thank Meyer. Something came out of that endless filing after all.

I parked haphazardly, shooting out and storming inside. Paunch said something to me that I barely heard. I was singularly focused on one person.

The elevator spat me out on the A and R floor. I rushed through the hall, belting out her name.

"Jaxson?"

Twisting around, I landed on her as she poked her head out of the conference room.

"Hey. Am I dying?" She laughed. "Why are you hollering for me?"

My jaw clenched so tight I was slow to answer. "We should talk, Gwen. Don't you agree?"

"Sure." She motioned to come inside. "The floor is meeting first thing to decide on a get-well gift for Mr. Meyer. I'm putting out cups and snacks. Help me out while we talk."

I followed her inside, eyes fixed on the back of her head. She fussed with a stack of cups, separating them on a tray, and chattering the entire time.

"—saw him yesterday. The next thing I know, I'm getting a text that Mr. Meyer was in an accident. He has a wife and three kids. I can only imagine what they're going through right now."

"It's terrible," I murmured.

Amazing. She actually sounds like a normal human being who feels real emotions. Nothing to reveal the true twisted psycho inside.

"I was thinking that instead of flowers, we pitch in for a stack of his favorite movies to watch while he's recovering. Ditto for a bag of treats. Something to brighten his day. What do you—"

"I'm sorry, Gwen," I broke in. "I'm not one hundred percent sure how we do this, but I'm betting small talk isn't it."

"What?"

"I think the apologies should go first," I continued. "So, I'll start with mine. I'm sorry, Gwen. Sorry that I snuck those recordings out of the studio and was responsible for your brother's album getting leaked."

Gwen went rigid. The water pitcher hung from her fingers almost comically, recalling memories of Greek statues. Their tales were tragedies too.

"Controlled Chaos. Guitarist and songwriter, James Sandoval. I didn't know his last name until I read the file."

Gwen shifted ever so slightly—her face cloaked in shadows.

"You still don't know anything, Jaxson."

"He's your brother, isn't he?"

"Yes."

"I don't have an excuse for what I did, Gwen."

"But you didn't do it, did you?" Gwen's rasp slipped into my ears and stood my hair on end. "Signing that contract was James's big break. He worked his ass off. Turned down good-paying jobs. Poured everything he had into the music and it finally paid off.

"Then their raw, uncut songs hit the internet and people trashed them. Their career hadn't started and it was already dead. James just... gave up. He signed your stupid contracts, quit the band, crawled back home and took over our father's feed store. Four years later and he's still the most miserable bastard I know."

"I remember them," I said. "Even those rough tracks were light-years ahead of people doing this for decades. I can still make this right, Gwen. End this—here and now. And your brother can have his dream."

"You make it right? Why should you?" she asked. "My second day of knowing you and I realized you'd never purposefully hurt the label. The songs were leaked by someone else, and I can guess by who."

"That's why you went after Val." I swallowed the distance between us. "You're not in love with me. You're just smart enough to have everyone looking for an obsessed stalker while you hide what this is really about."

"Went after Val?" She dropped the pitcher, finally turning to face me. "What are you talking about?"

I had to give it to her. She put on a hell of a confused mask.

"We're done playing games, Gwen. You ran her off the road. Busted up her car. Put those art skills to use with that sick flipbook. Tried to break us up and attacked Serena after the show."

"How could I have attacked Serena?" Gwen's normally cheerful face wiped blank. "I wasn't in New Orleans."

"Last I checked, planes still take off and land there every day."

"I see," she said, folding her arms. "So, four years after the fact, I came here on a desperate mission to kill, sabotage, and land myself in jail. All to get vengeance for my brother."

"Why else would you get a job here, Gwen? Interstellar Records can't be too popular with your family."

"It's not," she replied. "Even so, James made his choice. You guys didn't force him out. He quit. That didn't mean I had to do the same." She leaned off the table, moving around me. "I've wanted to work for a big record company since I was old enough to understand what a record label was. I've applied to a dozen all over the country. Scored an interview here and, I admit, I was curious. Were you a bunch of fuck-ups coasting on your good name, or was the leak just a freak accident? My brother deserved an explanation if nothing else."

I held still as she circled me. "I thought I'd spend a year here and then move on. I didn't expect us to become real friends."

"We're not friends." I flashed out, stopping her in her tracks. "You lied to me every fucking day and you're lying to me now. Admit what you did, and then get the hell out of my building."

"I'm not admitting anything." Gwen sounded amused. "I haven't done a thing wrong. Unless you've got proof saying otherwise, you need to back down."

I bent until our noses brushed. "No, you need to listen close. It'll never work, Gwen. Valentina is out of your reach and the two of us are stronger than ever. You can't break us up and you can't touch her. She's not going anywhere, but you are."

My voice dropped to a low growl. "I've got a private security detail that is now *your* detail. They will follow you everywhere you go from the moment you step out of your apartment until you walk back in. They'll clock everything you see, do, and eat. If you blow your nose funny, they'll report it to me."

"I'm pretty sure you can't do that."

I looked around. "Go ahead. Complain to someone. Call the police. While you're at it, be sure to explain the threats and attempted murders."

The corner of her mouth quirked into a smile. "Fine, Jaxson. We'll do it your way. When your hired guns come back and tell you that you've got it all wrong, I'll forgive you." She gripped my shoulder. "It's what friends do."

I stepped out of her grasp. "You're the one who has it wrong, Gwen. I'll do whatever I have to do to protect her even if it means following you myself."

Voices sounded in the hallway, signaling the start of the workday.

Gwen's eyes trailed me out of the door, that smile hanging on her lips.

VALENTINA

"I'm not surprised she didn't confess and let you lead her away in cuffs. That whole thing where you lay out the crime and the criminal gives themselves up out of respect for your genius, only happens in murder mysteries."

I was on the phone with Jaxson, coming out of my psych diversity class. I woke up, discovered he was gone, and knew instantly where he went.

"I told her that our guards would be following her from here on out and she acted like the whole thing was a joke."

"Where are you now?" I asked.

"Home. I'm picking up a change of clothes for Papa VZ and bringing him and Fernanda some decent food. They're supposed to be let in to see Meyer soon."

"Pick up some chocolates from me," I said.

"Where are you?"

"Flanked by my guards and on the way to the car. I'll be home in an hour, snuggling with Ryder, Maverick, and Adam on the couch. I'll have you next to me as soon as you finish looking after your dad. Love you."

"Love you too."

Hadley and Juliet drifted closer after I hung up the phone. They tried to give me as much space as possible. There was only so far they could go when an active threat to my life was still kicking around.

Guards on her or not, I won't stop driving with one eye on my rearview mirror until they put her away.

We arrived at my newest parking space. A small student lot behind the communications building.

My guards circled the car, peered inside, and checked beneath for good measure. They'd follow behind me in their cars and then head to their homes after I passed through my gates.

Peeling out of the parking lot, my mind turned to dinner. If I got in there quick, I could whip up my famous movie-night meal. Quesadillas, nachos, chicken wraps, and a plate of veggies, so my son had something healthy to munch on. We'd take it all into the theater and brighten this crappy week spending time together.

Yes, that is exactly what I'm going to do. I'll call Sofia too.

I rang her up and we talked on the drive.

"I'll bring dessert. What do you think of salted caramel popcorn bars?"

"I think I've always known you were my best friend, but now I see this friendship will last forever."

She laughed. "You're so weird, Moon. I'm going to claim the oven before someone gets there first. See you soon."

"Bye."

The mansion came into sight. I honked, waving out the window to my guards, and turned up my drive. The gate rumbled open at my keycode and I pulled in, killing the engine behind Ryder's car.

Adam will pass out an hour into the first movie. After I put him to bed, we'll watch—

A faint click broke into my thought.

I turned—mind consumed with comedies and caramel popcorn—and lit on the back as the seat came down. My heart stopped, locking on to a pair of eyes through the dark of the trunk.

I screamed.

Whipping around, I scrambled for the door handle, shouting for bodyguards I knew weren't there.

"Shut up!" A hand clamped over my mouth, yanking me back.

The thought to bite her crossed as she pressed the gun to my temple.

"Drive," she ordered. "Now."

My heart hammered on my rib cage, collecting dents I felt as well as heard. Driving off with this maniac was the worst possible thing I could do.

But staying here when Adam will be home from school any minute isn't an option.

Hands shaking, it took me three tries to start the car. The gun dug harder into my temple with each failed attempt.

Finally, the engine hummed to life. I put the car in reverse and drove out of the gates.

JAXSON

I pushed my dad onto a chair and shoved a coffee in his hand. He looked like he hadn't slept all night.

"How's Meyer?" I asked.

Dad propped himself up, rubbing the bridge of his nose. We were in the family visitor room. A sterile, windowless space. Flower pots and landscape paintings did their best to cheer up the room. It didn't work.

"He woke an hour ago. He'll be okay but we have another issue. Daniel told Fernanda that he was run off the road."

"What the hell? By who? Did he see the car?"

He shook his head. "It was dark. It all happened too fast."

I opened my mouth to tell him who it was, and then closed it. It was a rare and stressful moment when my dad looked his age. He had enough going on without discovering his assistant was a psychopath. Plus, there was the fact that I didn't have proof.

"You should go home and get some sleep," I said. "Now that we know he's going to be okay."

"I just found out someone tried to kill my partner. I'm not going anywhere." Dad bumped my knee with his fist. "You go home. Thanks for the coffee and clothes."

"I can stay with you, Dad."

"No need. We're good here." He stood up, drawing me in for a hug. "I'll be on the police, making sure they're doing everything they can. You take the rest of the day off."

"Are you sure?"

Nodding, he steered me toward the door and called bye as he headed back to the ICU.

I made for the elevator and dialed Val.

Voicemail.

I tried Ryder.

"Yeah?"

"Put Val on," I said. "Meyer was run off the road last night."

"Are you serious? Any chance it's not connected to Gwen?"

"Has to be her. She blames the label for screwing over her brother," I said. "Get Val. I have to tell her about this."

"Val's not here."

"Yes, she is." I got in and jabbed the button for the first floor. "I talked to her after class. She was going straight home. Get out of your office and look."

"Adam and I called for her when we got home." Alarm crept into his voice. "Her car wasn't in the driveway. She's not here, Jaxson."

"I'm calling Juliet."

I didn't waste breath on a goodbye. I hung up and dialed the bodyguard. She picked up on the second ring.

"We followed her home and watched as she drove through the gates," she said. "If she's not there, then she went out again and didn't inform us."

Panic rose like bile in my throat. *Calm down. For all I know, she swung by Ezra's mom's.*

I called Val again. And again. And again.

"Hey. This is Val. I can't get to the phone right now—"

Fingers stiff, I dialed the final number.

"Jacob, it's Jaxson."

"Yes, Mr. Van Zandt?"

"Tell me you're looking at Gwen right now."

"I am," he said. "She stopped at a café after work. She hasn't moved in the last two hours."

I breathed a sigh of relief. Gwen was nowhere near Val. She was okay.

"Thanks, Jacob. I can't get a hold of Val. I just had to be sure she was safe."

I heard a chair scrape the floor. "Should I come back?"

"Nah, it's cool. I know how to find her. Everything's okay."

VALENTINA

"Get out of the car."

My door flew open. She reached in, yanking me out, and shoved me in front of her. The gun jabbed my spine.

The deserted side road she forced me to drive to were plentiful in Evergreen. What they weren't was well used. It could take days for someone to stumble on my abandoned car.

"Walk," she ordered.

"Why are you doing this, B— Be—?" Her name finally came to me. "Bianca. What do you want from me? I don't even know you!"

Jaxson's boss shoved me, pushing me to the tree line. "You know what I want. I tried to get rid of you. I warned you to stay away from him!"

Another shove and I fell to my knees. Bianca hauled me up, strangling me with my collar, and put my ear to her lips.

"I'll make sure this time," she hissed. "Jaxson is mine. Finally, we'll be free of you."

We staggered through the trees, and Evergreen Forest swallowed us.

It was her. Jaxson's boss was behind it the entire time.

Fear blotted my mind. Discovering the true person after me should have brought the situation into clear focus, but none of this made sense.

"What are you going to do, Bianca?" My voice was a thick rasp forced out of my throttled throat. "Kill me? Bash me over the head and leave me here like you did Serena? Because that was you, wasn't it? Wasn't it?!"

Bianca tightened her hold, biting the collar deeper into my neck. Snarled roots rose out of the ground, grabbing at my ankles. I tripped, scraping my arm on bark and gasping in the stranglehold.

She let go to shove my back. "Move!"

Whipping around, I slapped her hand away. She struck just as fast.

Pain exploded in my temple and I fell, clutching my head, fingers dampening with blood.

Bianca brandished the gun. Hatred scorched in her eyes, warning that she would hit me again, and follow the act with worse.

"Why?" I was a notch below a scream. "You're risking everything, and for what? Jaxson will never be yours. Nothing you do to me will change that."

Her eyes flashed. "That's not true. You want me to believe it. That he's too young for me. That he loves you more. But Jaxson is my soul mate. We want the same things in life. He and I connect on a level I've never reached with another person. He'd see that if you weren't in the way."

Jaxson doesn't give a flying fuck about you other than bringing you coffee and sorted demo tapes.

I burned to lash her with the truth. She tormented me over a clearly imagined relationship with my boyfriend. I'd snatch it away from her like she took my safety and peace of mind.

I can't, common sense warned. *This woman has proven she's not above murder. I have to get out of this. Keep her talking.*

"Was Serena in the way too? Is that why you beat her head in?"

Bianca's lips peeled back. "She was another worthless slut throwing herself at him. Jaxson would never in a million years want her. I trusted him," she said. "Knew he'd be loyal to me, so I let him go to New Orleans. I followed to support him during his first festival and *you*"—she spat the word—"were there.

"You're always there. Tempting him. Seducing him. Filling his head with lies and pretending you love him."

"I do love him!"

"*I* love him," she roared. "Him and only him. You force him to grit his teeth and watch while you screw his friends. That's not what Jaxson wants. He wants a woman that will be there for him. Who'll support him in his dreams and who he doesn't have to fish out of someone else's bed every night.

"I know what he truly wants because I know his soul inside and out. As surely as I know his heart is too big. It's not easy for him to walk away from people he believes in, even if they don't deserve his time," she said. "No one noticed me among all the people backstage. I lifted his phone and texted you his true feelings."

"And Serena? Don't forget what you did to her."

She thrust the gun at me. "She can't have him either! And unlike you, she's gotten the message."

I pulled my hand away, tacky with blood, and gazed at the crimson liquid as the pounding in my skull scrambled my thoughts.

I have to find a way out of this. Wrestle the gun from her. Run to the car. Something!

"So, you put that thong in his car to break us up," I said, slowly getting my feet under me.

"That wasn't about you, conceited whore. I wanted Jaxson to have something of mine. Something intimate. Special."

"And the flipbook? Running me off the road? Am I being a conceited whore thinking that was about me?"

She smirked. "My biggest regret is not killing you that day. It was hard enough with all the barriers between us. Levi would fire me if he found out we were together, but still, I kept Jaxson close and promised myself I'd be patient until he dumped his girlfriend. When he did, I'd make him see that we could make it work in secret, and when he took over the company, all would be fine.

"I would've waited, but then I found out what kind of *relationship* you forced him into. He was unhappy with you and couldn't say it."

I stood, meeting her gaze. "Naturally, you decided to kill me and save Jaxson."

"You survived like the loathsome snake you are." She spat at my feet. "This time you won't slither away. I overheard him this morning talking to Gwen. Saying you're stronger than ever and he'd do anything to protect you."

Another thrust of the gun buried the muffle between my ribs. I staggered and fell against the tree.

"I should've realized you'd use my warnings like the manipulative bitch you are," she growled. "Play the damsel-in-distress and tie Jaxson to you even tighter. No more."

The air shifted. I witnessed her shoulders square—knuckles whitening on the gun.

She was psyching herself up to do the unthinkable and I wouldn't stand here and accept my fate. I bent my head, readying to charge.

"I'm the one who truly loves him. He'll see that when—"

"Val?"

My muscles turned to lead. *Voices? Am I hallucinating my love at the end?*

"Valentina, what are you doing out here?" Rustling sounded to our right. "Are you okay...?"

Jaxson broke through the tree line. The question died on his lips. "Bianca?"

Her snarl fled. The woman smoothed her hair back and tugged down her shirt—as if fixing herself up for him was most important.

"Bianca, what's going on?"

"Get out of here, Jaxson." She slashed her hand through the air. "I don't want you to see this."

His gaze flicked to the gun. "See this? What do you think you're going to do?"

"Get rid of her." She squared up, holding the gun with both hands, and training it between my eyes. "I love you. Your age. My job. None of that matters. You and I are meant to be together and we will be when *she* is no longer in the way."

"You love me," he repeated. Jaxson edged closer, looking me up and down, lingering on my bleeding forehead. "You... You sent me those gifts?"

"I knew you'd like them. I know everything about you, Jaxson. I'm the one that loves you!" She shouted it at him but snarled at me.

"You attacked Val, Serena... and Meyer, didn't you?"

"I had no choice! I heard him threaten you. Saying he'd never let you take over the label while he was vice president. I won't let anyone stand in the way of your dreams, Jaxson. I've always been there for you. I fight for you. Can't you see that?

"This bitch wouldn't let you go and Serena tried to steal you out from under me. I can't do it anymore, Jaxson." Tears spilled over her lids. "Waiting for you to leave her and see that I'm the only one for you. I'd never ask you to share," she said. "Never."

She seized me around the neck. I struck out, knocking the gun aside and lunged.

Bang!

"No!" Jaxson roared.

I crashed into her. Bianca quickly grabbed on and spun me, pinning me to her chest and allowing me to see the bullet hole in the bark. She pressed the gun to my head, promising where the next one would go.

"I won't wait another day."

Jaxson surged forward. "Bianca, stop!"

"No!" Her shrill shriek echoed through the forest. "Why won't you let her go? She doesn't love you!"

"I know she doesn't," he cried. "I've always known that."

"What?"

He straightened, looking me in the eyes. "I'm just another in her collection of rich, lovesick bastards willing to pamper and shower her in everything she wants. All Valentina cares about is money and sex."

My knees buckled. "Jaxson? How could you—?"

Bianca shook me. "Shut up! Jaxson, if you knew the truth, why didn't you leave her?"

"Because I loved her. Until I got those chocolates, keychain, and the album. I realized there was someone out there who loved me for me. Now I know it's you."

Her grip loosened slightly. "You do?"

"Yes," he said. "That's why you can't kill her."

"What?" She tightened her hold again. "But you said— I thought you understood!"

Jaxson put his hands up. "I do understand. But don't you see she doesn't matter anymore? I choose you, Bianca. We can walk out of here right now and start our life together." He leveled a finger at me. "If you kill her, that life will be on the run. Always looking over our shoulder. I'm set to take over Interstellar Records. I thought you supported that."

"I do," she said, voice quavering. "Of course I do."

"Don't force me to give up my home, family, job. If you love me, walk out of here with me right now, and let's have all of those things together."

"Jax-son." She cracked his name on a sob. Just like that, she shoved me away.

Bianca ran to his open arms. "I love you so much."

"I love y—"

She leaped for him. Jaxson whipped something out of his back pocket and jabbed her throat. Bianca went down, convulsing and writhing on the earth, the faint charged clicks of the taser echoing in my ear.

I gaped at her and then at him.

"Crazy bitch," Jaxson muttered. He stepped over her body. "Baby, are you okay?"

"You— How—"

"I'm sorry I said that stuff." Jaxson erased the distance and scooped me into his arms. I buried my face in his neck. "You're not with me for sex and money. You're with me because I'm never fucking letting you go."

I clutched him tight enough to break him, my own voice cracking. "How did you find me?"

"Ryder put a tracking app on your phone."

I reeled back. "He did what?"

My Jaxson grinned that grin. "I told him you'd be pissed even if it paid off. You had no reason to be hanging out in the forest. I broke the speed limit the whole way."

"I'm just glad you're here." I peered over his shoulder at the still body on the ground. "She was going to do it, Jaxson. I saw in her eyes she wasn't letting me out of here alive."

"I took your taser out of the nightstand in case Gwen decided to crack my skull open. I didn't for a second imagine Bianca..."

I hugged him tight. Jaxson liked and respected his boss. This betrayal cut him deeper than he'd let people outside of our family see.

"Let's call the police and go home," I said. "Cuddling on the couch with you, my loves, and my son in the next hour. That's where I want to be."

Chapter Ten

V*alentina*

"I'm not sure they want me there."

"This party wouldn't be happening if it wasn't for the hard work you put in." Maverick snaked his arm around my waist, resting his chin on my shoulder, and smiling at me in the mirror. "You're at the top of the guest list, Val."

"Don't think Ortega and Kessler feel the same way," I muttered. "Jade only deals with me for house business and Kessler doesn't return my calls."

"We're on to them now. We couldn't find a trace of half of those students who dropped out. They're avoiding you, so they can't be caught saying or doing anything incriminating."

I met his eyes in the mirror, a grim twist to my lips.

In the weeks since Bianca attacked, I retreated into the safety of my boys and friends, letting the police do their work. As a result, the rest of my semester was somewhere approaching normal—a word not often ascribed to my life. I say *approaching* normal because in the background was Maverick, searching for people who left no trace behind.

I smoothed the chiffon gown, rippling over the beaded bodice. The night of my charity dinner had arrived. The decorations I chose transformed the ballroom. The menu I approved was whipped up in the kitchen. Blair and I collected and organized the prizes. This was my party and Maverick was correct, I had every right to be there, but...

"It'll be hard to smile and trade small talk about the weather now that we know what we do. I just wish I knew what to do now."

"The only thing we can do is prove something awful happened to them," said Maverick. "The first step is getting into that file on Aiden's computer. We'll find Teagan and Sawyer, Val."

"If it's not too late," I whispered.

I finished getting ready and the two of us met Ezra, Jaxson, Ryder, Gwen, and her boyfriend Max downstairs.

Gwen was bouncing in her floor-length teal gown. "I can't believe we're going to a party at the Evergreen Country Club. Where are you taking me next week, Jaxson?"

He blew out a breath. "When do I trade my groveling for your forgiveness? Lunch has been on me every day for weeks."

"You accused me of being a violent, obsessed attempted killer because how could I not be in love with you?" She rolled her eyes, snuggling into Max. "You're going to be buying me paninis for a long time."

Jaxson mumbled something I couldn't hear but earned him a laugh and playful whack on the arm from Gwen.

Not only their friendship recovered from Bianca. Daniel Meyer was also on the mend. Banged up in the car crash, he took time off to rest with his family, but if the rumors were true, he planned to attend the charity dinner and snag that two-week tropical vacation.

We headed out to the cars, driving the short trip to the country club. The place was packed. The parking lot was fit to burst, and couples and coeds dressed in their finest streamed inside the club.

We drove up to the valet. Maverick got out and opened my door, holding his arm out to me.

"Ready?"

"I'm ready."

I climbed out and we melded into our group, passing through the frosted double doors and stepping on the red velvet carpet winding through the lobby for the ballroom. The carpet was Aiden's idea. Seeing it in action, I kind of liked it.

"Any prize in particular you want, Val?" Maverick asked. "We could snag that tropical vacation for ourselves."

"If this was one of those win-a-man auctions, I'd put a couple million on you." I covertly pinched his backside.

Maverick laughed. "I go for a lot more than that. Good thing you get all of this for free."

"Lucky me." I rose on tiptoe, claiming a kiss.

"Valentina? Oh, Valentina. There you are."

We broke apart. Jade scurried out of the ballroom, resplendent in a slinky black gown, and held her hands out for me.

"Is something wrong?" I asked as she took them. *There must be. Jade's barely spoken to me in weeks.*

"Yes, there is and it's me. I was wrong for how I reacted to your idea to invite all the past brothers and sisters."

I pulled a face. *What did she just say?*

"I'm sorry. What?"

"Tonight is about the Zeta Rho and Nu Alpha family coming together to do good for our community," she said. "And our family doesn't stop at those who graduated with us."

Jade tucked my hand under her arm and drew me inside. The ballroom was even more magnificent than I pictured. A wonderland of gold and white, draped in elegance for the mingling alumni to enjoy. I spotted Sofia among one such group, but Jade tugged me on before I could think to go to her.

"Once I realized I was being silly," Jade continued, "I took up your task."

"My task?"

Jade stopped behind a group of people and tapped a shoulder covered in blue ruffles. "Say hello to our new president."

The woman turned. My breath caught, held by the fist that punched my gut. Eyes gaping, I looked at her, connecting the person before me with the one I met over a year ago and coming up with one name.

Teagan Kainer.

"Teagan?"

"Hi," she said cheerily. "It's great to see you again. I can't believe the hopeful I talked to all those months ago is now the president who organized this. Isn't it amazing, babe?"

The guy next to her faced me, sliding his arm around her shoulder. Sawyer Burn smiled even wider than Teagan. "Incredible. Hey, is Ezra around?" he asked. "We've gotta catch up."

I couldn't answer. Couldn't think. Couldn't comprehend what I was seeing in front of me.

"I'm so happy they accepted the invite," Jade said. There was a blatant note of triumph lacing her voice. What she had won, I had no idea.

She gripped my hand tighter.

"Once a sister, always a sister."

Keep In Touch

Join Ruby's Mailing list for news, teasers, and more:
https://www.subscribepage.com/rubyvincentpage
Join Ruby's Facebook Reader Group:
https://bit.ly/3bNuCOq

ABOUT THE AUTHOR

Ruby Vincent is a published author with many novels under her belt but now she's taking a fun foray into contemporary romance. She loves saucy heroines, bold alpha males, and weaving a tale where both get their happy ever after.

www.ingramcontent.com/pod-product-compliance
Lightning Source LLC
Chambersburg PA
CBHW021313190726
48288CB00003B/831

* 9 7 8 1 9 5 9 2 9 7 0 7 9 *